Laundry

a novel by Suzane Adam

*translated from the Hebrew
by Becka Mara McKay*

D1569314

With the compliments of
Autumn Hill Books
www.autumnhillbooks.org

AB

Autumn Hill Books
Iowa City, Iowa

http://www.autumnhillbooks.org

Autumn Hill Books
P.O. Box 22
Iowa City, Iowa 52244

© 2008 by Autumn Hill Books
All Right Reserved. Published 2008

Printed in the United States of America

Originally Published as כביסה
© 2000 Suzan Adam and Keter Publishing House

Published by arrangement with The Institute for The
Translation of Hebrew Literature

Autumn Hill Books ISBN - 13 : 978 - 0 - 9754444 - 7 - 4
Autumn Hill Books ISBN - 10 : 0 - 9754444 - 7 – 6
Library of Congress Control Number: 2008925834

LAUNDRY

— *To Agi, my beloved mother, of blessed memory.*

one

For two days I've been running around, trying to understand, put things together, find some clarity, explain. Not
lose my mind. This isn't the time to lose it. I've been banging
my head against the wall, rifling through drawers, looking
for clues. I'm surrounded by this jigsaw puzzle, shattered
into a million pieces. How to sort it out, how to put it back
together. The telephone doesn't stop ringing. The house
reeks as if there's been a party, I can't air it out. The members of the moshav want to know what's going on. Our
neighbor Yochanan knocks on the door every time he sees
my car outside. He brings a pan of sweet-and-sour beef and
vegetables, something new his wife just learned to make in
her cooking class. I haven't got the strength to be polite. I
thank him and promise to keep him updated. I can't eat. It's
dark already. One more day.

At night I cry. In the morning I go to the grocery store
to buy a newspaper, maybe they've written something. Our
neighbors just shrug, such a tragedy. They ask me, do you
know how this happened? Nothing, no, I know nothing. I
want to run away from all the questions, go to Ashkelon, to
Queen Esther Street, to calm down Mrs. Rott. She cries, *Jaj
istenem, Oh my God*. She pleads with me, *Explain it to me,*

I don't understand at all, what is my daughter saying. I don't know, I don't know anything. Her sister Zsuzsi bursts into the house. Immediately she's on the phone, *Yes, yes, no, okay, Amnon says not to say anything, go tell your wife to stop speaking nonsense, they'll put her in the locked ward.* I'm on my way. She shouts after me, *Get her to calm down.* My head is pounding. Stay on the right side of the road, stop at the red light, pedestrians have the right of way, just no more police, please. The hospital, the smell of Lysol, in the corridor I hit my head against the wall. Nobody dies from this.

They haven't taken her away for observation, she's not crazy. After two days I take her home. She insists on sitting in the corner of the couch, where I found her. She's curled up, so tiny, how can she shrink into such a little lump? Every so often I ask her, do you want something to eat, something to drink? She doesn't want anything. For two days I've been trying to persuade her to speak, but she won't, she can't. There is so much despair in her eyes. She's not interested in anything, she doesn't ask questions. I take care of whatever needs to be done. I go out, I come back. She's in the corner, just breathing, nothing more. There's so little I can do for her now. Look me in the eye, I beg her quietly, I don't understand, you have to explain. She plucks lint from the checked wool blanket with great concentration. Silence. I know her silent stare. I've told her mother and her sister everything I know, which isn't much. She doesn't want to see them. Her sister phones all day long, pressing me for news, *So? So? Tell me what to do.* I don't know what to suggest. Her mother cries, *Oh my God, my God.* Me, I'm running around. Health insurance, Ashkelon, Mrs. Rott, I pass the police station, let them know she's home. *We know,* they say, *it's okay, we'll be in touch.* I need to deal with more paperwork. I need to tell my clients something. They know, they read the newspapers, *You have enough worries now, you need to stay home, with her.* My head is spinning, I'm being thrown from here to there, around and around, when will it end? She must explain. Her violet eyes blink through her chocolate-brown curls, wordless. I always understood all her gestures, but now, nothing. We began to create our own language long before I knew that she knew I was snooping around after her. Now I don't understand. She has to speak, I've told her a thousand times, don't worry, everything will be fine, if only you would say something. Should I shake her? Scream at her? It's nighttime. She lies on her back with her eyes open, scanning the ceiling. I give her half a sleeping pill so that maybe she can get some rest. In the morning she'll explain everything.

In the morning, she settles into the corner of the couch, silent. The house is locked, the telephone's off the hook. I sit on the other side of the couch. I tell her, put your head in my lap. She whispers, *I'd rather you sat farther away.* I jump up, landing in the armchair across from her. She is making pleats in the edge of the blanket, fold upon fold, her hands shaking. *I'll tell everything, from the beginning*, she says in a voice I don't recognize. It's not me she's talking to. I'm afraid to move, I don't want to disturb her concentration. Slowly, slowly, minutes pass, she lifts her head up, fixes her gaze on a corner of the ceiling. Syllables, letters. Sentences take shape from the words she is speaking. I hear; I don't understand, wait, from the beginning? No, from the end, the end is so terrible, she should start at the end, what is she talking about? Words, flat, monotonous, one after the other. She's reciting from inside herself, a story no one knows...

"At the age of five, I dreamed of being a belly washer. Three hills surrounded the town where I was born. The

3

slaughterhouse stood on one of the hills. The sloping path that transported the old and sick animals on their final journey appeared at almost every house. Cows, pigs, sheep, horses. Only the old and the sick, they told me.

"The age of five. *Beyond the forests*—that's what the name *Transylvania* means. Once, the Hungarians ruled; once, the Romanians. Like people any place, the people were happy, sad, strange, normal, sick, healthy, struggling, successful; I don't know what went on in their heads. They dressed as well as they could afford to dress and ate as well as they could afford to eat, depending on what kind of work they did. It rained, the springtime was ripe with wonderful scents. In the autumn, leaves changed color: red, gold, brown, the nakedness of the trees. Then the snow fell, the white queen, bells on the sleighs, a recipe for a fairy tale. People died like they do anywhere, and there was anger and sadness, and happiness—oh, such happiness, especially the Hungarians, when they danced the *Csárdás*. The Gypsies had bonfires. And the languages: Romanian, Hungarian, Russian, Polish, Czech, German; my mother knew English. Before World War II, there was culture: opera, concerts, and cabaret. The Hungarians especially longed for their roots, which were cut off when the Austro-Hungarian Empire was dismantled. There were simple peasants who could barely earn their daily bread. Then came the Russians, who made a new order in Transylvania, everyone equal—no rich, no poor, apparently: though some were closer to the dish than others. There was freedom of religion, but few Jews remained, the Satmar Chasidim were mostly wiped out, and the Christians didn't have the strength to pray to God after the war. This was Transylvania in the fifties.

"It seemed to me then that the Samush, which flowed a short walk from our house, was a wide river whose other bank I could barely see. My mother would laugh and say, what are you talking about, the Samush is a stream, like the Jordan, nothing more. I'll tell you the whole truth, it all began there, when I was five years old. The world was not my age, except for my friend Bijou and a few other children, we all understood each other, and at that age every millimeter counts. We played in the mud, and we threaded chains of butterflies on wires, a murderous gift for our mothers. In winter the snow kept us busy, snowball fights, even the ones who lost would laugh. My sister was small, my parents big, and I saw everyone from my height, even when I climbed the orgona tree with the purple flowers. I don't know what this tree is called in Hebrew. I'll tell you everything. It begins somewhere there, at the age of five, when I already knew how to stand up straight and walk on my own. I knew it wasn't polite to pick my nose. Nobody knows my stories.

"The slaughterhouse. Only the sick and the old, they told me. And only the sick and the old were fascinating to me. I loved to examine the many wrinkles the years had left on their skin, the bald scalps surrounded by a fringe of white hair, the special smell that leaked out of their mouths, their false teeth dancing in their gums, the many layers of clothes they wrapped around their creaking old bones. I was curious to see an old woman's underpants. I didn't have a grandfather or grandmother. I met old people at other people's homes. Sick people too. They were sick with the grippe, the flu—these were considered "healthy illnesses." There were also illnesses people died from.

"The sick gazed at me gently and hardly had the strength to pinch my cheeks. Sometimes they had treasures next to their beds, candy wrapped in crinkly paper, little squares of chocolate on pretty glass plates, arranged exactly in the center.

5

"I was visiting the sick son of one of our neighbors when I saw a real orange for the first time. The boy was sick with mumps, and all the mothers sent over their children to catch his illness. That day I sat alone at the foot of the bed, the sick boy snoring as he slept, groaning from time to time, his mouth gaping. I waited for his mumps to pass into me; in the meantime I collected a stack of unidentifiable crumbs from the rug and examined with boredom the other toys scattered about the room. His mother came and went, came and went, laying a hand on her son's cheek until it woke him and he asked for something to eat. This was the moment his mother had been waiting for. I, too, had been waiting for it. She brought a knife, a plate, and the orange. I knew it was an orange; I'd seen them in pictures, I'd been told that in Palestine they played soccer with oranges, and everywhere you went you could just reach up and pick one. The oranges in Palestine were as common as the potatoes in Transylvania, I was told.

"I didn't know that this place was called Israel, not Palestine, and that oranges were eight shekels a kilo. I had a card game, matching by countries, with four cards of Palestine: a woman with a jug on her head, the Tomb of Rachel or some other building with a round roof, a man riding a camel, and four golden oranges with green leaves. There was sand in the background of every picture. The people had dark skin, like people in the cards of Africa. Maybe not quite so dark. When I saw for the first time a three-dimensional orange, it looked just like the oranges from Palestine on my cards. The boy's mother took the orange in her hand and smelled it, closing her eyes. Then she turned it over several times, searching for the best place to injure it. When she found the right spot, she stuck the knife into the golden flesh. A spray of tiny droplets burst from the orange, moistening her

6

hand with a yellow mist. The air was filled with a pleasing new scent that was unlike anything I'd ever smelled before. Slowly, with careful, deliberate movements, she cut lines up and down, and where the lines met she stuck in a thumbnail and pulled the peel away in boat-shaped pieces. She left a peel on the plate, and for a brief moment it rocked gracefully back and forth. Beneath the peel was a transparent white skin, covered with white threads. The mother unwrapped the whole orange, arranging the peels in a careful stack. She pulled the white threads from her thumbnail; they looked like scattered hairs after she put them on the plate.

"The orange was from the boy's uncle, who had returned a few days earlier from the big city. He also brought a banana, which he divided up among the children in the family and presented to them together. Bananas and oranges from faraway lands. We didn't learn geography in kindergarten. Only I knew the Jews had Palestine. The mother again stuck a thumbnail into the middle of the naked orange. I heard a sound like paper tearing, but muffled. Now it was two halves of a ball. The mother put half delicately on the plate and said, this we'll save for your father and big brothers. The second half she divided into sections, offering me one. I put the prow of the little boat into my mouth and examined its texture between my tongue and cheek. The flavor was dry and disappointing. I pushed the section to the back of my mouth and bit down hard. A sweet, tart spray burst inside my mouth, pinching my tongue with its sharpness. While I chewed on the half of the section that I'd put in my mouth, I examined the second half. I peeled away the delicate membrane and separated the tiny, swollen vials, trying to find an imaginary cork, sucking the juice from each tiny bottle individually, until the mother scolded me and told me to eat nicely. I tried to stretch out that moment, but the section was gone and I wasn't given another. The sick boy got what was left. The next day I went back to try to catch the mumps again. This time the mother gave me three pieces of a strange, sticky candy that looked like yellow worms covered with clear nail polish, but its taste and smell reminded me of the orange from the day before…"

I get up from the armchair and start to pace a line along the edge of the carpet, back and forth. Her mother insisted we take that old carpet they had brought from Transylvania, meanwhile she'd clean it like new, so the living room would look warmer, so it wouldn't be so bare; meanwhile, meanwhile, she won't give up the carpet.

Now I understand why every time she peels an orange it's such a ceremony. She remembers it from then, she repeats each gesture. She is taking me to Transylvania, far away, but I want to talk about what happened a few days ago. More than twenty years have passed and she is telling me cute stories from when she was a girl of five, how can this be relevant? I return to my place across from her. There is time, patience, no shortcuts. I'm not leaving the house today, I'm attached to her. Every word is important. She's only five years old, if she just keeps talking it will all be clear in the end.

" … Interesting things happened around the sick. A five-year-old girl. A clever girl, they said to my mother. She doesn't say much, but you can see in her eyes she understands everything, the little imp, little devil, they said to my mother.

"A pretty girl, they told me, a head full of curls that couldn't be combed without tears. I hid my blushing cheeks in my hands when I laughed, my lips concealed my loose baby teeth. My eyes were violet, like Liz Taylor's, they told me .... violet. They only gave me problems, these special eyes. At the age of five I didn't know my violet eyes could make someone think bad things .... They called my mother Sophia Loren because she had big lips and big breasts. My father didn't look like any movie star, and my sister was too small to be anything but a sweet, smiling baby who cried whenever she needed something.

"At the age of five I was curious, investigating the contents of the yard, examining worms, beetles, processions of ants, what the dogs were doing when they were in heat. I went up and down our street; I was allowed to visit the streets next to ours as well. All the children spent their free time in the streets; the boys played with a ball or rolled a hoop back and forth, the girls pushed their dolls in strollers, everyone bragged about their birthday presents, or improvised something by putting four creaky wheels on a box. In the summer we hunted butterflies and threaded them on long wires, white butterflies, they were easy to catch. In the winter we built snowmen and had battles with soft, white snowballs, we even threw them at the grownups, and they laughed along with us, everyone knew everyone else, the children were the neighborhood messengers because nobody had a telephone. The streets were like a big nursery, our mothers only had to give us one look: Hey! Time to go home! Put on a sweater, eat, run to the bakery, go home to sleep. A girl of five.

And there was Yutzi, our neighbor ... "

Yutzi, I ask her, Yutzi? Wait, wait, what do you mean, I thought you didn't really remember her, why did you pretend? She looks at me as if I'm a stranger. She says, *Forget that you know me, I'm a five-year-old girl, I'm growing up in front of you, everything will be clear.* I need to take a break. I get up to make us some tea. Yutzi? I know I asked her to tell me everything, to explain, but I expected maybe three or four sentences, a condensed version, to make everything miraculously clear. This is more than she's ever said about the subject, and never with such seriousness. I'm not a big talker either. All these details, as if she's had them memorized for years, every word in place. She's not confused, she's not stammering, she's not stopping to think, to recall. I don't remember a thing from when I was five. In the kitchen I open the shutters a crack, take a deep breath. The morning air is warming up, there's chirping in the yard. I need to water the seedlings. Yochanan is in the field on his tractor. I should go apologize to him, the dogs have ruined his work boots again. I should tie them up, I should finish the fence and the gate, the workers are coming tomorrow, they shouldn't come. I need to go back to Transylvania, she's waiting. I go back and sit down across from her. She glances at me from her corner, she's there…

"…Yutzi was the prettiest of the girls. Seventeen years old, poised, with mischievous eyes. Yutzi was a belly washer, like many of the unmarried young girls who left school. The fate of whoever failed to marry. The veteran belly washers were aging virgins no man wanted. They stayed at their jobs for years, never lifting an eyebrow when a new crop of young girls started working.

"To me, Yutzi seemed like the earthly sister of the holy Virgin Mary, whose image glowed in the paintings that decorated the homes of the gentiles. I studied her every gesture. I tried to stretch my little neck, I stood on my tiptoes so for one sweet moment I could feel like the beautiful Yutzi. I was pretty, too, but not like her. I wanted to be a belly washer when I grew up, like Yutzi. Even though I had no idea what a belly washer did.

"Once a week, Anna came to help my mother with the washing and the ironing. I thought Yutzi was this kind of washer, too, only she just carefully washed bellies. Whenever anyone asked me what I wanted to be when I grew up, I said belly washer and everyone laughed. I thought if I persisted in my desire, I would grow up to be just like Yutzi, because Yutzi was the prettiest one of all. 'Yutzi, where are you going? I want to come with you.' I followed her like a stubborn suitor. I wanted to know where the belly washers went and what they did; I wanted her to teach me. Every chance I got I tagged along after her. Yutzi pinched my cheeks so hard they burned and my violet eyes watered. 'Go home, go home, little pest!' She used to shoo me away like she might shoo a dog in the street. '*Keeshta*! Go back to your mommy!' Yutzi would scream at me whenever she noticed I was following her, then she'd smooth her hair and continue on at her usual rapid pace, occasionally laughing out loud to herself without a backward glance, walking so fast that my small strides couldn't close the gap between us, even when I ran after her as fast as I could. I'd stop after a few minutes to catch my breath, checking to see how far I'd gotten during the chase. Sometimes my mother invited her to drink tea in our kitchen. Then I could study her. When she left I'd follow and watch her from the gate. In the winter my mother gave her a pair of gloves and a brown sweater that had shrunk in the wash. At the age of five I knew all the important things: going to kindergarten, getting to the neighbors' houses, visiting my friends on the next block, walking to the bakery to buy bread, standing by the gate with the empty milk bottles. I knew to fill a basket with the wild raspberries I picked; I knew to cross myself when I went to church with my friend Bijou and her family. I knew what dogs did when they were stuck together and that afterward there would be puppies. I knew my mother had given birth to my little sister; the stork didn't bring her. At the age of five I knew the old and sick died and when they were finished dying their families buried them in the ground and covered them with flowers and tears. I knew that when someone died you needed to cry, and then after a few days you could go on with your normal life. I sometimes saw the funeral cart and the procession, but I had never visited the slaughterhouse.

"A few buildings were scattered near the beginning of the path that led to the slaughterhouse. There was a tannery, a butcher shop, and a sausage factory, which was attached to the place where they washed the bellies—the place where Yutzi went to work every day. Children were forbidden to go near there. It's not a place for children, the grownups said. During her lunch breaks Yutzi always went home to fix something for her abandoned mother. Yutzi was the child of her parents' old age. Her five older siblings had all left home for the city. Her father had died of some illness, and her mother was so fat she could no longer leave the house, not even to go to church on Sundays.

"I saw Yutzi's mother just once, just a peek. She was lying in a high bed, her enormous body covering every inch of the mattress. I thought she looked like a soft, damp, pink pig, filling the room with her heavy gasps, accompanied by a smell that reminded me of rotting leaves. From where I stood I could only see the side of her face. She had a small nose that released tiny snoring sounds, her face was ringed with rolls of fat that began high on her forehead and cascaded in waves to her shoulders. I couldn't see her eyes. The rolls of fat ended at her throat, streaming gently inside a checked cloth that appeared to be an enormous pajama top. Her voice was like the echo that disappeared into our cellar, where my mother went to get potatoes, a cold, mossy-smelling darkness.

"Yutzi fed her mother soup one delicate spoonful at a time and wiped off the trembling mountain of her chin after each gulp, as if she were wiping off a fragile and expensive porcelain dish. 'Mamishka, how does it taste? Is it warm enough for you, Mamishka?' In a tender voice Yutzi urged her mother to eat a little more of the tasty soup she'd brought to her bed. Yutzi's mother was not satisfied. 'Don't slouch, get away from there, too slow, too fast, it's too hot, there's not enough salt, the carrots aren't fresh, get your hair out of there.' Yutzi hurried to gather her black hair into the large brown handkerchief that brought out the sparkle of her dark eyes, even in the room's struggling light. 'You're like St. Moritz!' I didn't know who this St. Moritz was. She spoke to Yutzi as if she were talking to an idiot or a donkey. She started to speak angrily about Satan's messengers, who had put her husband in the ground, all of them should be wiped off this earth, she groaned. 'There are more but they are hidden from us, we need to find them and wipe them off this earth.' Yutzi comforted her. 'Don't worry, Mamishka,' she said, 'I'll take care of all of them, one by one.' Her mother prayed to the ceiling, calling to Jesus to come and take her home. No matter how long she prayed her voice kept getting louder, until she was screaming at him and threatening him and her whole bed shook. I wasn't surprised that Jesus didn't come, although I was very curious to see what he looked like. She swore and screamed at Yutzi, scaring me.

"Five steps led up to the small entrance to Yutzi's house. It had a wooden door, a short, dark hallway; on one side wool coats and scarves hung from hooks. The kitchen had a tiny window with a stove beneath, a fire whispering in its iron belly. Yutzi's mother was lying in a big room that was separated from the hallway by a pair of doors. The day I saw her mother, Yutzi came home in the afternoon as usual.

I was on my way from the kindergarten back to my house. I tugged on Bijou's thick braid before we parted and continued on my way. Then I saw Yutzi and followed her.

"… My father was at work, my mother was at home, I was outside with the other children. There weren't even any cars around. I played in the mud with the dogs and cats, what did I know? We were children, running around all day, going home to sleep. What else was there to do at home? I had a doll with a stroller and everything, I loved to put my puppies in the stroller. I wasn't some waif running around in torn clothes, I was a normal little girl.

"I knew it was forbidden to disturb the fat woman. The children said she was really an enchanted pig who had put a spell on Yutzi as revenge because she didn't want to marry him. They said Yutzi's father had gone mad and jumped naked into the Samush in the middle of winter; my mother said that he was a sick, pitiful man and that it wasn't nice to speak badly of the dead. People told all kinds of stories, and the children added details from their imaginations, and oh, I had quite an imagination, they told me. Although I didn't speak much, they said I saw everything, I was five years old and that seemed like a good thing, I was a little imp and that sounded good to me.

"The day I saw how much Yutzi loved her mother, I wanted her to speak to me that way, so sweetly and nicely, to comb my hair gently the way she combed her mother's thin hair, and one day, instead of pinching my cheeks until they hurt, put her red lips gently to my skin and maybe even whisper a tender word…. I wanted Yutzi to love me, to pay attention to me, I don't know, maybe like something from a fairy tale, Yutzi a princess and I her escort, a wild little forest creature.

"When she finished taking care of her mother, she came out of the dark hallway, took her gray sweater from the hook, threw it over her shoulders, and then she saw me. A wicked smile spread across her beautiful face. She reached out two slender, nearly transparent fingers, and closed them around my earlobe. It burned between her fingers, and without hesitating she twisted the soft flesh in a brief, sudden gesture. 'You're following me again, little pest, I'll show you this time. This will teach you not to chase after me.' She slammed the door behind her, grabbing my arm tightly. I tripped along next to her with my tiny steps, trying not to fall behind, or fall down. She laughed the whole way, a strange laugh, almost like a horse whinnying, as if the laughter had got stuck in her throat and couldn't quite get out, and she muttered to herself. 'I'll show you something, little imp, little devil, I know ... I know.... I'm not afraid of you, little imp, you think I don't know? Every time you follow me something happens, I get screwed; I'm going to put an end to this, stinking little Jew with devil's eyes!'

"I didn't understand what she meant by stinking Jew. My clothes were clean, I hadn't stepped in any dog poop, I hadn't wet myself like one of the little girls at kindergarten always did, I didn't stink. A Jew? Everyone knew I was a Jew, but she said it like a curse, as if it was something bad to be a Jew.

"At first I wasn't really sure if she was even talking to me, she wasn't asking me any questions, she was talking so fast, without stopping, without waiting to hear what I had to say. I wasn't scared. Yutzi lived right on our street, four houses down on the other side. I knew Yutzi would take care of me, this was one of the things grownups were supposed to do, keep children safe.

"Finally she was taking me somewhere, finally I was going with her and not following after her. What did she mean, devil's eyes? I was a devil? She was confused, I was a good

SUZANE ADAM

devil, a little imp. There were many little imps in the forest, they kept small boys and girls from getting lost. The little imps kept the grapes in the vineyards from spoiling before the harvest. The little imps protected the baby storks who waited in their nests on the chimneys for their mothers to return. I was a little imp who could do everything efficiently. My mother said I was a little imp; my father tossed me in the air when he came home from work, laughing, saying I was his little imp.

"In the synagogues of the Jews there were no devils, only God, whom we called 'Adoynai,' He was everywhere, they told me, it was impossible to see Him; you could only speak to Him if you needed something from Him. In Bijou's church, there were terrible devils of Hell, they were naked, they had horns, and they had tails like rats; they were on fire, surrounding the skeletons of dead people, their eyes were red, and everyone—even grownups—was afraid of them.

"The good little imps wore bright green pants and had pink skin, red cheeks, and golden eyes, their ears were big and round like elephant ears. They always carried baskets filled with delicious treats—candy or fruit, sometimes flowers, too. Nobody was afraid of them; I was a little imp because I didn't drop things like Bijou always did. Whenever we had guests, my mother always asked me to bring the glasses to the table, nobody was as good at this as I was, gathering up all kinds of things: beads that scattered, peas that rolled under the table, blackberries, crumbs, cherries, I gathered them all up quickly and without squishing a single one. I was a little imp, they said.

"Yutzi dragged me along behind her, saying she would show me. I was full of curiosity. As she held my arm a tingly, itchy feeling spread through it, the same feeling I got when my foot fell asleep. I stumbled along after her, my curls

16

bouncing on my forehead, some of them plastered down from the sweat that was beginning to glisten on my skin. My legs were starting to get tired, but the intoxication I felt in her company, being connected to her, made me think that soon I'd be able to lift myself right off the ground and fly along beside her; I wouldn't keep stumbling on the stone path. In the spaces between the stones fresh grass grew, and everyone knew you had to be careful not to slip. Yutzi held onto me tightly. Farther and farther she took me, the path that led to the slaughterhouse widened before me. I could see the violets that decorated the edges of the tender green grass. She's taking me to the slaughterhouse, I thought in disbelief, this was forbidden, every child knew that...."

two

I sit slumped in a stupor, frightened as a five-year-old child, mumbling to myself, *Don't let this be.* She hears me and stops speaking. I had wanted to sit next to her, to curl up with her beneath the soft blanket, so that we wouldn't be afraid. She is limp, moving slowly, scared of the sounds all around us. The door creaks and she jumps. I am always trying to keep the atmosphere around her peaceful. I wanted to hold her, so she wouldn't be alone on this journey. More than twenty years have passed, how can she remember all these details? Where is she pulling all these words from? I get up, put my hand on her head. She shrinks away from me, lowering her head. I can't touch her, she stops me again. What can I do? I turn on a lamp, close the shutters. What about lunch, I'm hungry, she should eat something too, a sandwich? Maybe some cookies? Fruit, anything? She sits on the edge of the sofa. I cram a slice of bread, some cheese, half a tomato into my mouth, barely chewing, what can I do—I'm starving. Meanwhile, I check the messages on the machine: her sister asking me to call back immediately, her mother, crying; yesterday I told her I'd stop by in the evening, it doesn't seem like I'll be going anywhere soon. I need time for this story. Siddi Farkash announces in her chirping voice that they're home if we need anything; they heard what happened, their garden can wait, I shouldn't worry, the hell with the lawn, stay home with her, they understand. Gideon Weiler shouts his message, *When are you coming*?! I feel like I'm in a jail, a jungle. He's angry I didn't get to the pruning, because of his wife, Peninah, she wants me to plant more and more. I told her no more, Peninah, you've run out of room, in the end everything will die, but she's furious, she won't give up the philodendron that's overrunning their small yard. I have no solution to this overcrowding; they need to look for another gardener. The faucet in the bathroom is leaking, the pipe's damaged. I shoved an empty pickle jar under it, a temporary solution, how can I think about calling a plumber right now, I have a million other things I need to do, ask Sharabi to work on the fence next week, until then ... She coughs, I take the phone off the hook, I need to be with her, protect her, listen to her, understand her. The end is still far away, I am with her, go on, continue, please ...

"...Yutzi repeated that she would show me. My mother knew Yutzi, everyone knew everyone, everyone greeted each other with a hello, they told me to say hello like a nice girl. Everyone said Yutzi was beautiful, then they would groan and say, *Tsk, tsk, what a shame*, leaving school at the age of twelve, now she's a belly washer. This was a good job, she dressed well, her hair shone, the other girls her age hurried to put on their school uniforms: starched cotton with black pinafores, white pinafores on holidays, always being so careful not to get them dirty. I wanted to leave school, too.

"As we climbed higher, I could see the back of a cow that was wandering lazily down the middle of the path, a man in boots walking beside her. He held a thin branch in his hand, which he used to prod the cow from time to time, gently poking her loose skin. Old cows knew how to walk nicely, you just had to walk along with them patiently, they didn't make any trouble. I had seen cows like this many times, I knew where she was going, it was time for her to die. She was old, even the green, fragrant grass didn't distract her as she made her way, she already knew not to waste the farmer's valuable time. Smart old cows knew where to go, even little children could lead them along. But children were forbidden from going near the slaughterhouse, everyone knew that. It was not a place for children.

"I went with Yutzi without saying a word. Going up the hill was easy, the slope was gentle, but still I was beginning to feel weak. I was hanging from Yutzi's hand, she shook me sometimes, painfully closing the gap between us. But it had been a hard walk for Yutzi, too. By the end, as we reached the big gates of the slaughterhouse, she was breathing heavily, she put her hands on her slim hips, the way a mother does the moment before she starts to scold you about something. 'Now you'll see, you little pest, I'll show you!'

"...I'm talking about this for the first time, I was five years old, good Lord, she was seventeen...

"My mother remembers different things, but she spent most of her time in the house. She didn't follow me around, she didn't see what I saw. She would sit at home reading a book, my mother was an orphaned princess; my father was a poor orphan. He had been rich once, he had a big house, many rooms filled with fine rugs and porcelain; his parents were killed because they were Jews, then all his money was stolen because the Communists didn't like rich people. I knew that one day we'd go to Palestine to live with all the poor and orphaned Jews.

"Bijou was a Christian, she loved Jesus because he was the savior of the whole world, except for the Jews, he was angry with them. Nothing bad would ever happen to Bijou because

Jesus watched over her. Every Sunday she got dressed up and went to Jesus' house to thank him. I knew Jesus, he knew I was a Jew and wasn't angry with me, I loved the songs they sang to him. My mother told me there was a God higher than Jesus who loved everyone and didn't care who was Jewish and who was Christian. I didn't know the songs for the Jewish God. Except for my family, Dr. Ontel's family, and a few old people, everyone seemed to prefer Jesus. I didn't know why I was Jewish, or why Jesus couldn't watch over me, too, especially when I visited him and told him what a nice house he had, and made sure to be extra polite when I was there, and kneeled to pray and showed him I thought he was important. Jesus died even though he was young and healthy, but he died for everyone, so that young people could give birth to healthy children, who would only die when they were very old. Bijou spoke to Jesus, promising him she would be his bride. She knew how to say a lot of things, she learned all her declamations by heart, she could repeat long messages. 'Tell your mother that tomorrow I'm coming over to finish pasting the labels on the jam jars, and tell her that she should soak the cabbage in salt water so it will be ready the next day.' Bijou could remember all of this. I didn't like to talk very much, only when I absolutely had to—hello, good-bye, thank you, yes, no. Instead of speaking I would shrug or make faces that were apparently amusing to grownups. *You're adorable, you're a cutie, you're a little imp*, they told me.

"Even though everyone always called us best friends, Bijou got on my nerves. I could do whatever I wanted at home, I could go anywhere in the house. Bijou was always very busy, and I found the list of dos and don'ts at her house quite strange. She couldn't sit on the floor, because worms might crawl into her underpants. She couldn't play with my puppies because they might have dangerous diseases. She

22

couldn't come to synagogue with me on Rosh Hashanah because she wasn't Jewish.

"I went to synagogue with my parents on special occasions. It was boring. Old men were always mumbling, *Shmoy yisroyel* and *adonoy ehad*. There was no singing, there were no paintings on the walls. There was a big closet with embroidered blue curtains they would open with great emotion and take out heavy scrolls that they could barely hold onto. They explained to me that this was the Torah, where all the prayers of the Jews were written. I found this very strange and troubling. Sometimes they kissed the scroll, but children were forbidden to touch it. My mother had to sit alone on a special balcony hidden behind a curtain, and I ran back and forth between my mother upstairs and my father downstairs, the old men didn't like this. Bijou wasn't allowed to come with me even when I told her there was a Jewish holiday when they danced with the scroll and threw candy.

"In Palestine I'd have a friend who would be allowed to do everything with me.

"Above Yutzi's mother's bed hung a wooden crucifix; around Yutzi's neck dangled a cross, without the nails or Jesus on it. The little cross hung from a thin, short chain. You could see the cross no matter which blouse she wore. Jesus wasn't on this cross, so I couldn't ask him to protect me from Yutzi's anger.

"Yutzi stood with a hand on her hip, stretching her neck forward a little, like a nervous goose. She stood like that across from me, hesitating for a moment as she considered the severity of the punishment she was about to give me.

"In the meantime, the cow and the man walking with her reached the place where Yutzi and I stood facing each other. The cow stopped in front of the gate. The man stood in front of her with his back to us and placed his large hands on the wooden gate. He lifted his hands over his head, as if he were surrendering to the cow, or to the gate. He turned his head toward us and gave Yutzi a sharp glance. He looked down at me and something softened in his eyes; I smiled at him but he just made a tsking sound in his mouth and pushed on the gate, whose broad wings opened wide, the cow started walking into the yard in the same calm way she had walked along the path. Just before the man closed the large doors behind the cow, Yutzi slipped in after them, leaving me standing across from the closed gate.

"...Where could I go? I had never been so high up before. I could see the roofs of the houses, the chimneys and the storks' nests—they came from another country. The chimneys seemed like something extra sticking out of the roofs. In the surrounding quiet, on the top of the hill, next to the slaughterhouse gates, I heard sounds coming from the other side of the fence. I was five years old. They told me only the sick and the old went to the slaughterhouse.

"A mixture of mooing, bleating, and screaming. I pressed my ear to the gate to hear better, I peered through the cracks in the wooden boards. I couldn't see where the sounds were coming from—just the edge of a white-walled building, dirt, yellowish puddles, and a wooden fence. I walked a few steps over to the long fence, my insides fluttering with a rising fear. I saw the wall of the building. I could also see some tall, barred windows, the wall ended. It seemed to me I could hear the cry of a hungry calf, through the next crack I saw a yard. The old cow stood in the middle of it, a few calves running around her, frantic, trying to nurse from her dried-up teats. The cow stood, indifferent, as the calves grew more desperate, the whites of their eyes bulging with terror. They were alone, without their mothers, and the old cow couldn't help them.

"Two men in boots and overalls came and led the cow somewhere else. The calves milled around her anxiously; they didn't want her to leave. The men pushed the calves away and disappeared. I called to them from the other side of the fence, pushing my little finger into the crack. 'Come here, come, come,' I pleaded. They came, and I said, 'Your mother will be here in a little while, you're not allowed to be in the slaughterhouse, you're too little, only the old and the sick. Come here, come.' One of them started suckling vigorously on my finger, then they all began pushing, trying to get to my finger. One calf had a large wound on its hind leg; he was trying to get closer to the fence, hopping on three legs, the others all pushed against him inconsiderately and he almost fell down. They were so hungry. With my other hand I pulled up some long stalks of grass that were growing nearby and offered them through the cracks, but they were still babies, they didn't know how to eat grass, like my baby sister who only knew how to nurse. I thought she was hungry once when my mother was busy, and I put a piece of bread in her mouth, and even though I made sure to give her a soft, tiny piece she didn't eat it, she just turned red, and then blue, until my mother came and slapped her hard on the back and explained to me, a bit distressed, about feeding babies.

"I couldn't get the calves to eat, either. They were still hungry, they lost all interest in befriending me and scattered in the yard. A man came and picked up the calf with the hurt leg. I was happy. They'll take care of it, I thought. I walked a few more steps along the fence. At the very end of the building, inside, in the darkness, at the very back, I saw that the old and sick cows didn't die alone.

"So much blood—more blood than came out of my finger when I tried to slice bread with a sharp knife, the one my mother never let me touch, but I'd wanted to anyway, and she wasn't angry, she just wrapped it in a bandage and said now I'd learned my lesson. So much blood came out of me — it hadn't stopped by the time my father came home from work. He said maybe I needed to go to the hospital and get stitches, but I was tired and the last bandage was still dry, so they gave in and let me stay home.

"Cows had even more blood. Their blood streamed onto the floor and into a groove. The men's boots were red, their hands were red, one of them was rinsing the concrete floor with water the whole time, keeping it clean. Then they brought in a cow with a rope around its neck; it stood quietly while they tied its four legs together. When the cow was all tied up, the men left it standing there and another man came in, dressed in overalls and boots. The cow watched, sniffing at him a little. He stood directly opposite her, returning her gaze, then took a step back and lifted a big, shiny, steel hammer with a long wooden handle straight over his head. The hammer hung in the air for just a moment, and then came down on the cow's head. The moment the hammer's head pierced the exact middle of the cow's skull, she collapsed like a tower of wooden blocks. Her legs were still under her big body, her head was still raised, propped up by the handle of the hammer that now rested on the floor, its other end stuck in her head. Her large eyes protruded, and a small stream of blood trickled from her nose, like a child with the sniffles, but red. She lay there quietly. The man left for a moment and came back with a long knife. He bent over her and briefly ran his hand under her neck, then stood up, pointed the knife, and with a single movement slit her throat. I heard a final sound leave the cow, the sound of air leaking from a punctured tire. All the air came out at once, along with the blood that was again covering the wet floor. The two men

26

came back and together they pushed the cow onto her side. One of them pulled the hammer out of her head. A steel chain came down from the ceiling, and the men attached it to the rope around the cow's legs. Now she was on her back with her legs in the air. Slowly they lifted her with the chain until she was at their eye level, her head falling backward, almost drained of blood. Hanging upside-down like that she was conveyed inside the building until she vanished into the dark.

"Next to the track that had carried away the cow hung a row of lambs, also upside-down, their hind legs pierced by hooks, leg by leg, like the nails that pierced Jesus' legs. Their heads bobbed back and forth, and they cried, tongues protruding from their mouths until a man with a knife came and cut their throats. One by one they were all quiet, and their blood filled the groove, mixing with the cow's blood. The row of lambs also traveled into the distance, like train cars disappearing in a tunnel. The dark was too dense for me to see inside, and everything seemed jumbled together, and I was cold, and I didn't know if it would be okay to fall asleep or if I needed to try to stay awake until Yutzi came back.

"Suddenly I saw Pishta, Bijou's father. I knew he worked at the slaughterhouse. Many people I knew worked there, but I'd never seen them in their stained work clothes. He came out of a passageway that ended between two long, tall tables made of shiny stainless steel. Flung across his shoulders was half of a calf. It was the one with the injured leg. I could see its ribs from the inside. It had already stopped bleeding.

"Bijou's father whistled; I knew this was a sign that he was in a good mood. Whistling or singing, Bijou's father was a happy man. And then suddenly, mysteriously, there was Yutzi right next to him. They stood facing each other on either side of the calf whose leg had not been taken care of. They stood close to each other, Yutzi licking her lips the whole time, standing a little crookedly with her weight shifted to one leg, her head cocked to the side, one hand playing with her hair. Then she shifted to the other leg, her hair falling over her shoulder as she continued to comb her fingers through it. Bijou's father burst out laughing, pinching her cheek and then reaching down to slap her behind when she turned around to leave. The man with the big hammer came and stood beside them; he pinched Yutzi, too. I wanted to rescue Yutzi, to make them stop hitting her, but their blows were apparently weak, maybe even pleasant, because Yutzi laughed, turning back to them, and Pishta gave her another smack. Then they disappeared into the dark and I couldn't see anything.

"Only three hungry calves remained in the yard. I was hungry, too. The wind burrowed into my ears and froze my reddening cheeks. My violet eyes burned, I wanted to go home, but I couldn't feel my legs, and I couldn't remember the way, and I couldn't make a sound, and I couldn't examine my neck to see if they'd cut my throat, too, because I couldn't find my hands, and I thought for a moment maybe I was tied up and that was why I couldn't move.

"'Ildiko! Illlldiko! Where have you disappeared to, little brat?! Come here! Ildiko… I'm going to kill you… where are you? Aha—here you are! Brat! I'm not finished with you yet.' She found me standing frozen, my nose running with a watery mixture of snot and the saliva I'd been unable to swallow, my red sweater wet beneath my neck like my little sister when they forgot to wipe her chin. I was happy to see Yutzi, she had come to take me home, she would explain everything on the way. She grabbed my hand, dragging me stumbling behind her down the sloping path; I tripped and fell to my knees but she kept going, marching along with her huge steps and never looking back.

"The beautiful Yutzi was angry with me because I was always following her. She knew that I saw and she didn't care. I wanted to ask her if she knew it wasn't just the old and the sick that were taken to the slaughterhouse, and I wanted her to explain to me why they were tied up and cut, and what happened to them after that, but she wasn't in the mood for children's questions. Many times I'd been told that when I grew up I'd understand, so I shouldn't ask, because some things were not discussed with children, and maybe Yutzi wouldn't know because after all she wasn't a woman yet, she wasn't married and she didn't have any children. 'A thousand times I told you not to follow me. You have Satan in your purple eyes, I know … He's following me, I'm not afraid of anyone, I'll show you, Satan.' I didn't understand what she was talking about, I just wanted to be like her, like Yutzi. Bijou wanted to be the bride of Jesus, Andrash wanted to be a policeman, I hadn't done anything wrong, why was she so angry? Why did she want me to be afraid of her? I didn't know what I could say to her to make her stop, make her take me home. She seemed to have her mind made up, and I didn't want to make her angrier. We went down the hill, turned off of the path, went behind some tall bushes, and at the end of the path we arrived at the place where they washed the bellies.

"'*Csókolom, csókolom*,' Yutzi greeted the old belly washers; '*Szervusz, szervusz*,' she said to the younger ones. She seemed cheerful; her anger had vanished. I stood in the doorway, dozens of eyes twinkled at me in gentle curiosity. Yutzi introduced me to the belly washers. 'This is Ildiko, Leona's little imp. I found her wandering around.'

"A smell of rotting quinces hung in the air; I recognized the smell even though I'd never been to the belly laundry and even though I couldn't see any quinces. The younger girls sat on long benches next to steel tables like the ones in the slaughterhouse, but not as tall. In the middle of each table were large, brown enamel pails with white enamel interiors. We had pails just like them at home. There was a greasy, gray dough inside the pails. The girls pulled thick, twisted strings of it out from the pails and made small heaps, searching for the beginning of each string and then delicately using four fingers to turn them inside out, reaching inside and threading them through as if they were threading elastic into a new pair of underpants. 'Take her away, she's pale, the little girl doesn't feel well, this isn't a place for children, take her home — her parents must be worried,' said the girls. Yutzi replied, 'She wants to be a belly washer. I'm showing her, so she'll know. She's always following me around; this isn't the first time.' Yutzi winked and continued to joke with them.

"When the guts were all turned inside out, another group of girls carefully scraped away the remaining material that still clung to the sides, using wooden knives. Then each string looked like the peeled skin of a transparent snake. Gently dropping the strings into another pail of water, the girls handed these pails to another group of girls who sat at the end of the bench. There was a large machine that looked like my mother's meat grinder, which children weren't allowed to touch. A fat, older woman with an apron that looked like it had been smeared with mud took a red-brown dough from a large bowl and poured it into an opening on top of the machine. Then, without wiping her hands, she slowly turned a wooden handle, while another woman threaded the end into the machine. With every turn of the handle, the machine expelled the dough into the transparent sleeve. The women's movements were synchronized. One turned the handle, one made knots. My mother always made delicious hamburgers when she was finished using her meat grinder.

I didn't understand what they were making. This was far away from the place where Yutzi had deposited me when we first arrived.

"Yutzi hovered among the girls, touching this one and that, tidying, scolding, making little comments the way our kindergarten teacher did when we sat down to draw or to use scissors and glue. She announced to the girls that up in the main building there'd been an announcement: the next day a delivery would arrive, and they needed to work quickly. It was torn up and they needed to be careful or else their wages would be cut; they needed to be precise, neat, and at the end of the week they'd be able to take home anything left over if they did their work right. One skinny, pale girl with a yellow kerchief tied neatly over her hair touched my shoulder. She pushed a slice of soft *kabanos* into my frozen fingers. 'Just a little longer, sweetheart, and Yutzi will take you home. Eat, eat—it's good.' Usually I loved *kabanos*, with black bread and green onions, but not this time. The women laughed, their voices chorusing as they urged me to put the tangy piece in my mouth, but I couldn't. I just watched them, no longer able to see Yutzi as the most beautiful of them all.

"I stood in one place, my head spinning, my mouth full of saliva, dripping onto my red sweater, my knees skinned, my head itching, and in my stomach a large lump of something painful that wanted to get out. I wanted so much to go to sleep. I couldn't see my bed, and I knew everyone sleeps in their own bed, and maybe my mother would be angry if I fell asleep on the wet floor of the belly laundry. I waited for Yutzi to take me home to my bed, Yutzi didn't care about me, I didn't care about anything anymore, I just wanted to leave already, to go home to my mother who would lay me down on my pillow, under my soft blanket, to my mother who was a kind, sweet-smelling princess who always smiled at me and patted my head, who always relaxed with a book in her hand when she wasn't busy cooking, straightening up the house, or taking care of my little sister. She moved calmly, serenely; she had a big smile and a warm lap, but Yutzi was more beautiful.

"This happened years ago, my mother remembers other things ... I'd vanished from the house for three hours, I was so far away, Yutzi returned me battered and drained, and all the way home she told me, 'If you say one word, you hear me, little witch? I'll rip out your guts and fill them with minced dog meat, you hear me? Not one word!' With every word she spoke she yanked my hand with her cold fingers.

"I saw my mother standing at our gate, her hands clasped beneath her Sophia Loren bosom, her dress clinging to her legs in front and fluttering in her wake, her dress the color of butter and decorated with pink and yellow flowers, small and delicate. On her feet she wore her soft brown slippers, her white wool socks folded neatly. She shouldn't be standing outside in the cold wind, she should at least have a shawl over her shoulders, she never lets me leave the house half-naked, I have to have a sweater, a jacket and a hat, what is she thinking? She's going to catch cold, she'll get a terrible flu. My father appeared at the end of the block, his hair a mess; as he came running toward us I could see his eyes were red, like my mother's. 'Mrs. Leona, I found Ildiko wandering around near the hill. How did she get all the way over there? I needed to get to the laundry right away, it was only a moment's delay.... nothing happened to her; she's just a little tired ...' We stood there, the four of us, my mother, my father, Yutzi, and me.

"Yutzi dug her fingernails into the frozen flesh of my palms, her head erect, her words passing into the space between my father's and mother's heads. They felt me all over, looked searchingly into my eyes. My mother examined my pants—my knees were smudged with red and brown. I didn't say a word, but my breath came quickly, my chin trembled, I wanted to shut my eyes, but I was afraid of not seeing my mother. Maybe this only took a second and maybe they talked for more than an hour; I saw thin clouds floating around me, and I was astonished at how they came down from the sky to wrap themselves around me, as if I were one of Jesus' little angels. I wanted to say to Yutzi, do you see? I'm a good little imp, Jesus isn't mad at me, he's embracing me with his clouds. As I thought this the clouds tangled themselves around me, whirling and turning gray, dimming, until there was only blackness.

"When I opened my eyes I knew I was sick. A clear glass of water stood on the nightstand next to my bed, along with a damp white kitchen towel. My throat felt dry, my blanket was smothering me. I tried to lift my chin to rest it on top of the blanket. The harder I tried to pull the blanket away from my neck, the more it covered me; I could barely see my mother's shadow hovering beside the bed, circling around and around until it landed like a large bird on the floor next to me. I turned my head away; I was worried that if she fell she'd be injured, like the baby storks sometimes when they lost their balance learning how to fly. My mother knelt down, leaning her arms on the edge of the bed, her fingers interlocked, the fingers of her right hand over the fingers of her left, making a little gate of her hands. I'd never been able to do this, even though I tried every Sunday at church. I thought my mother had decided to stop being Jewish, now that Jesus had somehow rescued me from Yutzi. I heard her whisper to herself, 'It's a blessing from heaven, the good Lord has heard my prayers.' I understood then that God Himself had intervened on my behalf, and that I was still Jewish.

"Yutzi had baked *pogácsa* for me, sweet-salty little rolls. Even though they'd dried out after a few days, they were still tasty; Yutzi knew I loved *pogácsa*. My mother said she'd come to visit me because I'd been sick, and you shouldn't visit the sick empty-handed.

"When I saw Yutzi, I wondered if I was just sick, or if I was going to die like the cows and calves, and I thought maybe Yutzi was going to rip out my guts and bring them to the laundry, where the girls would do what they needed to do to make them clean.

"My mother stayed by my side all the time, comforting me and caressing my forehead, straightening my curls so they wouldn't get in my eyes, playing with the ringlets next to my ears, at the same time tickling my damp neck, wiping the sweat from my forehead. 'Come on, one more little sip, one for me, one for Daddy, one for Yutzi.' Yutzi smiled at me warmly, the way I had always wanted her to, reaching out a hand with those transparent fingers of hers and gently pinching my cheek. I flinched, pulling away, burying my face in the pillow to get as far as I could from her hands. My mother laughed in embarrassment. 'She has a fever,' she said, justifying my behavior, and turned away to bring something from the other side of the room. Oh, how frightened I was of Yutzi's gaze at that moment. She pinched her lips together so tightly that her mouth looked like a dog's bottom after it makes poop. From between her wrinkled lips she hissed, 'Satan! One word out of your mouth and you're finished!' She drew a finger across her throat, like the man at the slaughterhouse had drawn the big knife across the cow's throat. I understood this gesture perfectly.

"Mother returned, in her hand a porcelain figurine of a cat with a pink ribbon around its neck. I was forbidden to play with or even touch the porcelain figurines that decorated the buffet. 'I want to give you this—we're so grateful to you for finding Ildiko and bringing her home safely. You can't refuse, it's the least I can do...' My mother sobbed. Yutzi placed an arm around her trembling shoulders. And I didn't understand any of it. I'd been in bed for two days, I'd gotten apples, a cheesecake that Bijou's mother had baked especially for me; my mother had been waiting on me hand and foot all day long, my father had been coming home early from work—everyone said what luck it was that Yutzi had found me, what a hero she was. I stayed quiet. I didn't want Yutzi to rip out my guts.

"The images from the slaughterhouse didn't occupy my thoughts. It was the belly washers and the old women who still smiled at me every time I shut my eyes. My mother made me promise I would never, ever, wander so far from the house, and I would never go off without telling her. She didn't ask me what I'd seen; she just insisted with all her strength that anywhere near the slaughterhouse was not a place for children, and I was absolutely forbidden to go there, it was a place for grownups. My father was angry; he said I was a big girl and smart and I should understand how I'd worried them when I disappeared, it was only luck that Yutzi had found me, because girls like me who wandered away from their homes could get into all kinds of terrible trouble, and oy vavoy how disastrously this could have ended. I understood something much worse could have happened, and I needed to watch out for Yutzi because she was the greatest danger to me, but I said nothing about this, because nobody would have believed me, especially now, with all those hugs and kisses they were giving her.

"When I was seized by fear, I preferred to throw up and make myself fall asleep by fainting, yet I didn't even realize I was doing this—it simply happened, releasing me from all the bad feelings. My house was warm and clean, Bijou came every day to play with me, and although I wanted very badly to tell her I had seen her father with half of a calf slung over his shoulder, I stopped myself, because she was a blabbermouth and didn't know how to keep secrets … and if Yutzi knew I had said anything…

"Afterward I ate the hot soup my mother had made for me and some bread spread generously with goose fat and sprinkled with small pieces of white onion and salt. How I loved the feeling of a full stomach, there was no food that didn't seem delicious to me, and it seemed as though the more I ate, the farther away I could push my dream of being like Yutzi. At first they affectionately nicknamed me Little Pogácska, then I was Honeycake, I was also Sweet Doughball. Whenever I sat down there were five rolls of fat on my belly, my thighs rubbed together when I walked, and I started to think Yutzi was casting a spell on me, so I would grow up to be like her mother and not like her. They told me I was round, they told me my cheeks were a good color, healthy, and that was the most important thing. My mother told me I was beautiful and maybe I should eat a little less bread. It was impossible for me to eat without bread: goulash with thick gravy; mashed beans with sausage and fried onions; egg yolks — the soft bread soaked up the warm yellow of the egg, it melted in my mouth, and the crisp crusts of fresh bread just out of the oven, and the sweet cherry preserves from old Dontchi Neini — impossible without bread.

"My mother was very delicate, and she could no longer carry me over big puddles of water; my father said I was already too big for him to lift into the air; he laughed and called me a little imp. I grew and I grew. My mother kept my clothes in a closet until they would fit my little sister; I got some new shoes and mittens. I could easily sit on my chair at dinner without needing pillows to make me tall enough.

"The bigger I grew, the more beautiful Yutzi became. Her body filled out, grew curves, her eyes sparkled, her hair flowed to her waist, and she swayed her hips when she walked, as though she wore high-heeled shoes instead of plain lace-up boots. I kept following her. They said she'd come to no good, only my mother said she was a good girl and they should let her be because she hadn't had an easy life.

"Ever since Yutzi had taken me back to my house, my mother hadn't stopped showering her with gratitude. At lunchtime she helped Yutzi by feeding her mother so Yutzi wouldn't have to walk all the way home from work. My father brought her women's magazines from the big city, and countless times they invited her to sit with them on our comfortable sofa and listen to the pleasant music that spilled out of the elegant gramophone that had once belonged to my grandfather.

"Every chance Yutzi got to come near me—if nobody could see—she pinched me. On my shoulders, my ears, my back, especially my belly. She loved to grab the soft flesh of my belly between her fingers, squeezing hard and, if there was time, twisting it right and left. My mother scolded me and said I needed to watch where I was going and stop tripping over things all the time, because my whole body was covered with black-and-blue marks. I didn't cry. What could I do? Grownups loved to pinch children, with affection, everyone knew this custom. My mother and father also pinched me, gently, with a smile.

"I kept following Yutzi. I wanted to stay behind her so she couldn't come after me; I wanted to know where she was so she couldn't sneak up and surprise me. I hid behind the tree trunks in the yards of neighbors who'd forgotten to lock their gates, I could identify her footsteps from far away. She wasn't actually doing anything bad, just coming and going from the market weighed down with bags. More than once I almost convinced myself to run to her, to ask if I could help. She went to the laundry every day and returned as fresh as if she hadn't spent the whole day working, but I knew she'd been there because she was always accompanied by the faint odor of rotting quinces. Sometimes she'd whisper to me, 'I'm not through with you yet.' Even though I was afraid she'd catch me and finish me off like she threatened, I often stole after her until she reached the edge of the path that led to the slaughterhouse. She used to skip lightly up the hill and disappear behind the gate; she didn't work up there but nonetheless she had some task that took her there instead. Bijou's father worked there, but I couldn't say anything to Bijou—or to anyone—about the slaughterhouse. I was afraid Yutzi would make my guts into sausages if she knew that I was investigating her. About what went on in the slaughterhouse I only understood later. My mother never knew this because I wasn't allowed to tell…"

A knock on the door. She jumps, startled. I leap up to calm her, she lifts a hand to her face in a gesture of self-defense, leaning to the side. My God, she's afraid of me. More knocking on the door. I feel as though it's the middle of the night, who could it be at this hour? No—it's still daylight, they should come back tomorrow, they should leave us in peace. I don't want to take a break, I can't turn away from her gaze, I don't know whether to come closer or back off, to scream, *Have you gone mad? You're afraid of me?* Her eyes have no spark, they're not even violet anymore, they're red, so is her nose, her lips are dry and cracked, pale. Where has her beauty gone? More knocking. I have no choice but

to open; outside the light is blinding, it hurts my eyes, it's not yet sunset. Messiah the plumber stands there sweating, breathing hard, I'm frozen stiff, he wants to come in, I tell him, *I'm sorry, Messiah, you've come at a bad time.* He says, *You said it was urgent so I came without calling. You've solved the problem?*
No, I say, *but...* He looks at me, asks in a fatherly voice, *Are you crying? Did something happen?* I say, *Is another time okay?* If I weren't crying, I'd laugh: the Messiah comes and I've told him to leave. The house is locked again, the telephone is off the hook, she can't be interrupted, it's torture to go back inside her story—for me, too. I hope the hard part is over. Yutzi? I didn't know, I want to be angry, but at whom? We were blind, she was mute. Yutzi the lame. Damn her. What would I have done, I'm not such a big hero, either. I'm crying, she's telling me a story, I'm crying, once I didn't have the courage to cry, boys don't cry, they told me. I ran away, I ran away—from my mother, from her screaming, from my father's flood of curses at her, from the beatings, I was afraid, I ran away, this was a long time ago, now we're grown, together, why is she alone? I want to ask her, *Who should I ask?* She's talking to herself, summing it up, and what about me? Where am I? Why don't I know anything? It's all scattered in pieces, a shudder, these thoughts are churning me up like a cement mixer. Ildiko? Soft, kind, reserved, polite, quiet—now everyone is in hysterics because of her, it's too late, I'm afraid again, of going on, I don't want to hear anymore, enough, I don't want to know, but I've forbidden myself from drawing a conclusion. First she should explain how all this will lead to the end; maybe later questions won't be necessary. I sit down. Is it cold or does it just seem that way to me? I'm sweating and I'm cold; I check to see if she's covered up, I just look, so as not to frighten her

again. We're shut inside the house, I won't open the door again for anyone, so she can speak without interruption, so we can get to the end. Batya is looking for her too, the friend she sees every couple of months. Maybe she knows what happened. She's even quieter, afraid of her own shadow, she'd faint for sure if she were sitting here with us, listening to this story; she has young children. I'd prefer it if she didn't come, if nobody came, not her mother, not her sister, we're not home, we've gone to Transylvania. I tell her, *Keep going, keep going, at this hour nobody will disturb us.*

" ... Yutzi quickly became part of the family. She didn't knock before she blew in like a storm, and my mother always smiled at her and persuaded her with pleasant conversation that she should read her books, and my father played nice music for her, and they gave her my mother's extra clothes, and the down blanket we kept for guests, and three jars of jam from the ten jars we'd bought from Madancsi Néni, and she got medicine for her mother, and meat and potatoes, and a pail full of black plums, and my mother wrote letters for her to her brothers who lived far away, and to the government, asking if they could send someone to take her mother to the hospital because she was so sick and couldn't stand on her own legs and there was nobody to lift her heavy body. What could I do? My parents had decided to take care of Yutzi as if she were one of their own, my big sister, and one night I heard them whispering that maybe after Yutzi's mother had been taken to the hospital, she could come and sleep at our house, so that she wouldn't be alone. I was silent; I wasn't much of a talker anyway.

Yutzi grew more beautiful and my mother spoiled her, giving her manicures, braiding her hair, letting her use her rouge and expensive perfume. I kept an eye on her while she enjoyed herself in my family's embrace. I went out into the yard, or I went to Bijou's. I didn't want to speak with Yutzi. My mother scolded me, telling me I wasn't polite.

My little sister was already learning to walk, and I watched her, making sure she didn't leave the house, making sure she didn't wander out of my sight—especially when Yutzi was around. But she wasn't in any danger. Now she was the little imp, growing taller, she had curls too, and a sweet, warbling laugh, and she did somersaults and other funny things, and everyone clapped their hands. Yutzi used to put her on her knees, *hőtz hőtz katona ketten űlűnk a lóra hárman meg a csikora*, and she sang to her, *az a szép, az a szép, akinek a szeme kék*. They told me I was already grown, they explained to me how a big girl needed to behave, and even though every evening my mother sat next to me and kissed my forehead and stroked my curls and told me a little story about a princess, I felt that everything was temporary, soon something terrible would happen, and even though mornings and evenings started and ended in the same way, I expected something to change, and it did…

"In first grade, our uniforms were beautiful and made everyone seem festive. Elementary school was just like kindergarten, but bigger and without games. Mr. Felush, our teacher, was a serious man, gray-haired but not bald, who wore a suit and tie. He was tall, maybe because we were short. Every morning he sent one of the boys from the senior class to ring a gold bell in the hallways until all the children disappeared into their classrooms. We would stand at attention, every child next to a chair. Mr. Felush entered calmly, blessing us all with a 'Good morning,' which we answered with a chorus of '*Zdrastya tovarishch*.' My father explained to me that we needed to greet our teacher in Russian because of Communism. I thought that it was enough to be Jewish and that there was no need for Communism at school. Communism was something for grownups. There was another Jewish child in my class, Joschka Ontel, whose father was a respected doctor and whose mother was a senior official at city hall, and even though they were Jews they never had any problems with the government. My father had once been a rich man, and my grandfather on my mother's side had been a titled aristocrat; the Communists did not like this, so they took away his big house and his carpets and special paintings. One time my father showed me a photograph of the house they'd taken away, now five families lived there and we lived in a house with three rooms and a kitchen—this was relatively well-off, they told me, and my mother still had almost all her books except for the ones with words that were insulting to the people in charge.

"Our teacher never said anything bad to Joschka or me, but I knew my behavior had to be exemplary because I was a Jew and not a Christian like Bijou, even though the Communist rules said everyone was the same. Our teacher used a wooden ruler to point at the letters he wrote on the blackboard. He banged it on the table when we were noisy; he used it to punish stubborn children.

"He would ask a child to stand on the little platform next to his orderly desk. If the child didn't know the answers to the questions he was asked, he would be scolded and sent in shame back to his seat, or he would have to hold out his hands in front of the class, and the teacher would smack the pink skin with the ruler until it grew red from the beating. But this hurt less than the second method of punishment, for which the scolded student had to clasp his hands tight, thumb and four fingers stuck together. The teacher raised the ruler over them, striking the fingernails and the soft flesh of the hands. I was careful and didn't get into trouble, I did

42

my homework, I learned my declamations by heart, and at recess I helped wipe off the blackboard and carry all the books back to the teachers' room.

"Day by day I heard the word Palestine more often at home. My father would disappear from the house for days at a time. They explained to me that he was trying to make arrangements for exit documents, passports, but *shhhh*, I wasn't allowed to say anything, this was a secret.

"One day my father returned home excited and confused, looking like he hadn't slept a single minute in all the days he'd been away from home. My mother was also gripped by anxiety; for hours they were busy with paperwork, writing, conferring with each other. I was playing with my sister, and when she fell down as she ran around mischievously, I hugged her and whispered, 'It's okay, everything will be better when we get to Palestine.' Even at night my parents continued to whisper, and between *Palestine, passport*, and *visa*, I also heard *Yutzi*.

"It was dark in the room I shared with my sister. The blinds were lowered almost completely, white moonlight penetrating the cracks between slats, illuminating the glass eyes of the doll that lay beside her. When it seemed to me that everyone had fallen asleep and I alone remained awake, I got out of bed and crept with hesitant steps toward my father's side of my parents' double bed. I stood there next to him; he was apparently not sleeping very deeply, he stretched out his arms and I sank into his firm embrace. He made a groaning sound in his throat that woke up my mother, she also turned to me and I was pulled between them. It was warm, my mother on my left and my father on my right. My mother kissed my cheeks, my father kissed my fingers, and I was overcome with terror, something terrible had happened, my mother and father were hugging and kiss-

43

ing me, caressing me, letting me fall asleep with them. Even my little sister wasn't allowed in their bed anymore because it would spoil her. When she cried in the middle of the night, someone would go to her and tell her not to be afraid and go back to sleep. I was wrapped in their arms, and a feeling of joy filled me and then a great fear. They breathed peacefully. When the moon was covered by a cloud and the room was completely dark, I asked in a thin, shrill voice, 'Is Yutzi coming to Palestine with us, too?' My mother turned to me slowly, raising herself up a bit beneath the blanket, leaned on one elbow and said in her gentlest voice, 'No, my little *pogatchka*, it would be wonderful if it were possible, but she can't come with us.' I was warm and comfortable, my mother had called me her little *pogácska* and Yutzi wasn't coming with us. I drifted into a deep sleep with a smile of delight adorning my face.

"The first snowfall arrived the next day. The pale flakes softly blanketed the sidewalks, the streets, the tree branches standing naked in the yard, the triangular edges of the fence posts; the flakes fluttered in a drunken dance in the air, falling in clump after wild clump until they found a place to rest. I leapt out of the big bed; the house was empty and I thought everyone had gone to Palestine and left me behind. I ran around barefoot among the three rooms of the house. When I went into the hall, I saw Yutzi standing at the stove in the kitchen, vigorously stirring a small pot of my sister's porridge with a wooden spoon, her body following the movements of her hand. I cocked my head the way dogs do in a moment of confusion, and then I realized she was holding my sister on her hip and playing a game with the chain that held her cross. Quietly, so she wouldn't notice me, I went to my bed and buried myself under the cold blanket.

"Most of the time my mother was at home, and when

44

she went to the market or to a neighbor's house, she took
me with her or left me at Bijou's. I always knew where my
mother was. Although I was a big girl, I was afraid she
would leave me alone, I was afraid she would give my sister
to Yutzi as a gift, I was afraid Yutzi would grind up our
white dog, Bokshi, who was going to have puppies again,
and she would fill my guts with the red dough, like the girls
who sat at the end of the long table at the laundry.

"Apparently I fell asleep, or fainted from lack of oxygen
under the blanket. Hours passed, the snow stopped falling.
When I opened my eyes the light in the room was growing
dim. My mother, my father, and Yutzi were busy folding
clothes and putting them in boxes. I was surprised because
my mother had already switched the clothes in the closets;
winter had just begun. Maybe they were making shelf space
for Yutzi's clothes? Maybe she was coming to live with us?
There was no room—where would she sleep? My sister was
sleeping peacefully, holding her doll. Yutzi was standing on
a chair, reaching a hand up to the highest shelf in the closet,
pulling out the embroidered white shirt that my mother usually wore for special occasions. She held the delicate fabric
carefully; when she turned around to step down from the
chair, she saw I was awake. Immediately she pursed her
mouth and widened her eyes; I knew right away I wasn't
supposed to say a word. After that hard gaze, Yutzi turned
to my parents and continued chatting pleasantly with them
as she kept folding.

"In the meantime my sister had started to stir in her bed,
and my mother went to her immediately, making comforting
sounds. 'Pitzi, Pitzi, look how wet you are, come, come to
Mama, shhhh....my itsy-bitsy baby.' She made a fuss over
my sister, who buried her head in my mother's soft neck,
her cheeks flushed from sleep, her blue eyes sparkling with

the last bit of daylight coming in from the street. My mother untangled a lock of curls from my sister's head. I watched this wonderful picture, my sister wrapped in my mother's loving embrace. My mother's back was to me; I smiled at my sister, and she smiled back and extended a finger toward me, calling, 'Diko...Diko.' My mother, father, sister, and Yutzi—all of them looked at me. My father came over first, pressing his lips to my forehead to check for fever. Yutzi stood near the edge of the bed, my sister crawled onto my belly, and my mother stroked my hair. I wondered how sick people felt before they died—certainly not like this. All the faces looking at me seemed happy—even Yutzi was relaxed. 'Finally the princess awakens. How are you feeling, Kitschi?' I'm a princess? I'm Kitschi? My sister is Pitzi, and I'm still small, too, my mother calls me Kitschi—a sign she has understood I can't be left all alone. 'Are we going to Palestine today?' I asked. Everyone laughed, what was I talking about, there was still time until we got permission. Many more arrangements had to be made, first my father had to travel for a few days, and my mother, too, next week. They had to finish the paperwork. They hoped I would feel better next week so they could go, they said; Yutzi had agreed to take care of us, and Bijou's parents would help out, too. Four or five days in all, why was I crying all of a sudden? *Kitschi, you're not a baby anymore, Yutzi will play with you, and if it's not too cold out you can go see if the Samush is frozen yet, last year you almost learned to skate on the ice, maybe this year you'll learn to ski.* They promised to bring me special presents, but I had to get better fast, maybe I could get out of bed now. *Come look, Kitschi, everything is white outside.*

"My pajamas were soaked from my waist to my knees. I was ashamed to get up; the wetness wasn't sweat. I lay there without moving, waiting for everyone to be busy again so I could take care of my embarrassment by myself, but Yutzi was making sounds of mischief, and with an *uh-oh*! she pulled away the blanket, revealing my frozen limbs and the wetness. 'Tsk, tsk, Kitschi, what is going on with you? It's not so terrible, these things happen, you slept so soundly all day, don't worry, get up and we'll fix everything.' My mother calmed me and Yutzi giggled and only I saw that she was happy for my misfortune. I wasn't dead, but I was turning into a baby who wet the bed, and if Bijou found out, all the children would know; Yutzi would tell the women at the laundry and they would laugh until the guts shook in their hands.

"My father brought a pail of warm water. He put it next to the fireplace, and I had to take off my smelly pajamas, exposing my body in front of Yutzi. This was hard, very hard. She sat on the rug on the other side of the room, legs apart, rolling a ball back and forth with my gleeful sister. From the corner of my eye I saw that she was looking at me, even though everyone knows it isn't polite to stare, I wanted to tell on her, *Mommy, see how she is looking at me, she wants to rip out my guts.* I was scared, but even to me this didn't sound logical—beautiful Yutzi was playing patiently with my baby sister, my parents showered her with affection as if she were their own daughter, she took care of things, helped with the housework, spoke politely with the grownups. ... Tell on her? *What kind of nonsense is this,* they would tell me, *come here and let's see if you still have a fever...* I slipped into my clothes and went to press my nose against the window. It was silent outside, the snow covered the street in a soft, heavy layer, the moon shone through a hole in the clouds. Tomorrow we would make a snowman, like every year, I wasn't sick, I didn't have a runny nose. Tomorrow I could wear my new boots and my red mittens, the air would be cold, it would invade my nose and my throat like the mint candy I once got from a man who came to talk about business with my father. Tomorrow Yutzi would go to the laundry, and I would convince my parents they should take me and my sister with them on all of their errands.

"And except for Yutzi, everything was fine. Bijou and I played with dolls, I knew how to make the sounds of a baby crying or a puppy whining in distress, and we had snowball fights. My sister was bundled up from head to toe, I carefully gave her rides on the sled, we laughed and had fun, I loved being a child after it snowed. Yutzi was at work, like my father. My mother checked on us from time to time and called for us to come in the house on time, later it snowed again, and the fireplaces were lit in all the rooms, a thick soup bubbled on the kitchen stove, and everything was clean and tidy. My mother wore her long, wine-colored robe with the white collar and her brown slippers. She read a book under the lamp with the transparent lampshade trimmed in gold flowers. My sister was worn out by the snow, and as soon as she was out of her layers of clothing and under her blankets, she fell asleep.

"I wore brown slippers, too. I went to embrace my mother; she put down her book and gathered me into her arms, kissing me many times all over my face. 'Come sit with me for a little while, you don't let me pamper you anymore.' It took a little while before we found a comfortable position—her Sophia Loren bosom made it hard for me to get my arms around her neck. I was big and heavy on her delicate knees, who did I take after? My mother was thin, my father was thin, my sister well-padded with baby fat that would disappear when she turned two. Maybe Yutzi was right and she had put some sort of curse on me, the little Satan who followed her, I would end up like her mother, a fat pink pig. She would take me to be slaughtered, and that would remove the curse. She was beautiful and good, the unlucky princess, and maybe if I just ate less bread everything would be fine. I didn't want to think about her during this wonderful moment when my mother's scent was dulling my senses. 'Mommy … don't go … don't leave me alone,' I begged, whispering in her ear. 'Kitschi, what kind of silliness is this, you won't be alone, Yutzi loves you and your sister.' I wondered why she wasn't paying attention, she had perfectly good vision. More than once I had heard conversations between her and my father. She used lots of words I didn't understand, and my father needed to think for a long time before answering her, and the neighborhood women also came over all the time to consult with her, and she could quote long, lovely sentences from the expensive books that only she read, and she knew what we needed to buy at the market, and how to fry the eggplant perfectly, and how much salt each dish needed, and which words to use to convince my sister to behave. My mother knew everything.

"I had my arms around her, my head sunk into the curve of her neck. We sat glued together, holding onto each other. With one hand I played with the fine curls at her nape that had escaped from the long braid wrapped around her head. We were quiet. I tried to match the rhythm of my breathing to hers, finally I managed to empty my lungs when I could feel her breath caressing my ear, warming the hair that covered the back of my neck. We breathed together. I was certain that if I stopped breathing she would keep breathing for me, and this feeling filled me with peace, like after a pleasant nap, a warm bath, or a good meal…

"'Kitschi, I met with your teacher and he told me that lately you've been behaving oddly—you're a good girl, he told me, but you don't smile and you don't speak up, you're daydreaming. What are you daydreaming about? It's going to be a while before we go to Palestine, you know that. Is it worrying you? You'll have friends there, don't worry about it now. And Kitschi, try to work on your attitude toward Yutzi, you're insulting to her and that isn't like you. See how nicely she plays with your sister. Yutzi is practically an orphan, her mother is very sick, and I'll never forget how she found you when you were lost, you could have drowned in the Samush or some other terrible thing if she hadn't found you…' I didn't want to ruin the magic that surrounded us, so I just said *Okay*, and *I'll try*, and then we were quiet again, I tried to match my breath to hers, the fire burned in the fireplace, whispering steadily, I was about to fall asleep in her arms, I was daydreaming about summer, imagining my mother with wings, floating with me in a blue sky with no top or bottom or sides, I wondered how we could be flying and standing at the same time, and why she wasn't tired, and how I could be so light….

"Yutzi burst into the house with her coat and her boots covered in mud and snow. I slid from my mother's lap and landed on my butt on the hard floor—or maybe she had actually dropped me, because she jumped up and ran to Yutzi, who seemed to be as furious as the snowstorm that was developing outside. *What happened? Come, warm up, relax.* Yutzi was crying in a loud, ugly voice, tearing at her hair like a villager in a funeral procession. She threw herself down, rolling from side to side, beating her icy hands against the shiny parquet floor, screaming, '*Jaj istenem, segits meg*, oh my God!' My mother took Yutzi in her arms like a stork spreading its wing to protect her chick, murmuring words of comfort in her ear. I sat on the floor next to my mother's armchair inside the circle of lamplight. My sister woke up with a fuss—she wanted attention, too.

"Yutzi's mother was very sick and needed to go to the

hospital. The government had not yet replied to my parents' letter. *Mrs. Leona, help me,* begged Yutzi. I tried to picture Yutzi's fat mother dying, and I didn't know whether to be good like I'd promised and feel sorry, or to take pleasure in the sweet taste of revenge now that Yutzi was suffering, or even worse, if I should start to worry Yutzi would accuse me of this disaster that had befallen her. My mother told me I was a big girl, I could stay with my sister for a few minutes while she went to see what could be done, until help arrived. I was afraid my mother wouldn't come back, but I didn't say anything. I just went to my sister, who was crying. My mother left. A few minutes later my father came home, and even though he had a long walk from the train station and he was tired after working all day, when he heard Yutzi was in trouble he turned right around and left the house again without saying a word to me, leaving me and my sister alone. We sat on the carpet in the large room that we used for both family and guests. One large rug covered most of the parquet floor. My sister was watching me. For some reason the rug caught my eye; with concentration I methodically traced the patterns. A wine-colored border two fingers wide, a thin black stripe, a thin white stripe crossed by black lines like the teeth of people in the pictures I drew. Flowers and stems twisted in a wonderful pattern in the middle of the rug, leaves streamed from the flowers in stripes and circles, each shape changing and turning into a new shape, burgundy, black, brown, white, gold, green—an expensive Persian rug, they'd explained to me. I wasn't allowed to walk on it in my dirty shoes like Yutzi had just done. Only in the summertime did they take up the heavy rug—my mother, my father, and Anna, too, who only came to clean and iron—hanging it on the wooden fence outside, and all the neighbors passing by would stop and marvel at its beauty. My mother would put a kerchief on so she wouldn't get dust in her braid, then she'd beat both sides of the rug with a carpet-beater made from a bundle of reeds. When she was finished, a cloud of dust was created with every sigh that came from her body. Then she brought buckets of vinegar diluted with water, and with a soft brush she gently scrubbed the silk fibers of the rug until they sparkled and gleamed in the sunlight.

"It was hard to clean the rug, and I thought about this as I traced the curling flowers between me and my sister. A strange trembling seized me, as if I'd been turned upside-down by one of the winding vines, a cold wind shook me from the inside, a cave formed in my body, even though I'd only heard of caves in stories and folktales, I was certain this cave I felt inside me was made from heavy whirlpools of mud, like the ones I saw once when the Samush overflowed its banks. I wanted to sleep, I was so tired, I was cold, and I was hot, and my sister was crying. I turned my body toward her, I didn't stop saying her name, then from deep inside the cave a clap of thunder burst out, drenching my sister and the rug with a pink dough filled with little chunks in colors that seemed to be absorbed into the pattern of flowers and leaves. My sister, who was almost three, opened and closed her mouth like a dying fish that has washed ashore. My last thought was that I was supposed to be responsible for her, but my sister kept disappearing and reappearing as I sank slowly into the warm dough that was closing around me like fresh apple strudel.

"When I woke up, I was naked from the waist up. Dr. Ontel, Joschka's father, was pressing his fingers to my neck and under my armpits, placing a palm on my chest. With his other hand he tapped steadily, his ears trying to interpret the echo inside my ribs. I was cold, and when Joschka's father turned me over onto my belly and started tapping on my back, the curls that fell on my face had a faintly sour smell. The sheet and mattress were soaked with cold urine. I turned my head from side to side, examining my surroundings in terror. Beside me my mother whispered, *Hush, hush, everything is fine,* but I was looking for my guts. I thought they were hanging from a rope, waiting to dry before being filled with the ground meat of Bokshi and her puppies.

"I heard all kinds of words: *sickly, circulation, low blood pressure, sugar, epilepsy, tests, hospital.* Dr. Ontel knew about my father's hemorrhoids, my mother's monthly cycle, and he was an expert in my sister's poop. He said I had to go to the hospital for blood tests. I thought I was dying, like Yutzi's mother, I heard *drága jo istenem* and *Kitschi.* My mother was crying, my father bit down on his lower lip, I heard my sister singing to her doll, *chippi chippi chippi choka.* My father's strong hands carried me to his big bed. I looked for Yutzi. Maybe I was thinking out loud, because my mother answered my question, *Yutzi's fine, she's gone with her mother to the hospital, she'll be back in a few days, you'll get better, my darling daughter, Dr. Ontel said you'll be fine, you just need to rest and take this medicine.*

"I'm not dead, my guts are still intact, and Yutzi is far away. I could again sink into a clean, dry sleep.

"The next day, after I'd fainted once more, I was taken away to a hospital that specialized in children's diseases.... My father said we would travel to Bucharest, Pishta would take us as far as the train station, but that really wasn't important..."

three

"My mother bundled me up in a fur jacket that barely buttoned over my woolen underwear and two sweaters. My father's thick scarf was wrapped around my head, I wore flannel pajama bottoms under my itchy wool pants that I hated, plus gloves and boots. I sat like that on the edge of the kitchen chair, my body sealed up, beads of sweat dripping from my forehead and blurring my vision, waiting for Pishta, Bijou's father, to come with the slaughterhouse truck.

"The slaughterhouse truck was coming for me, I was sick, the sick went to the slaughterhouse. The truck, like Yutzi said. Even though I recognized it, its color, the sound of its engine, and even though Pishta, my best friend's father, sat in the driver's seat, and even though my mother stood anxiously at the open door of the truck's cab, and even though the truck seemed to be innocent of anything wicked and evil, I refused to climb in and sit on the bouncy, brown leather seat. Bijou's mother held my crying sister on her hip, comforting her. All the children were at school, the neighbors were busy. The street was white except for the tire tracks of the snowplows, whose blades had turned the white snow into a brownish porridge. I saw footprints people had left on the sidewalk, naturally they were big and small, blurred, deep. I tried to guess which of them belonged to Yutzi. My mother was getting angry, Pishta was in a hurry, and again I felt as though I were about to take flight. Before I collapsed again I had enough time to look at the roof of my family's house melting into the branches of the tree that stood like a naked sentry.

"In the big hospital, they put me in the second bed to the left of the door. There were ten beds in all. The large windows had bars. It was the eighth floor of the ten-storey building. A hospital just for children. The regulations were strict: we could only leave the room to use the bathrooms and once a day for a shower, according to a schedule devised by the nurses. The children were listless. Some were bald, some bloated, some gaunt. The smell of Lysol was new to me. I felt as healthy as a horse, I had an appetite, thankfully. I was pink and chubby, a stain of health among the sick. My mother felt guilty for years for leaving me there. They took a lot of my blood in glass syringes. I stared at the floor the whole time, making sure my blood wasn't dripping into a groove next to my bed. My mother didn't understand, the doctors were not as nice as Dr. Ontel, always scolding me, insisting I lie quiet. Some of the other children slept, some of them groaned, tossing restlessly. They were quiet; they didn't act like any children I knew. Their visitors were sent home. According to the regulations, patients were allowed visitors once a day for two hours, even if the patients were frightened, crying children. My mother rented a room from a family nearby; this was very expensive. She promised me she would come back the next day. I didn't believe her. I was sure she was abandoning me. I was sure Yutzi had engineered this plot to get rid of me. The next day I was shocked when my mother's worried face found me beneath the covers.

"And there was a girl there, fragile as a baby chick, whose age I couldn't guess. She sat rigidly straight. Her hair was not like a girl's hair—it was just a yellowish-white down that seemed to float like a halo above her scalp. This was Marishka the artist. From her I learned that I could draw instead of faint.

"The doctors bandaged my veins and went to see what was wrong with my blood. The thin, smiling nurse who always patted the children walked by the big room at all hours, peeking in to make sure everyone was quiet. I cried and cried, and when I finished crying beneath the covers and couldn't faint from fear, and didn't see colors swirling together, and didn't feel any caves in my belly, I got up from the bed with its squeaky steel springs. With my healthy steps I approached Marishka's creaky bed and sat down.

"She was very thin, the skin of her hands nearly transparent—through it I could see bluish scribbles, and yellow, pink, even blotches of purple, as if the colors of the drawings scattered around her were staining her from the inside. Her eyes were two sunken brown holes. She didn't have any eyelashes, the only color on her face that wasn't somewhere between gray and white was her pinkish lips. From the corner of her mouth her pale tongue stuck out, decorated with little white dots. Her head tilted toward the same side as her tongue pointed, and when she moved her tongue to the opposite corner of her mouth, her head also leaned to that side, as if her tongue were helping her head keep her balance. It seemed to me that her bed was bigger than mine because she only took up as much room as a pillow, at the very top. I sat on the edge of the bed, at the end of a path of colored pencils strewn across the white bedspread. She didn't speak, just kept drawing with surprising concentration, ignoring her guest. Maybe she hadn't seen me.

'What are you drawing?' I asked in a whisper, so as not to disturb her, and also so I wouldn't break one of the hospital regulations — I still didn't know them all. She raised her head from her notebook and stared at me the way my teacher used to look at students who disturbed him when he was in the middle of reading a book, except that Marishka didn't have glasses, and her gaze wasn't threatening or scary. She lifted up her notebook and turned it around so I could see the results of her labors, and said in an older girl's voice, 'I'm drawing a picture. Isn't it pretty?' The page was crowded with lines, smudges, colors streaming into each other to make more colors and more lines. There were no blue skies, or houses with red roofs, or flowers coming out of brown earth, like in the pictures Bijou and I drew. 'Is it pretty?' she asked again. Yes, the picture was pretty. She turned the page and showed me the picture upside down. 'Isn't it pretty?' I thought this upside-down picture was pretty, too. I didn't say it out loud, but I nodded, and she carefully tore off a page and held it out to me. 'You draw something, too,' she commanded. I picked up a blue pencil, the color I loved, and thought about what to draw as I chewed on the end of it. 'Draw,' she insisted. 'Close your eyes and draw,' she said in the firm voice of a teacher. I thought this was a silly suggestion. If I closed my eyes, how could I see what I was drawing? I tried anyway, if only out of curiosity. With my eyes shut, I scribbled with the blue pencil, then felt around for other colors without opening my eyes, until I was completely frustrated. 'You're not drawing, you're doodling. Draw!' she said. She was so small and fragile, more so even than the porcelain girl with the goose that decorated the high shelf of the buffet at my house. She gave me another page and coolly turned back to her own drawing.

I understood she was giving me another chance. I closed my eyes and saw my mother's smile, the snow, the rug, the Samush overflowing its banks, Yutzi's hair cascading in waves, moving from side to side as she walked. I drew black lines, crowding together. Beside them I drew many more in sky blue, between them paths of red and brown and two purple circles above them, from which pointed yellow horns that blended with the green at the bottom of the page. I don't know how much time passed; when I lifted my head I felt the way I felt every time I woke up after fainting. Marishka watched me, her mouth forming a smile. 'You drew a beautiful picture,' she said, and collected all the colors in a small wooden box, where she also put the notebook, without having to fold the pages. She put the closed box next to the pillow she was leaning on, groaned like a woman exhausted by a long day of work, and slid under her blanket, disappearing. Her body made such a small lump in the covers that it seemed as though the bed hadn't reacted to the fact that someone was lying there.

"The next day, during visiting hours, I asked my mother to bring me a notebook and many colored pencils. For hours that day, between the needles and the examinations, I lay on my back staring at the ceiling. For ten days the doctors tried to solve the mystery of my fainting spells. They only talked to me when they wanted me to lie quiet while they did their daily tests. I said nothing, I didn't tell them a thing.

"From Marishka I learned how to mix colors. I never figured out the secrets of her drawings, and she didn't examine the contents of mine. Two days before my mother bundled me up and took me home, Marishka's bed was empty, neatly made, without her wooden box. 'Where is Marishka?' I asked the nurse. 'She's gone.' I was afraid to ask where she'd gone.

"To this day I regret not knowing what happened to her. Maybe she died, maybe today she has children. She taught me to draw...."

She gets up heavily from her place. I go to help her. She goes to the toilet, I wait by the door. No, nothing, I don't know this about her. She's always healthy, never even a little flu. And her drawings? It's true, I never asked her where she learned to draw. I thought that she was born with that talent, that it was her hobby. She's always saying to me, *You know me so well*. Know her? The last person whose name I expected to see in the newspaper? I haven't shown her: a small article, a moshav near Ashkelon, they didn't even mention the name of the moshav. But at the grocery store they shrug. *What a tragedy*. They ask me, *Do you know how this happened*? I don't know. She turns off the tap, comes out, goes into the bathroom, washes her face, drinks some water, returns to the living room, saying to me in a hoarse voice, *Let's keep going*. It seems to me she has gotten used to these short breaks; settled back in her regular spot, she continues as if she'd never stopped. For me it's difficult to return without interrupting the flow. I take advantage of every chance to ask questions, I say to her, *Yutzi I can understand, but how does this lead to the end*? She says, *I'm seven years old, it's not possible to skip anything if you want to understand the end. You're always asking, why didn't I tell you, why didn't I say anything? Is this hard for you to hear? My sister wants to be done with this lickety-split, my mother is in tears, you're running out of patience, maybe it would have been better for me to stay quiet, what's the point? The truth is hard to hear, who would believe me? The end, the end, just the end, the end doesn't explain anything*. She's right. Talking about it calms her. I need to be slapped out of my panic, I'm always pushing her with why, why. She sees my anxiety, speaks faster, it doesn't help. She pays attention to every detail—smells, colors, how does she remember it all so clearly? I'm looking at the rug, the same rug she threw up on so many years ago. Tomorrow I'm going to throw it out, even though it's not stained, for years it's been a reminder shoved under her nose. Outside it's dark, I know, the end of the workday. I can hear Yochanan parking his tractor, the cars of the farm workers pass by the house. The neighbors among them are sure to peek into our yard, everyone knows us. We were accepted some time ago here. They're certainly shocked, everything seems changed to them. *Boom*, everything is changed. I hope they keep going, they don't stop by to ask how we are. Yesterday they cornered me in the grocery store, asking, wanting to know. I told them to take it easy, it would be fine, she needs to rest, they shouldn't come visit, she needs quiet. I'm watching her, afraid of losing the connection, so she won't get tired and fall asleep. I'm ready to go on.

"At home, everything was normal. Yutzi still hadn't returned from her dying mother. My sweet sister was excited to see me. I suddenly felt so big next to her, she was like a doll come to life.

"Bokshi had five puppies in the cellar. Two of them froze, or just died somehow; the remaining three were fuzzy and full of life. We brought them into the house, and my sister and I took them into our beds, under the covers, until my mother caught us. I was sure she was going to be angry, but instead she brought us an old sweater and a box and settled them in a corner near the fireplace until they started to pee on the rugs and the parquet floor, and this was too much for my father, so he exiled them to a space beneath the shelves in the pantry, near the kitchen, where it was still warmer than the cellar.

"And there was the crow. We called him something like *Korom Fekete*, which maybe meant 'black as coal,' I'm not sure. We found the baby crow beneath the orgona tree in the yard, his wing broken. We nursed him back to health using an eyedropper to feed him lukewarm water mixed with ground meat, drop by drop into his beak. He had a box on the top of the cellar roof. We didn't know that after we'd touched him he would never be able to rejoin the other crows, that we had imprinted him. We thought that one day he'd spread his wings and fly away. He became part of the family, taking short flights to accompany us to the end of the road, then returning to his box. People raised all kinds of animals—rabbits, pigeons, pigs, ducks. We had four hens that laid eggs for our breakfasts and a rooster that made sure to wake us in the mornings, along with the rest of the roosters on our street. And we had our crow, this wasn't so strange. We took care of him and he stayed, the other children envied me and wanted to feed him, but he would only take food from people in my family. Yutzi didn't like the crow; she was afraid of him. The crow didn't like her either.

"I had violet eyes, and a black crow hovered over my head when I wandered around outside. One day he disappeared. We searched for him, we called for him, my mother reassured me, saying he must have found himself a wife and maybe one day he'd come back with his children. I knew something else had happened to him, because Yutzi told me someone had finally taken care of that damn crow, and I was next in line. From this I concluded that the crow's guts had been ripped out, because that was how Yutzi wanted to take care of me.

"Years later my mother admitted that one of our neighbors had shot the crow because of the terrible noise that woke him every morning at six o'clock, but at the age of seven I couldn't have been told this, so my mother told me something else. The crow never learned to eat on his own, and someone needed to give him pieces of sausage to keep him quiet. He was a skilled thief, managing to pluck out the glass eyes of my sister's teddy bear, and he pecked holes into the hard plastic cheeks of my antique doll with his beak. He wasn't able to tear out her marble eyes because this was the treasured doll Shatzi had given me as a present before they arrested him.

"Shatzi disappeared from my childhood just like the crow. He was a neighbor, he didn't have any children, and he and his wife heaped presents and affection on us. He was also connected to the slaughterhouse somehow, he was responsible for wholesale supplies or something like that. He was close to the meat pile, along with some hungry friends. The Securitate accused him of theft and put him under investigation. In jail he was found to be innocent of all charges, but he was a Jew, and the Securitate preferred Jewish criminals. They wouldn't drop the charges, so he hanged himself, and his wife committed suicide afterward. They told me Shatzi and his wife had gone on a trip somewhere far away, I was sure we'd meet them again in Palestine even though his wife was Christian, and that confused me a little, but the main thing was that they left their Great Dane, Teddy, in our care. He ate too much and went crazy when Bokshi was in heat. He was enormous, and Bokshi was just a little terrier, but they had this impossible love for each other, until my parents sent him to live with the family of Anna, our maid, who lived in a small village.

"Anna ... At the end of that winter events took place at a dizzying speed. I felt wonderful, I drew and drew, I didn't faint. I worried a lot about my sister, I watched over her, I played with her, I sang to her. My parents were very anxious and distracted, behind the curtains they spoke about the errands and last-minute arrangements before we left for Israel. I wasn't prepared. Whenever my parents were home I didn't worry. Yutzi was living at home with two of her brothers who had been offered work at one of the many factories that were beginning to appear in the area. They kept an eye on her the way Shatzi's dog Teddy used to keep an eye on Bokshi, I felt protected from her, she no longer spent evenings at our house. My parents still spoiled her with their warmth and attention, but her brothers weren't pleased with her connection to my family, though they didn't turn down the gifts. My sister missed her. I tried to change her mind about Yutzi. I played with her for hours, I sang to her. I stopped following Yutzi around. Instead, I drew.

"When the sun had melted the piles of snow, and turned the streets and the fields to swamps that swallowed our shoes, we spent a week in Anna's village, near Bucharest, so my parents could get our paperwork in order. I didn't ask about the urgent trip that had apparently been cancelled, when Yutzi was supposed to stay with my sister and me. I thought that I'd managed to convince my parents not to go without me.

"Anna's family's house had a hayloft they climbed up to by using a tall ladder that leaned against one of the building's bleached walls. From up there we could see the old Jewish cemetery, which was no longer used and was surrounded by thorny fields that bordered the pastures, whose edges we could barely make out. I was almost eight, my sister was almost four, and Imre, Anna's younger brother, was almost ten.

"Imre's grandfather took all of us children to catch storks. One Sunday morning he dressed in his good clothes and packed black bread, sausages, and a small, flat bottle that from time to time he placed to his lips, above which grew a heavy gray moustache that quivered after every swallow. He loved children, and I thought that if either of my own grandfathers were still alive they would surely be like Imre's grandfather. We sat in the bed of a wagon pulled by a brown horse and took turns sitting next to Imre's grandfather in the driver's seat and holding the reins. He whistled and sang as we jounced along a dusty road that passed between plowed fields waiting to be sown. This was where the storks came. Each child was armed with a cone of old newspaper filled with grains of coarse salt. At the edge of the field, where the storks' tracks were most abundant, he parked the wagon next to a tree, unharnessed the horse, and took out his bottle. We scattered with unmistakable joy, running around in the soft clods of earth, trying to get close to the storks, who circled and landed in large groups. Imre's grandfather told us whoever could manage to sprinkle a little salt on a stork's tail would make the stork stand still, quiet and calm, and then we'd be able to stroke the soft feathers on its neck. I believed him, my sister believed him, and Imre apparently just enjoyed running around with us. Once Imre took me and my sister to play cops and robbers among the graves in the old cemetery. One day when the grownups were busy and didn't need to supervise us, we ran wild, field after field, no cars around, playing secretly, and then Imre showed us his treasure—a collection of matches, a rarity for children. We collected dry twigs, and Imre said we were on a deserted island, captured by pirate ships. We lit a beautiful bonfire, and then we saw how a little bonfire can be swallowed by huge flames. The fire was put out with buckets of water, I don't remember how they got control of the flames, which had spread through the dilapidated graves in the cemetery.

What did they do to us? We hid in the hayloft and waited for Imre's grandfather to return. He climbed the ladder and the scraping sounds his steps made on the old wood made my heart race. His head appeared in the doorway of the hayloft, he glanced at Imre and at me; he didn't look at my sister, just shook his head from side to side and said that after dinner we wouldn't be given any desert, nor would we get to have the candy he'd been saving as a surprise for us. I had a good childhood."

Nights are quiet on the moshav. Even though the houses are fifty meters apart, I can hear Yochanan's television. It's already midnight. I think maybe this is a good time to go to sleep, to come back from Transylvania for a rest, until morning, then we'll continue. She needs to rest for a few hours, I need to pull myself together, get organized. I'll need to go out tomorrow, run errands. I tell her gently, *Enough, we'll continue tomorrow.* She doesn't object, takes half of a sleeping pill. I take a whole one. She wants to sleep on the couch. I don't argue, I fall asleep across from her, in the armchair.

The dogs are barking. Yochanan's tractor is going out to the field, six o'clock in the morning. I jump up from my place; she's still sleeping. Her eyes are closed, she's wrapped in the wool blanket, breathing evenly, a doll with faded cheeks. She should rest, she's sleeping, as I'm used to seeing her. I need to go out, just for an hour or so, she'll be fine, asleep. In my head I organize a checklist—only the most urgent matters: the Weilers, Form 17 for our health insurance, milk, dog food, do something about the leak at the Debretznys', my mother. As always, I'm the connection, going from house to house, to her mother, her sister, passing messages along. *You know her best*, they say. I do the pruning, watering, and planting, so everything will be clean, pretty, sweet-smelling. I go back and check every week, taking each season into account. What now? Roots are coming in, the soil needs tilling, outside summer is sparkling. According to the trees it's autumn, in our garden, seedlings, the rest of the building's a mess, the lawn is coming in nicely. Now concentrate on your driving, go slowly, remember the traffic laws, stop! Red light, the road is jammed, crowded, honking, go home, everyone! What are they all doing out here? Is everything okay at home? I hope she'll sleep until I get back and no well-meaning neighbor comes knocking at the door. She's so weak, maybe I didn't need to go out, I should have woken her up, told her I was going, promised I'd come back soon. I'm worried she'll panic, she shouldn't be left alone, I'll make a U-turn here and go back. I open the door quietly, tiptoe inside, I didn't need to leave her. She's not sleeping, she's sitting folded up on the edge of the couch, frightened, crying. *It's just me, I left and I came back*, she's wringing her hands, a weak smile catches the corner of her mouth. She's happy to see me. I approach her slowly, she doesn't push me away. I embrace her, she hugs me tightly for a second, and again turns to stone, lowers her head, avoiding my kiss. I say to her, *You're not alone, I'm here, do you want something to drink? Something to eat? You want to keep going?* She nods, I run to the kitchen: hard-boiled egg, toast, the cottage cheese has gone bad, cucumber, slices of green pepper, coffee, better she should have some tea with lemon, quick, before she loses her appetite, she needs to eat. I place the tray in front of her, she doesn't touch a thing, I knew it. Suddenly I remember her vitamins, the iron pills, she hardly swallows a thing, then buries herself back in the blanket, rocking a little. This is hard for her, I can't help her, she takes a deep breath, shuts her eyes, opens them. I encourage her with mute gestures, like a mother who opens her own mouth wide when she wants to feed her baby a spoonful of cereal.

four

"When we returned from Anna's village, Bokshi wagged her tail with joy to see us. And there was Yutzi.

"Two weeks later we left for Israel. I didn't know the time was at hand; the holiday in the village had filled my dreams with new visions, I had so much to tell Bijou. I felt older. Yutzi seemed like a woman to me now, and this changed her status in my eyes. When I'd been smaller I had related to her as though she were a big girl. She wasn't married, even though she was now a strikingly beautiful young woman. I thought she was doomed to the same fate as most of the old belly washers, whose smiles were already blurry in my memory. I wasn't afraid of Yutzi, and I didn't hate her either. When I followed her now it was only with my eyes, a sense of disappointment and sourness filling me, as if I were somehow being prevented from a kind of pleasure. And maybe only now I feel this way, in place of that girl. My parents were busy—they weren't a part of this. I was no longer terrified by every unusual incident. I thought, that's it. What happened, happened. My parents were making arrangements for our journey to Palestine, I waited patiently. It wasn't so simple to just leave, everything was hush-hush, a secret, *shhhh*, I understood this … Yes, we're going to Palestine but don't say a word about it to anyone.

"I don't blame my parents for what happened next, they had enough troubles. They didn't have the energy to follow my every changing mood …

"I didn't throw up, I didn't faint. I took good care of my sister, I played with Bijou, I kept my distance from Yutzi. One day, like a thunderclap in clear weather—and those days had been bright and clear, filled with springtime smells—in the evening, my father and mother sat down on the couch next to each other, across from the fireplace that still burned on cool evenings. They sat me down in my mother's armchair under the light of the floor lamp. I knew they had something important to announce, their expressions told me this as well. We're going to Palestine, I thought. 'Kitschi, Daddy and I need to go away tomorrow morning, only for one day, you'll look after your sister, and Yutzi will come and sleep here at night.' My mother spoke very slowly. Maybe she was afraid I'd be sick, like the last time when they'd almost gone. I was stunned. My father thought I had guessed the purpose of their trip and said that soon we'd leave for Palestine, but in the meantime it was a secret, and they needed to sign the final papers and then, if everything went well, we'd get our passports. I stared at them in shock; everything they were saying sounded like the distant murmuring of strangers.

"My mother knelt down at my feet and wrapped her arms around my hips, pressing her head against my knees. This felt so strange, my mother and I in reversed positions. I tried to count each section of the long braid that circled her head. I noticed some white hairs woven in, decorating the dark brown that was always shiny and fragrant. She had a soft neck with a small beauty mark under her earlobe. Her eyebrows formed two perfect arcs. The skin above her closed eyelids was smooth and transparent; below them were the brown circles of her gaze. The rest of her face was dominated by her Sophia Loren lips, large, heavy, red without any lipstick. The curved corners of her mouth ended in two small dimples, always hinting at the possibility of a smile. My father patted the back of the armchair and stood up as if released by some kind of internal spring, 'Na jo,' he said, as if agreeing with himself. My mother also stirred, releasing herself from this moment of indulging me. I remained seated under the light, blinking hard to fight back the burning in my eyes, which my parents didn't notice. My lips were dry and I couldn't swallow a growing lump of spit.

"The whole time I kept encouraging myself: *I'm a big girl, I'm a big girl*, everything would soon be in order and we could leave for Palestine, and that would be the end of my problems with Yutzi. *Let them go, I'm a big girl.* I needed to look after my sister. It had been a long time since I had heard Yutzi call me Satan and tell me she was going to rip out my guts. Her brothers kept an eye on her.

"'Can we sleep at Bijou's house?' I asked. I tried, but I knew it wasn't a good idea. Bijou's house was even smaller than ours, three children and a baby on the way. My mother turned to me and shook her head without saying a word, a signal that this wasn't going to work, there was nothing left to discuss, Yutzi would come take care of us at night, a simple solution, we didn't have to disturb half the world just because they were going to be gone for a single night. I was a big girl, I would draw, I would play with my sister. Yutzi would be busy making the beds and fixing dinner. I would be fine.

"My parents didn't sleep for days before we left for Israel; they had many worries. What was I going to tell them?

Don't leave me alone because Yutzi scared me with stories of Satan and ripped-out guts? I believed she was telling the truth, but they believed in her, too. They also told me I had an overactive imagination. Dr. Ontel had determined that my fainting was the result of my overtired and overworked mind. At school I was a quiet child, a good student. I had an appetite and this proved everything was fine, I was fine. They left. Early in the morning they left.

"They woke me early in the morning, kisses and hugs, and *Kitschi be a good girl, we'll be back soon, you won't even know we were gone.* My mother's cheeks were cold, my father was scattered, trying to organize their papers in a large envelope he put in his polished leather briefcase with the buckles that rattled with a metallic clink-clank when he walked.

"I got out of bed, my bladder full, urgent. I wanted to smile at them so they would remember me like that. I wanted to wake up my sister, so her doll-like face would accompany them on their way. Yutzi was at the stove, wearing my mother's apron, stirring the porridge. Everything had been arranged to the last detail while I'd slept. Cold air penetrated the house as my parents disappeared across the threshold. I released my bladder. I felt the wetness dripping down the inside of my thigh, collecting inside my slippers, soaking into the fur, overflowing and spilling into a little puddle, marking the place where I stood. I was afraid, I wanted to run after them, but I was wet, I was afraid that Yutzi would notice the warm vapor rising from my pajama bottoms. I raced back to my room, stripped off my pajamas, rolled them into a ball and hid them under the bed. Every time I heard the wooden spoon knocking against the side of the pot I knew I was safe; if Yutzi left the porridge it would burn and there would be nothing to give my sister for breakfast, and Yutzi didn't have anything against my sister.

"I crawled under the bed and took out the wet lump of cloth, crept back to the puddle and mopped it up, folding up the cloth and wiping, being careful not to let it drip until I had put it back under the bed. I grabbed a clean pair of underpants and a warm undershirt and put them on just as Yutzi appeared, heading straight to my sister's bed, ignoring me. I thought it was polite of her to give me some privacy while I got dressed. 'Pitzi, Pitzika, good morning! Who wants to come to Yutzi?' She sweetly coaxed my sister out of bed. I sighed with relief. She looked at me and just said, in a normal voice, that it was already late and I needed to get moving.

"Later, I sat at the kitchen table with my head lowered, the smell of the porridge warming my nose, and I had to look up to remind myself of the fact that it was Yutzi who had prepared our breakfast, not my mother. My sister was giggling and babbling nonsense, without a care in the world. Outside the light was clear and bright, a sign that we could expect pleasant weather. Yutzi took our spring jackets from the coat rack, handed me mine and patiently pushed my sister's small hands into her pink jacket, carefully holding the sleeves of her sweater so they wouldn't bunch up uncomfortably. She helped me thread my arms through the straps of my knapsack, and around my neck hung my lunch bag with its slice of fresh bread spread with goose fat. This she'd quickly prepared while I was putting my shoes on and tying them. 'After school go to Bijou's; I'll come get you in the evening,' she said, before turning toward the nursery school with my sister. I followed them to make sure she wouldn't kidnap my sister, or show her anything, until I saw the teacher patting my sister on the head. Yutzi wouldn't do anything bad to my sister, my sister didn't have Satan's violet eyes. The nursery school teacher would bring her to

Bijou's house in the afternoon; I would look after her. I hurried on to school, breathing in the clear, cool morning air, filling my lungs. I thought, something's changed in Yutzi, without a doubt, maybe because I'm older, maybe the spell has been lifted, maybe I'm not Satan anymore, maybe, maybe. These thoughts were running through my mind as my teacher wrote math problems on the blackboard.

"All day I played with Bijou and prayed to Jesus, to our forefather Moses, who I knew from Passover, to God, that just this once the sun wouldn't set. I prayed that my parents would return as a surprise, or just return; I prayed that something would happen to Yutzi so she wouldn't be able to come get me and my sister. But evening closed in; it was barely light outside when Bijou's mother crowded us around the kitchen table and gave us a treat of sweet *palachinta* filled with white cheese and cups of clear, strong tea.

"It began to rain, the clouds pulling a dark curtain across the sky. It was evening, Yutzi was knocking on the door and calling for us to come out; she didn't want to come in with her wet coat. It was getting late, she said, and we needed to gather up our things quickly and go home. All the while I tried to ease the sleeping fears stubbornly raising their heads inside me. She didn't pinch me anymore, she didn't stab me with her hard gaze, maybe it was over. Still, this was the first time I'd ever felt that my own house wasn't a safe place to go.

"My sister crowed with glee when she saw Yutzi, all day she'd been dying for Yutzi to come and take us home, to play with her, spin her around on the rug, tell her bedtime stories. The house was cold and smelled empty. I helped Yutzi bring in firewood from the shed, which was nearly emptied of the stacks that had been piled up at the beginning of winter. I thought, I'm really grown up—Yutzi let me try to light the fire in the fireplace in our room, and when I

74

spilled the ashes from the night before she wasn't angry with me. She walked through all three rooms just like my parents did every evening. My sister raced through the house, shouting *Yutzi, Yutzi come here*!

"Yutzi was busy in the kitchen, heating up water, then she undressed my sister, bathed her in a tub with the warm water, put her pajamas on, combed out her curls, kissed her many times and put her to bed. I stood by my bed in my underwear, resting a hand on the dresser and waiting. When she finished taking care of my sister, she turned to me and in a voice that was almost gentle said, 'You're not in bed yet? Hurry and wash up before the water gets cold. Why are you standing there half-naked, do you want to catch cold?' I didn't want to catch anything; I did everything with quick, mechanical movements until I could feel the blankets and sheets starting to absorb the warmth of my body. Only then did I allow myself to relax my muscles, but my eyes didn't close. Yutzi told my sister about once upon a time in a faraway land, palaces, a prince and a princess, elves and carriages and everything ending happily ever after. I wanted her to tell another, my sister had fallen asleep, I was afraid that my turn had come. I shrank as much as I could and made myself sleep. Yutzi tucked the covers around me, just like my mother and father did before they turned off the light, and went into the living room to take care of grownup things, later, quietly, they would sit on the divan whispering. Sometimes they listened to soft music.

"Yutzi had already left the room, I knew, because her scent had faded. Quiet. Why wasn't she bothering me anymore? Maybe she was going to come to Palestine with us after all, and she would start up again there, but now she didn't want to arouse any suspicion, or maybe she'd found a different Satan. I could hear her washing the dishes. She was making the pleasant, familiar sounds of a house preparing for nighttime. Maybe it was simply done with, and that was all. I was tired. The sound of my sister's breathing was soon matched by my own, which deepened and eased. I fell asleep.

"I knew I was dreaming because my father's gramophone was playing. On my mother's armchair, beneath the light of the floor lamp, sat Pishta, Bijou's father, smoke curling from the cigarette he held between his large fingers. He was sitting in my mother's armchair without a shirt or pants, and Yutzi danced in front of him, naked.

"In the main room, a fire burned behind the grate. The steel barrier that circled the fireplace and kept the embers from burning the parquet floor was open. Three logs were a part of this vision, two large ones with a smaller one propped on top. The two logs on the bottom were wrapped in living creases of red and white. In some places long tongues of glittery new colors burst from the creases, orange and blue and a transparent yellow. As the triangles of flame burned in the crevices and folds, a kind of competition began among them. The smaller ones that burned in the lower logs and couldn't seem to burn under their own power merged with the flames around them, which were also shorter and weaker. Thus they formed another, larger tongue that was able to leap straight up to the highest peak of the veteran flames at the top, and even higher. The smaller log lay in the middle, cloaked in the same fire that enfolded and strangled the small, burning, wrinkling embers of dark blue-gray that turned clear, dissolving on their way up the chimney, outside, toward the sky. Anyone walking by could easily have seen, on one side of the window, in the direct light of the floor lamp beside the lowered shutter, ovals of light inside, earthbound stars shining between the slats of the wooden blinds, arranged in fixed spaces one after another beneath a third. On the other side of the window there was a movement of orange and red lightning, pale, gleaming, ignited and then doused by the motion of the blinds. The smaller log surrendered in the end to the flames of the larger ones, the burning accompanied by the sound of a strong exhalation when little drops of water were released in angry black steam. After this struggle, the fire straightened and burned with a peaceful unity, decorated by the activity of the gleaming sparks. The sky was clear, the street was quiet, my sister floated peacefully in the world of dreams, I lay curled up beneath my blanket. Only my eyes saw through the tiny slit between the blanket and the white sheet.

"Pishta sat in my mother's armchair, still smoking. When the long tower of ash collapsed, scattering softly on the rug's burgundy border, he tossed the butt in the exact center of the fire, which now burned indifferently. He sat back as if a kind of paralysis had spread through his body. Only his tongue moved from side to side, wetting his top lip and then his bottom lip, making sounds in his throat like a man who smells something tasty to eat. Yutzi also licked her lips, as she did at the slaughterhouse. Her lips looked like butter cookies, crescent-shaped, swollen, coated with clear strawberry jam.

"The door to the children's room opened into the living room, a door like two white wings with geometric designs carved into them, squares inside squares. On the rare occasion when the doors were closed, these designs formed a raised, symmetrical pattern of a flower with six petals in each corner, one centered flower with two gilded handles attached to it, extending out and down as if they were the flower's leaves. When the doors were open, each handle took the shape of half a flower on the open side. From where I lay I could see that a gentle push on both doors into the living room would have closed the gap between the two halves and created the perfectly formed flower with its two gilded handles.

"In the space between the doors sat Pishta, and Yutzi danced before him, naked. The flames danced behind her, decorating her body with a costume of red, orange, and yellow light. She was enchanting, as if a good fairy had gently tapped her on the head with a magic wand. Her hands swayed over her head, and her body swirled with the graceful movements of riverbank reeds. Her bare feet were entwined in the nap of the rug; she twisted her hips in circles that matched the spiraling movements of her shoulders. She glided closer to the armchair, bending her body in the shadowy space between them to take Pishta's face between her branchlike hands, offering the two apples of her breasts to his hands. Something snakelike awoke in his body; he wrapped his arms around her torso, clinging to her flesh, moving his head back and forth, licking the drops of sweat that gleamed on her skin like fire. His head was trapped, buried in her arms as though he were caught in a thicket of vines. He breathed hoarsely in the space between her breasts, quenching his thirst by sucking noisily on one of her pink nipples, which shrank into a small point that he needed to grip with his teeth to keep it from slipping out of his wet lips and escaping. Yutzi suckled him on the right side and then the left as she moved her head back and forth, making sounds that were at once pained and laughing. She put her arms beneath his armpits and pulled him effortlessly to a standing position. He was a large man. The illumination of the fire had almost no effect on the dark color of his skin, which was as shiny and wet as if he'd just stepped out of a warm bath. Yutzi drew away from him, gathering up her hair, blowing as if she were trying to extinguish an imaginary candle that burned between them. She blew on her breasts, under her arms, toward Pishta, directing the air from between her pursed lips up then down. He reached out his large hands without moving from where he stood, taking a handful of her hair in each and drawing her near. She lost her balance and fell to her knees in front of him. In one hand he continued to grasp a handful of her hair, stretching it away from the pale skin of her forehead. In his other he held a black cucumber that had appeared between his legs and put it close to her lips. She tasted it with the tip of her tongue, licked around and around it and then swallowed it, almost all of it.

The room echoed with sounds made mostly of the letter M, as if they'd been stopped right behind clenched teeth. The cucumber went in and out of Yutzi's mouth in a steady tempo, it glistened in the firelight. Pishta loosened his grip on Yutzi's head, she slid away from him on her back, straddling his knees. He burst out laughing and asked her something in a bossy tone. She reared up toward him as if she were angry, grabbed the nape of his neck and pulled his head between her legs with a willful gesture. His head twisted back and forth between her thighs. In a choked voice she cried out to him not to stop. Pishta laughed again and stood up. They wrestled for a moment, until he collapsed on top of her, preventing her from moving, pressing her down, although she didn't try to escape. She fought against him with her hips, flipping him over. They struggled like this, Yutzi writhing, biting, scratching him. He laughed at her, sticking his tongue into her mouth and her ear. Yutzi yelped like a dog that's accidentally been stepped on, she tossed her head from side to side, biting her fingers. Her hands flew uncontrollably over her head. Suddenly she arched her back, her face crumpled up, and she closed her eyes tight. Her mouth opened wide with an *ahhh* that burst from deep in her throat. Then her body was completely still, except for her rising and falling breasts, which quivered like vanilla pudding with cherries on it. Pishta was satisfied with her swoon; he got up, lit a cigarette, and sat next to her, hiding the fire that was beginning to die down behind him. From where I lay, they seemed like a black stain surrounded by a red halo, like a dangerous rain cloud hovering insolently in front of the sun when it has just begun to set.

"I raised myself up to a seated position. I was beginning to think I wasn't dreaming. They were laughing and whispering. Pishta finished smoking and turned to throw the cigarette butt into the dying pile of embers that still burned weakly. Yutzi turned her back to him, lying on her side, resting her head in one hand, stroking the rug with the other. With a thick finger Pishta traced circles on her shoulders, then drew an imaginary line down her stomach and made circles on her thighs. Yutzi laughed and started to wriggle around again on the rug. Even though my room was almost completely dark, and the light of the floor lamp could barely illuminate the dim living room, her eyes met mine. Like an arrow she shot toward me, passing through the narrow gap in the doors without touching them. Pishta ordered her to come back, but she was already standing across from my terrified violet gaze. Her hair stuck to her shoulders in dark clumps, her breasts lifted and fell, growing and shrinking with her rapid breaths. I thought she was going to start screaming, her lips shrank into a pale noose of a scowl below her nose. Her nostrils flared as if she were an upset mare. She stood right next to me, her hands gripping the soft flesh of her hips; from the curly black patch of hair that grew between her legs dripped something transparent that smelled pungent and slightly sour.

"I knew I wasn't dreaming. Yutzi had an expression on her face that even in my worst dreams I had never seen, even worse than when she saw me by the slaughterhouse, worse than all the times she'd threatened me to keep quiet. I couldn't faint—she paralyzed me with her eyes, skewered my stomach to the wall as she stood there. Pishta called to her, she was distracted for a split second. I took the opportunity to escape, pulling my blanket over my head, she shrieked at Pishta to shut his mouth and turned back to me. She was nearly foaming at the mouth with fury, yanking away the blanket. 'Satan, you are dead now,' she hissed between her teeth. I managed to raise my hands and cover my face with my arms, my pajama top came untucked, my belly was exposed. I was already prepared to feel Yutzi ripping out my guts. I curled up and waited for the pain. Instead of ripping out my guts, she jerked away my down pillow, which was already soaked with my sweat. She pounded it, as if she were about to refresh the wrinkled bedding. When the feathers expanded into a single shape, she lifted the pillow over my head as if she were about to strike a gong with it, and with a quick, sharp movement she lowered the pillow over my face and pressed down and pressed down and pressed down with all her strength, she pressed that pillow onto my face as hard as she could. She wasn't laughing, she wasn't just trying to scare me, she pressed down with all of her strength because she wanted me to stop breathing, she wanted me to die, I knew this, even though I'd never seen how someone acted when they wanted to kill someone else, I knew. And even though this was the exact kind of situation in which I would have thrown up and fainted, I struggled to stay awake, I knew she was killing me, and like the cows who didn't know what to do when they were killed, I didn't know what to do either. I tried to kick my legs and move my head, but she was much stronger than I was, and I was already running out of air.

"I saw the white feathers hovering in a black hole opening up beneath my body. The feathers spiraled down peacefully, silently, without touching. I was already beginning to relax, when suddenly a heavy, prickly lump of feathers landed inside me and exploded into a million glass eyelashes. She released me. I was breathing.

"I heard my sister crying, I heard Pishta's voice nearby, screaming, *Are you insane? Have you completely lost your mind?* I heard Yutzi growl in response, *She's the devil, did you see how she was watching us?* Pishta said, *I'm leaving, get a hold of yourself. You want to make this kind of mess for us? Your brothers would murder us. She's just a little girl who doesn't understand, she didn't see anything, give her a little* pàlinka, *and she'll go back to sleep. You said she wouldn't wake up,* Pishta said scornfully. Yutzi screamed at him, *Get out of my sight,* meny a frantzba! My sister cried, Yutzi screamed at her to shut up. I breathed with my eyes shut, they left the room. I heard Pishta's belt buckle; Yutzi kept hissing, 'I'm not through with her yet,' Pishta told her to take it easy, the door slammed shut. Later she came back and quietly poured something sweet and fiery into my mouth. I must have fallen asleep."

five

"Slowly, slowly, I came back to life, I regained consciousness. At first I felt my body. In my mind I counted my toes—to this day I can still do that, imagine my toes separate from my body, one by one. Now it just seems stupid, even embarrassing, but then, when I was aware of myself counting my toes I knew I wasn't dead. I heard my sister running around, my parents' voices. I could smell Yutzi. Everyone was home. It was morning.

"A week later I left behind almost everything of my eight-and-a-half years. I took with me the love of my mother and my father, a feeling of responsibility for my little sister, the ability to separate my toes from the rest of my body and count them, and strength—at the age of eight, I felt very strong. At the age of eight someone had tried to kill me, and I had survived.

"'Kitschi, Kitschi,' I heard my mother whispering in my ear, her tears wetting the new nightgown I'd put on the night before. '*Drága jo istenem.*' I felt my father beside me; he was crying, too. '*Drágám, drága kislányom.*' My sister pushed her way between them. 'Ildy, look what I got, they brought you something too, don't sleep all day.' My mother embraced me, pulling the upper half of my body right out of the bed, then resettling me. The window was open, the orgona tree was decorated with tiny, bright-green leaves, the air in the room was cool and fresh, the fireplace in the living room was clean, with three logs in the middle—two below and one on top, the yellow rings in its heart wrapped by rough brown wrinkles.

"When my mother lifted me out of bed and into her arms, I was sure it had all been a bad dream. Wrapping paper was scattered on the floor. Yutzi was clapping her hands like an excited little girl—she had received a flowered dress made of an expensive fabric. Her eyes glittered with tears of happiness, she hugged and kissed each of my parents in turn, waving the gift in front of my sister. 'Look how pretty, Pitzi…don't worry, Ildiko will be fine, you have nothing to apologize for, everything is fine, I had to change the bedding twice, she threw up and wet herself, it's lucky Pishta was passing by, he peeked in to see if we were all okay. He helped me clean her up. Pishta is a good man, he wanted to call Dr. Ontel. She'll be fine, already she has more color in her face.'

"They had returned. They had our passports and exit papers. I wanted to show them how happy I was. I got out of bed and made an effort to be swept away by the excitement of their return, and by the presents: a fancy doll with eyes that opened and closed and real eyelashes and long blond hair I could comb with a brush that came in a jeweled box; a set of necklaces made from brightly colored beads, with matching earrings; pink silk underwear; shiny white boat shoes with appliqués of butterflies; a dress with lace ruffles; and chewing gum. Chewing gum from America, explained my parents, and we chewed and chewed. The sweet taste vanished quickly but the stuff stayed in my mouth, a rubbery plasticine that my saliva couldn't dissolve. We rolled the rubbery material into balls, and my sister challenged me to a stretching contest: We stuck a white lump to the handle of the closet and with our front teeth we pulled the gum into doughy strings, taking small steps backward. I won—I managed to pull the gum into a thin thread ten steps away from the closet. My sister's piece tore apart in the middle, and when she bent down to collect the threads they stuck to her curls and her fingers. My mother had to cut off a chunk of her hair. She told us that if we wanted more gum we had to promise not to take it out of our mouths. At dinner that night everyone got a whole orange for dessert, even Yutzi got one, which she took home. Before we went to sleep, my father said I wouldn't be going to school anymore because I was still weak and I needed to start packing—we were leaving for Palestine in a week, we had passports, exit papers, we could go.

"I had only one more week to hold on, and I had to be on guard for my life. Yutzi was a daily threat, if only she wouldn't finish me now. For another week I needed to watch out for her, I wouldn't let myself be alone with her. She was buzzing around the rooms of my house like an industrious bee, helping, deceiving my anxious parents. The neighbor women came crying to my mother, telling her how strange it was that we would no longer be neighbors, giving each other final words of advice, and mementos. Yutzi served coffee and butter cookies. Whenever she flitted past me I was perfectly still, just as I'd been told to behave around wasps.

"All week the hectic preparations went on around me while I stayed in bed. Everyone said that even if I felt well, it was better that I stay in bed and save my strength for the journey. Some of the children from my class came to say good-bye; others sent a letter they'd written with the teacher in which they wished me health and a good life.

All the children signed it. Bijou came almost every day and talked and talked to me endlessly.

"All I remember from that week is sitting in my bed while all the commotion went on around me. I thought about all the reasons that I must have been awake that night—that it couldn't have been a dream.

"I couldn't have invented those scenes. The breasts of the women I knew were like my mother's—huge, sagging, with large brown nipples like chocolate cookies. Yutzi's breasts were like two little clown hats with pink buttons instead of pompoms. How could I have dreamed of something like that if I'd never seen such breasts in the daytime? I wasn't dreaming.

"Many times I'd see the little whistles that boys had between their legs in the summer when we walked by the Samush where the younger children swam naked. I knew exactly what they looked like, and they didn't look anything like what Pishta had, how could I have imagined that Pishta had a whistle that looked like a black cucumber? And everything they had done—I had never seen anything like that, anywhere. Dogs did something like what Yutzi and Pishta had been doing, moving together like that, except without the licking, but what they had done beside the fireplace was stranger.

"I knew that old and sick cows died, but until I'd seen with my own eyes how they died I'd never dreamed about it, because until I'd seen it, how would I know what to dream about? Afterward she'd stood next to my bed and wanted to kill me. I wasn't sleeping, I hadn't fainted, I wasn't confused—I had seen the whole thing, I hadn't dreamed it. Neither had the cows been a dream. My dreams were like sinking into warm pastry. I dreamed I was going to the bakery to buy a round loaf of brown bread and I needed to take a towel from home with me so I wouldn't burn my hands, because the bread was coming right out of the oven, and once Bijou didn't want to do something so I dragged her by her braids and she kicked me in the knee, then we went to hunt storks and I threw salt on her hair. These were the kinds of dreams I had. Nobody ever danced naked in my dreams, so in the end I knew without a doubt that everything I had seen had happened, and that she had wanted to kill me.

"I didn't say anything. A child of eight doesn't think logically like an adult. I was afraid. In Yutzi's eyes I was the devil's messenger, following her around after the bad things she had done. I didn't tell on her—I have no proof that anything happened. I woke up to this reality as if after a peaceful sleep. The activities in my house made sense, we were packing up, excited about the unknown adventure before us. What if I had stood in the middle of the room and said to everyone, *Stop! This and this and this happened, please punish the criminals!* And if somebody believed me, what then? I preferred to remain in a place where everything was okay, and everything that was not okay I packed in my chest of paints between the pages of drawing paper.

"I understood that life can take place between two planes: on one side we got up, got dressed, ate, spoke politely, came and went, made arrangements, played, laughed, packed, got excited; on the other side everyone was by themselves, and what went out into the world wasn't necessarily what we kept packed inside our chests of paints.

"Yutzi was like this, too. It seemed like I could only be certain of my sister—her behavior concealed nothing. I wasn't even sure I understood the words I'm using now. At any rate I didn't speak, I didn't arouse any suspicion, I waited for time to come, when we would leave for Palestine and leave Yutzi behind, and this would be best of all—I wouldn't see her anymore...

"Parting from Yutzi was hard for my parents. She had been my savior, taken care of me and my sister, she was a wonderful young woman. My parents had a difficult time leaving her with her two brothers and dying mother. A wretched orphan, who would worry about her when the whole village said that she would never amount to anything? My parents would send her money when they could, they promised. In the meantime Bijou's parents would see to her welfare; I almost told my parents there was nothing for them to worry about since Pishta and Yutzi were already good friends. I stood back when everyone exchanged kisses and final words of good-bye. Yutzi came over to say good-bye to me. She came close, her back to everyone else. In her eyes I saw the same look—the look she reserved just for me. 'I'm not finished with you yet,' she spat between her teeth as she put her cold lips against my burning cheek, grabbing the hair at the nape of my neck with one hand without twisting my head back. In her other hand she pinched my cheek hard, until the flesh stung and my eyes watered with pain. My mother came to comfort me, telling me I shouldn't be so sad to be leaving because who could say, maybe we'd be able to come back and visit Yutzi, or maybe she'd be able to come visit us in Palestine, and she promised that we'd be able to write letters when we missed her. This is how she comforted me. Nobody noticed one of my cheeks was much redder than the other.

"I don't remember Bijou's final words, I don't remember saying good-bye to our old dog Bokshi, who we were leaving with Dr. Ontel. He promised to take care of her until her very last days. I don't remember the train to Bucharest, or getting on the airplane, or the Vienna station, or the large sleeping room in which a deluge of Jewish families on their way to Israel slept, more paperwork, the grownups discussing it nervously. I'm sure there were children there, I don't remember that, or flying over the Mediterranean, or disembarking at the airport at Lod. I was escaping, hurry, hurry, only in Palestine would I be safe. I felt like a fugitive.

"On the way from the airplane to the terminal I must have woken up, I saw people kissing the asphalt, mumbling words from synagogue, *shehechiyanu v'keamanu*, my father said we were on holy ground and even he had tears of excitement in his eyes.

"It was Hamsin season—a heat wave. The first night of Passover. At first I thought we had arrived at a furnace in Hell, the Hell of the Jews, not like in Jesus' church. This Hell had people who smiled and shook hands and helped us carry our belongings. In a large room there were tables set to honor us, with white paper and sweet red wine. People sang *Hava Nagilah*, and *Hevanu Shalom Aleichem*, we ate lettuce, hard-boiled eggs, matzo. The children were given sweets wrapped in brown paper, red candy shaped like a chicken standing on a white stick, chewing gum, raspberry-flavored soda. Later the families dispersed, we got into a wonderful car that had "Taxi" written on its roof, and my father sat next to the mustached driver, who had a little hat on his head like the black yarmulkes they passed out at our synagogue to anyone who came to pray on Friday nights, except the driver's yarmulke was knit from brightly colored yarn. He was a nice man; the whole time he kept saying *shalom, shalom* and *welcome, welcome, good Israel, yes?* in English, which only my mother understood.

"In Transylvania we'd also had hot summer days, but I'd never before felt as though I were breathing fire. We traveled to Ashkelon. On the way we saw big signs with all kinds of lines and shapes on them, and also words written in the Roman alphabet. I could read those: Rishon Letzion, Ashdod, Ashkelon. On the side of the road were yellow hills like those in the pictures from my card game. Farther on we passed trees that grew in a straight and orderly line, they weren't tall, they had dark-green leaves and millions of tiny white flowers, and the smell ... The windows were open, the fiery wind dried my lips and the inside of my nose, the smell, the smell was sweeter than any perfume I'd ever known. This was the Garden of Eden, not Hell, a Garden of Eden with a wonderful smell.

"My father explained that this was a modern country. *Look at these good roads*, he said, and the power lines, and the houses, every floor had running water and steel pipes, and the cars and trucks. We passed by stores with fancy displays in their windows, very modern, all the people were dressed in light, cool clothing. Some of them wore funny hats on their heads, especially the men, the children ran around barefoot in white undershirts and puffy blue underpants, everyone seemed relaxed and hospitable, and spoke to each other with many hand gestures. I thought, maybe this helps them understand each other better. The smell, what a wonderful smell accompanied everything. I looked for oranges rolling around in the streets; instead I saw fences of cactus with large, flat leaves growing alongside the roads; their thorns I came to know later.

"We had arrived in Israel. I quickly learned the colors and the smells. Next I tried to absorb my first words of Hebrew. Every night I returned to Transylvania in my dreams. After two months they told me I was a 'Sabra,' a native, like the cactuses, except instead of being thorny on the outside and sweet in the middle, I was sweet on the outside while inside the thorns pricked me ..."

I am wiped out, exhausted. Yutzi, she's a little bird planted in my brain, chirping, pecking, piercing my thoughts. Yutzi,

LAUNDRY

Yutzi, dear God, I can't think of anything else, *jaj istenem*, this isn't over, where has she been storing it all? I don't know anything about her. It's as if the electricity has failed, we're groping around in a blackout, getting pricked, stumbling, until we find the lights, even then it's still dark. When will she come back from there? She's a new immigrant; the ending is so far away. I call to her, plead with her, I'm not a magician, a Superman who can turn the world around. I can't rescue her. I feel more like a Cyclops, everything focused on a single point in my forehead, everything draining into it, absorbing her words, her pain.

She speaks without stopping, in a monotone, her body stone-like in the corner of the sofa, her eyes dry. I know her body language well, those frowns, the tone of her voice. She asked me to sit far away so I wouldn't be tempted to touch her, to offer her useless comfort. What happened, happened, it's impossible to change. She's speaking like a lab technician pointing out the contents of a test tube under a microscope, she's putting it beneath the magnifying lens again and again. Hidden materials are assembled and becoming clearer, sharper, much to my astonishment. I know her, know how to read her facial expressions, her body language. She's like a poem I know by heart. Now she's reading me the invisible words written between the lines, explaining to me with the logic of poetry, of rhyme and meter, like my sixth-grade teacher who taught us the poems of Rachel. I'm sorry I wasn't listening then, it was beyond my powers and seriousness to get caught up in a poet whose happiness was wrapped up in her great suffering.

I'm in shock. I always had a feeling we were transparent, layer upon layer, blended together like her watercolors, lines emphasized here and there, but everything clear. What did I know; watercolors aren't opaque. Suddenly she is peeling

91

away, revealing the white paper beneath that absorbs the liquid shades of her I know, opening up a hole, or a vacuum, or a box, or a sleeve, or a tunnel. She has burst free from there, and I remember she was always clear, clean and full of light, how could I have known? She rid herself of all the evidence, all the signs, every crumb.

She's in control, it's true—she's always in complete control. She's not the kind of person who likes surprise parties. She always knows who is in front of her and who is behind. Now I understand she works hard to keep things in order: yes, no, safe, dangerous, always alone. Can it be that she's always alone? Where am I? Or her mother and her sister? This whole time she's been asking me not to blame anyone, this was how things were, and there's no point in asking how or why. She lays out the facts like a pattern: if not her it would have been her sister, and maybe everything would be different. She says that in her story there's no room for the words *if* and *maybe*, but for me this is torture, because if I'd known maybe I could have helped her. Her mother sits at home on Queen Esther Street and cries; she doesn't insist on seeing her daughter. She didn't know a thing either, she is also tortured by *if* and *maybe*, I'll see if I can unburden her of some of that pain; I've never seen her mother so upset, so sad, so hopeless.

Her sister comes and goes. She's not used to situations that don't have immediate solutions. She found the best lawyer to help her sister, this lawyer Amnon Meiri, who said it's important to keep it together, we shouldn't talk about it too much until it's completely clear what we're dealing with, according to all the advice we've been given it's still possible to come out of this somehow.

I'm the connection. She talks to me, I pass it on to the rest of the family, they react. I tell her *your mother's in shock,*

she doesn't understand, your sister is angry, pressuring me, I
myself don't know what to think. Even an experienced poli-
tician would be at a loss, shuttling back and forth like this.
She hasn't touched her breakfast. The neighbors are undoubtedly already eating dinner; I'm hungry, too. Although
I've been drinking, my throat is dry. I remember I haven't
done the shopping, the refrigerator is empty, we have some
sweet-and-sour chicken. I miss her schnitzel, her chicken
soup with egg noodles, she's feeling sick to her stomach,
that's normal in her condition. She wants to wash up, good,
maybe a warm bath, later she'll have an appetite. Carefully
I help her into the warm water, I leave the bathroom door
open. I go to cook some potatoes, she'll eat them if I mash
them up.

six

She's wearing the blue robe I bought her last winter, she always says it's too dressy and doesn't wear it. The robe enfolds her softly, bringing out the special hue of her eyes, that's exactly why I chose that color. I haven't finished building the fireplace I was planning. It's raining. Some chicken soup, and still no end to the story. Outside it's a late-summer night, I open the blinds and windows—I need to air this place out a little. Nobody will come by at this hour. Her hair is still wet, her bandaged hand rests limp in her lap. I ask if she's in any pain, she says no, just her back feels a little twinge. I know she's suffering. A large purplish-green bruise circled in yellow is still painted on her hip, there's nothing for it; it just has to heal on its own, the x-rays showed no internal damage. She doesn't want to take any pills for the pain, she says this way it's easier for her to speak. I've been sitting across from her for hours, waiting for her to keep going, another long night ahead of us...

"In Ashkelon the taxi driver dropped us off in one of three new developments. A little wooden hut with cold stone floors surrounded by other huts. A transit camp. There were two rooms in the cottage, a shower and toilet, a kitchen with a sink above a cupboard. Little brown creatures streaked across the floor, surprising my mother, who began to shriek with alarm; my father danced around, smashing the poor little things. They made an unpleasant crunching sound between the soles of his leather shoes and the hard stone floor. Black eyes peeked at us through the windows, they belonged to brown-faced children with short, dark, curly hair. My father said they were from Yemen, that they were good Jews, and that Jews came to Israel from all over the world, they were all brothers, and this was a democracy in which everyone was equal, and everyone could do what they wanted. This I understood. An hour later, a man came from the Immigration Agency. He brought a square wooden table and four chairs, four steel beds with springs and thin mattresses, four cups, silverware, plates. And four scratchy gray blankets and bedspreads, my mother said that soon our trunk with our own things would arrive, and then we could make the house nice and clean and comfortable. She said now we could breathe free. I thought, yes, it's all over, there is one God who watches over all the Jews, no more Jesus, no more slaughterhouse, no more Yutzi.

"At home we speak about our new life. I tell myself, Ildiko, what happened, happened. I want to turn over a new leaf. A million times my mother says *wonderful, amazing*, and at night when she thinks I'm asleep, I hear the worry in her voice as she speaks with my father. I am also haunted by fears at night. We needed to be careful, to pay attention. In the morning my mother always wears her Sophia Loren smile, bringing me back from the Transylvanian night. She tells me to have a good day and sends me off to school.

"A white building stood in a large, dusty field. Round brown columns supported a large roof that jutted out over three gray doors—the teachers' room, the secretary's room,

96

and the room that belonged to the principal, Mr. Chaim Ben-Amram. Beside this building, spread out in precise intervals, stood ten huts. Each hut held four classrooms. Between the building stretched a bleached field of carefully tended grass we weren't allowed to walk on. My teacher's name was Dina, she was tall and thin, she had a short, stiff haircut with a ponytail shaped like the number 6 and twin curls over her ears that never moved, even in the wind. She changed her hairstyle every few months; my favorite was when she parted it exactly down the middle and it flowed down either side like a waterfall when the water splashes up to the highest point, pointing outward, swinging from side to side in her ponytail holders like a boat on the water in time with the tick-tick sound of her high heels.

"On Friday during our lesson on citizenship there is a stormy discussion that all the children participate in, shouting and rolling with laughter, and the teacher always says *yofi*, good, which I don't understand. The children keep moving around and swinging from their chairs and even the table is pushed from its place when they jump up in excitement and say some word that she again responds to with *yofi*, and turns to the blackboard to scribble lines and circles with chalk from right to left. She doesn't have a ruler in her hand. The children never sit up straight or keep their hands in their laps; they burst out one after the other to speak, without permission. This is all very confusing to me; I can't understand what kind of rules would allow them to behave this way.

"Batya sat next to me, she had already been in Israel for two years, she had come from Czechoslovakia and she knew a few words in Hungarian. I understood that the other children had chosen a new name for me, because my name was impossible to say in Hebrew, and anyway what kind of name was Ildiko? By a majority vote they chose my new

name, Chavatzelet. Batya explained to me that this wasn't
too bad, they had changed her name, too, as they did with
anyone who didn't have an Israeli name, and Chavatzelet
was the name of a kind of lily. This suited me, since we had
come to Israel in the spring, when the lilies were bloom-
ing. Some of the children had suggested Rakefet, but the
teacher said those were winter flowers, and other children
said Rakefet was too delicate for me. Chavatzelet was a
nice name, Batya assured me. I was just worried my parents
wouldn't be able to pronounce the "ch" sound, because in
Hungarian we didn't have letters that needed to be gargled
in the throat before they were spoken. In her kindergarten
my sister also received a Hebrew name, she too was told
that Zsuzsa sounded strange in Hebrew. The kindergarten
teacher gave her the name of another spring flower, Shoshana. Zsusza was actually short for Zsuzsana, which was
like Suzanna, which was like Shoshana, or Shosh for short,
although this meant "salty" in Hungarian. My mother said
we were young and we would adjust. She herself was not
adjusting. I said to my parents, *I'm not Ildiko anymore, I'm
Chavatzelet.* My mother said, laughing, *It's just a name.*

"Nissim Pitosi was the strongest boy in my class, and
he loved to beat me up. Moshe Kadosh was his happy ac-
complice. The teacher used to punish them by making them
stand in the corner, but at recess they'd beat me up even
worse, so I learned not to complain about them. During our
art lesson we learned about cave paintings, during the next
recess I got beaten up by Nissim Pitosi and Moshe Kadosh,
kicking and spitting and punching me and calling me by my
new nickname, 'Mammoth.' I didn't know how to swear or
to hit, so I just took it.

"My parents were worried about how we were going
to manage, there was a recession, and they also had heated

discussions about money. Take it from the Germans, don't take it—I suggested that if the money was owed to us, they should take it. My parents hadn't explained to me exactly what kind of money they were talking about.

"After school Batya and I would walk to the sea, at first I was afraid of the waves, I was afraid the waves that shattered on the shore were angry, and they whipped the sand back and forth to warn me that if I went in the water they would carry me away beyond the horizon. I was afraid of their power. The sun burned me until I had little balloons filled with water all over my shoulders and my mother had to spread yogurt on them all night. I learned to be careful and not step on the asphalt. And we had fruit and vegetables and chicken almost every night. My mother sewed yellow and orange patterns on the gray blankets we received from the Immigration Agency, we covered the floor with the big rug we'd been allowed to bring to Israel, and there were always flowers in a vase on the table.

"I learned a system of defense: not to get mixed up in things, not to stand out, to give in, back off, speak only when spoken to. Most of the time I looked for an empty corner and drew. At first I felt like I'd fallen from the frying pan into the fire. There was never any quiet. In Transylvania I was a stinking Jew, Satan's messenger; in the Garden of Eden of the Jews I found no shelter. My parents were busy, working late. I took care of my sister, bought the groceries, swept the floors. I was a big girl. I quickly learned to control what happened to me, I felt like I had strength, self-control. I learned to answer questions with sufficient, polite responses, to smile, agree, and not complain. I never complained. My sister grew up to be the ambitious one, and she got almost everything she wanted by stamping her feet. Even today she is like that, she has more friends than you can count, always dropping by; they have this loyalty that's incomprehensible to me. I love her ability to control others.

"Later we moved into an apartment and things improved. One night I heard my mother crying. She and my father were arguing again about the German money. My father was for it, why not? Everyone was taking it, work was difficult, we had many expenses. My mother insisted that she didn't want to go to the grocery store and buy a liter of milk in exchange for a liter of her parents' blood, she couldn't do it, she couldn't take their money. My father said idealism never brought anyone back from the dead, and we were alive, and that was the only important thing now. *We have children*, he told her, *we need to build a future for them and this will help*. I knew something about this war. I was in bed the first time I heard the siren. I was home sick with the chicken pox. I jumped out of bed, frightened. My parents explained that it was Remembrance Day for all the Jews who had died. This reassured me because I'd known about death for a long time, and as long as my guts were in their place I wasn't worried. Not until two years later, when my class was preparing for a Holocaust commemoration, did I really understand. I came home and—as my teacher had requested—I asked my parents if they had also survived the Holocaust. My mother said what happened, happened; my father explained to me about how the Nazis spread their ideas, and summed up by saying that his parents and my mother's parents had not come back from the camps, but he and my mother were alive and that was what was important, and we didn't need to talk about it too much because it was part of history. Then I understood that my parents had been in Hitler's slaughterhouse, and they didn't want to speak of it for the exact reasons that I didn't want to speak of my own slaughterhouse. Someone had wanted to kill them and the important thing was that they'd survived, just as I had survived Yutzi's wanting to kill me. This only strengthened the feeling I had that I wasn't the only one who carried hidden parcels of fears inside. I didn't ask questions, I understood that this was life: don't ask, don't speak of the past, look forward, keep your eyes focused on the future.

"In the end they took the money, and my father used it to buy a home, not milk. It was an old house, in good condition, in Afridar, an established neighborhood with many Hungarians. It had stucco walls, windows and blinds that opened outward; I could stand at the window and view the orchards that reminded me of the Transylvanian forests, of the open fields around Imre's house. Suddenly I longed for cold air and snow, but not for people. I didn't even miss Bijou.

"The new house was spacious, with a big bathroom, a kitchen with many cupboards, a refrigerator and a stove with five burners. Sabbath evenings were quiet, lovely, greeted by the aroma of chicken soup. My mother and father rested, reading *Uj Kelet*, the Hungarian newspaper. My mother had found a library in Tel Aviv that had books in Hungarian; every month she came home with four new books. On Saturdays she enjoyed her books, and my father tried his hand at gardening. He had started an herb garden in the empty lot beyond our fence, where he'd taken out the grass. I loved our little yard with its three barren fruit trees. And the cypress tree. I sat for hours at its base. I thought if I focused hard enough on its upper leaves, if I dedicated enough time and patience, I'd be able to see it grow, centimeter by centimeter. I was proud of our cypress—despite my father's attempts at caring for it, despite the strong winds that blew it around until it creaked, despite the burning sun, it kept growing. It didn't struggle or compete or show any sign of difficulty. It simply grew.

"After some time, when I'd gotten used to the logic of the world around me, I settled into a routine. It wasn't anything unusual. My mother would have said I was very happy in school. I was a good and responsible girl, a good student, I helped around the house, I was close to my sister, I was fine. At conferences with my teachers, my parents were told I was disciplined, a model student, I was fitting in well with the rest of the class, and in general I understood things easily, they said, they said, everyone said, this was convenient for everyone. I was not asked, but everyone could see I was fine. My sister was the terror. Even in kindergarten she wanted to rearrange the whole world, why were things this way and not that way. When she wanted something she fought for it until she got her way, and there was always something she wanted. To turn things upside-down, move things around, attack, change, go, come back—most of all she wanted things to be done the way she wanted them done, and she succeeded. She was brilliant, a little ball of energy that would explode often and without warning. I think my parents even encouraged her to be this way, a fighter, and between them they said good, it's good she's stubborn and won't compromise. At a certain stage, although this was much later, she tried to fight my battles, but I wouldn't cooperate. I wanted to be completely in control of my own life, and I reacted to her desire to get mixed up in it with hugs and kisses only, and all the while I told her not to forget that I was the elder sister and there was no logical reason for her to try to manage my life at the same breakneck pace she lived hers.

"For two years I was the punching bag for Nissim Pitosi and Moshe Kadosh, and I didn't understand how they could spit on me, how boys could beat girls up so hard, how Jews could beat up other Jews. My mother worked hard at a packing plant and broke all her fingernails. She didn't have time to read, she was pale and tired. There were other women who didn't look like this, they were dressed up, pampered, went for leisurely walks on beautiful days, didn't have to carry heavy bags, their faces were made up nicely, not red and sweaty. Not all the Jews were poor orphans. Just like in Transylvania, there were bad people in Israel, too. In Israel there were Jewish Yutzis. I had to be careful.

"At the time I thought there was something in me that attracted evil. My violet eyes, or my body, which was ballooning out of control, fat and ugly. My mother would say I was as pretty as a doll. Long ago I made peace with the fact that I was no longer a little imp who stirred everyone's affections. I lacked the desire to resist, so I never complained. I knew I needed to settle my problems on my own, I had to decide to think and act according to my own judgment. I understood this—not everyone thought and felt and spoke in a clear way. My parents had been hiding the truth about the slaughterhouse in Transylvania, and about Hitler, and maybe they were hiding other things. They weren't there when Yutzi wanted to kill me, and my teacher couldn't be with me at recess. I needed to watch out for myself.

"I didn't pity myself. I didn't know I could complain with these kinds of questions—why did this happen to me, why me? Even now I don't pity that girl. That's how things were, I held myself responsible for the way things had developed. I adapted to a set of internal rules, monotonous, with few changes. I tried to see without being seen. Sadness? Depression? Crying? What good would those have done? I loved to laugh, I laughed when my sister didn't succeed at something, and that was rare enough. She would scream and shout and stamp her feet and tear things up. This made me laugh—when she lost control and devoted herself to swearing and loudly expressing her feelings. I drew. Dozens, hundreds of drawings, I didn't think I was making art. I drew the way Marishka had taught me. I closed my eyes, the colors and shapes flowed from inside me, without criticizing, without stopping, without needing to explain. I spilled my heart onto those white pages. I spoke with the sea, with my parents; I explained to Nissim that it hurt, I told the cypress it was beautiful. Maybe a good psychologist would have understood that I wasn't just a girl with some talent, and maybe if I'd been forced to express myself in words I wouldn't have ended up where I ended up.

"In the end I took care of things, I was satisfied with the way I built things around me. My silence didn't disturb anyone. I didn't know there were other possibilities. I just didn't know it was possible to air one's grievances, that someone could change things. People thought and felt however they wanted, explaining it to themselves as best they could. I couldn't change this, but I could control myself, that's how I felt, that it was safest for me to be in control of myself and not to depend on the desires and feelings of others. My mother is confused now, she's busy justifying herself. She chose to live her life inside pictures that have been precisely cleaned of all ugliness and wickedness. This worked wonderfully for my sister, it strengthened her. It tore me to pieces. So I preferred to form my own conclusions, and I stopped learning from the experiences of others, and I stayed silent…"

I know her silences well. And I always thought they came from the same place as my own. It's not clear anymore, she's not letting me intervene with questions, even though I've told her I get lost from moment to moment. She said I need to find the way myself, this isn't within her control. The more she proceeds with the chronology, the more I am

LAUNDRY

assaulted by fears. Soon she'll be telling about me. She'll be
standing somewhere I didn't know existed until now, she'll
reveal what she sees from the same angle.
    Like her, I didn't like to talk. I didn't lie, I didn't contra-
dict, I didn't ask. Self-control—I loved this quality of hers, it
made me feel safe. We are lost, frightened children, how will
we get up tomorrow? She's dozing off. I don't even want to
offer to take her to bed. I cover her with two blankets, the
nights are chilly. I can't spend another night in the armchair,
but I can't leave her alone in the living room. I go to rinse off
the dishes. The phone is practically bursting with messages,
seven from her sister, *Are you both crazy? You want to kill
Mother? Call right away! Oh, knock some sense into my sister's thick head and tell her tomorrow I'm coming over there,
and Amnon says he has to speak with her as well, there's not
much time, hello? Hello? At least call Mother! Have you
forgotten that we're a family?* I have no choice—tomorrow
I'll go to her mother. I won't ask permission. I've decided
to tell her mother the whole story, about Yutzi, about the
slaughterhouse, and there's more—she should know that I
don't know everything yet, poor Mrs. Rott. But she needs
to know, I can't bear this alone anymore. I need to give her
sister an update, she'll tell Amnon, or maybe not, maybe
it's better not to. There's no hot water, I forgot to tell Messiah to check the water heater. I need to explain to him so
he won't be afraid to come by. Maybe he's already heard.
I wash up, shaking with cold, crying quietly so she won't
hear. How do we go on? How do we sleep? Where will I lay
my head down? I take another blanket from the chest and
curl up on the floor next to her. She's sleeping, that's what's
important, she's sleeping. So am I.
    I wake up to the delicate sensation of her caressing my
forehead. I open my eyes, see her, she is lying curled up on

the couch, her bandaged hand reaching toward me, she's stroking my forehead, playing with my hair. Her touch is such a relief to me, good morning, my woman. She's relaxed, I'm surprised, but instead of being happy I'm frightened: Maybe she's gone mad? No, she's as sad as she was yesterday, her gaze is unfocused. She gets up suddenly, goes to the bathroom, the magic vanishes, there's been no miracle. She comes back, sits on the edge of the couch. Another day lies ahead of us. I go to the kitchen. I have no choice—I need to get groceries today. They'll ask questions; I don't care. Coffee, tea with mint, she agrees to a bite of toast, quietly we sit down, like any normal morning. *I'm going to Ashkelon, to your mother, will you be okay? I need to reassure them, at any rate, you know they're very worried about you, your sister is out of her mind.* She says, *I'm fine, really, go, go, I'm fine.* Already I can't leave the house, the moment the screen door shuts behind me I'm seized with fear, what else can happen when my back is turned? No, no, I tell myself to relax, it's all over, I'm beginning to understand, I need to explain it to the others. I'll go to her mother; like an urgent telegram I'm bringing all these images she's filled my ears with.

seven

I'm barely at the threshold and Mrs. Rott falls into my arms, weeping. She grabs me in a strangling, unfamiliar embrace and won't let go. She trembles and sobs in my arms for a long time. Over her shoulder I can see a pillow and blanket on the couch; she hasn't been sleeping in her own bed either. The blinds are drawn shut here, too. Her sobs grow weaker, her cries farther apart, she loosens her grip, her hands fall to her sides. Suddenly she is like the Mrs. Rott I know. She takes a dozen tiny steps in no particular direction, stops, turns around, clasps her hands together, pinches her lips tight, pushes me into the living room, closes the door quietly behind us as if someone were sleeping in the other room, and all the while she's talking on and on in her broken Hebrew.

"Good you are here, *jaj istenem*, I have nothing patience, you are a gold man, *nu*, sit, sit. I bring a little like this of something for the mouth, maybe a little cup? At this time, maybe something alcohol? No, you're to driving, something more easier, sit, please you don't hurry, *nu*, sit. Soon I bring you, you saw my daughter, she say something? My God, *istenem*, you know her, what you say on my daughter? How this happened? I stick a knife in my stomach, I die myself, if I am knowing to tell why she is like this. She was a doll, you

know, I took her in a stroller like a doll. This people saw
down and said what a doll baby she is, good, she is eating
good, she is sleeping good, *nu*, what you are to saying with
my daughter? Why she is like this?"

I ask her to sit next to me, I take her hands in mine, this
makes her burst into tears again. She takes a tissue from
her pocket. I tell her in a quiet, calm voice, *Ildiko has been
telling me about Transylvania.* Mrs. Rott is completely silent. I recite everything I have heard, without stopping, in a
monotone. A long, trembling groan drains from her lungs,
she inhales as if she's swallowing every word, her eyes dart
around, when I'm quiet she clutches my shoulders, weeping,
letting go, speaking, and then beginning the cycle again.

"I am mother no good! I am mother no good! I don't see
with my eyes my daughter has difficult. *Istenem* ... I am not
to speaking bad about my daughter, she is never lying, she's
quiet, yes, not to speaking too much, now she is to speaking you stories, I don't know. Yutzi? *Istenem*, how Yutzi?
She was sick, so sick. She had much water in her body, not
pee good. You know how much *protectzia* was for we take
her to hospital in Bucharest? *Nu*, this is Communism, no
money. My husband was much money all taken by Communism, I am no *princessa*, but Communism doesn't loves
people like this, only to work in the ground, the Securitate
ask my husband, where is money, where is money, my husband not has money, no money in Switzerland bank. How
much sorrows, they think we have money, that my husband
hides the money, so they don't to let us go to Israel, no, no,
my family are good people, father mother, this is the family
of Meyer Changre, very famous my family. Communism
doesn't love people with much money, the Securitate wants
simple people, I to give my books, necklaces, everything to
Hell, after I to go to Auschwitz with my family, neighbors to

steal everything in the house, we were finished with no house. I said I am the daughter of Meyer Changre, they *shhhh* ... you don't to speak more, now Communism everyone same thing. I was a girl, alone, alone, not crying, this is hard to tell the story in Hebrew, I to speak Hungarian, good? I want you to understand very well ...

"I met her father on the train that collected the surviving souls scattered across Europe after the camps were liberated. I sat next to the opening of the train car. The wind was cold and he sheltered me in his bony arms. After we'd traveled for eight hours, the train stopped on the outskirts of an abandoned village, the residents had fled in fear of the oncoming force of the liberation. They were afraid the Americans would take revenge on them for what they'd all known. We were hungry and we searched for food, he wouldn't let go of my hand. I was very weak, still dressed in my striped uniform and of course I was bald. We broke into one of the houses that still had some heat in its walls. There were embers still burning in the fireplace, the pantry was full of good things, I started to wolf down a leg of smoked pork, but he snatched the food from my mouth and allowed me only a bit of sweet tea and bread spread with jam. He saved my life, who knows how many people died because they gorged themselves with food after years of starvation, the food simply killed them. We stayed there almost a week, until the train was full again, ready to move along with the survivors. He bathed me, fed me, kept me warm, took care of me like a big brother. We didn't speak much, what was there to talk about? When my stomach was full I saw that he was a young man, handsome, such eyes he had. His gaze went right through my skin. At night, when the cold wind blew through the cracks in the wooden shutters, he kept my spirits up with stories of the famous Rott family, known all over Transylvania. They had money, fields, and barns, storerooms full of grain and three automobiles. He saw his parents and three sisters led to the building with the chimney, and he was the heir to all this property. He wanted me to come with him. I didn't know anything of the fate of my own family, and began to have the disturbing thought that my family would not look kindly upon this refugee who had found me, even if he was the son of wealthy traders. Such nonsense swirled around in my head. I thought about the dramatic scenes between us if I convinced my family to allow me to truly love this man who had rescued me. But nothing remained of them. My status, his property, the Communists took it all, I had no home. I traveled to my town and he waited for me. From that moment we were together.

"When we returned from the camps, young and alive, we had only one thing in mind—to be happy. We were a young couple and the government settled us in the house where our daughters were born. We played music, sang, danced, happy that it was all over. I never looked back. He was also very practical. We started over again, from the beginning. We had love for each other, love for life, this was our strength. Our love grew with our two daughters. We weren't Zionists. For us Israel was Palestine, with sand and camels and women carrying jugs of water on their heads. Until we started to hear of the offers of the Jewish Immigration Agency that was paying bribes to get permission to leave for the few Jewish families who remained. We were interested. They were making my husband's life impossible. He was investigated endlessly in the cells of the Securitate—they watched him, threatened him, made sure he lost his job, ensured that he could only find work in a shoe factory, barred him from the university on charges that he was against the government. They thought his parents had smuggled money into Swiss banks. You think I needed to talk about these troubles? To burden a little girl with stories of atrocities? I never said I'd been in Auschwitz, but everyone knew we were Jews and what had happened to us. Why did I need to keep my girls in this kind of prison? We thought about the Jewish state, we heard stories that oranges rolled down the streets, that there was plenty for everyone, and most important, freedom. The same freedom we'd hoped to teach to our daughters.

"Although the government wasn't pleased with our new interest in the Jewish state, they weren't anti-Semitic. Kill me if I ever manage to understand from where my daughter's stories come from. Satan, guts, Jesus? On our street there were no anti-Semites. We lived in peace with the gentiles; they were good neighbors. We were young and all the *shmoy-yisroel* meant nothing to us. My daughter went to church with her friends on Sunday, who thinks of such things? I was always careful to say it was all a matter of belief, the Christians had Jesus, and the Jews something else. She played with her friends. She never said anything about Jesus, or that he wouldn't watch over her. Satan and Yutzi? Yutzi brought her home very sick, I'll never forget that day. My husband and I looked for her for hours. A girl that young gone missing, what could we have thought? We were afraid she'd been kidnapped by gypsies, that she'd somehow managed to get all the way to the Samush and fallen into the water. It's possible that she'd wandered to the slaughterhouse and seen something. Good Lord, I'm her mother, people used to come and tell me all their sorrows, and we helped them all, all of them. Yutzi was a poor girl, miserable. Her brothers were hooligans, her father killed himself. He was crazy, as was her mother. I helped her, and you're telling me my daughter was suffering? She was a sick girl! These are all fantasies from a high fever, the best doctors examined her.

They said she was epileptic, it was not so severe, she would be fine, but she was sick. She had seizures, she used to faint and vomit, a sick child, I was ready to sell my soul to whoever could cure her. Her father got down on his knees and begged them to help her, but she got better. When we came to Israel, she got better. The weather, we thought, it had a good effect on her. You say all these things are true? I was blind? Yutzi and Pishta? And after? Everything that happened after? How could she keep this all inside and never say a word? Is this possible? Am I not her mother? Don't I know her? Can I say she's right, and that all of it is true? What is true? These things she alleges happened during her childhood? And now? She's a grown woman, not a helpless little girl. Why didn't she come to me? Why didn't she go to her sister? Why didn't she pound on the table, make a fuss? We're here, in a democracy, a free country, everyone loves her. Suddenly she speaks, she tells you everything, insists that she's responsible for a disaster. No one understands how this happened, or why, why does she insist? Never mind me, but she and her sister were always like a single soul. Ask her sister if she understands. Maybe she wants attention? No, no, she always wanted to be left alone, and now to pay such a price for it, if this is all true. No, I can't think about this..."

Another story. I tell Mrs. Rott about the childhood of her firstborn daughter, and how does she react? Yet another story I didn't know. It's true I never asked, and Mrs. Rott is not the kind of person who talks much about herself. She's quiet and shy, she likes things to be clean, fresh flowers decorating every corner of the house.

I feel almost like an archaeologist, chipping away at a widening pit, descending into it, into another room, a maze. I don't understand anything. I didn't know any of it, violating the oath of years of silence. In my family we always screamed the truth in each other's faces. This did not make me any happier, though at least we knew each other's sore points; her family is partitioned, everyone nursing his own pain. Her mother wants to talk, too, about herself. She explains, she justifies, maybe this is an opportunity to discover everything, to weep together. I don't know what the connection is, what to do with all these stories, I'm not a mailman. It's already noon, I have to get going, Mrs. Rott hurries to the refrigerator, packs me a nylon sack of food, says, "This is a little something warm to put in stomach, now there is no mind for to cook, go, go, sweetheart. I'm fine, sorry I'm to talking this way, you don't need my story on your head also, there is enough with my daughter, go, she isn't good to be alone. Zsuzsi will come soon, I to speak with her on her sister, never mind I am cry, this good, everything outside now, you are gold for my daughter, this is luck for everyone, you are strong, later you come back again, go, my daughter need you, *Istenem, istenem, segits meg.*"

eight

A twenty-minute drive between Ashkelon and the moshav. Where do I fit in? She's on the couch, facing away from me. Even if she weren't in pain, I doubt she'd have the energy to greet me. Her mother is weeping; her sister will take care of her. I give her a short report, she reacts with a shrug. I know she cares, in any other situation she'd rush to be with her mother if she heard she was upset. I can tell she's waiting for me to sit down, to forget about everyone else; she wants to continue speaking. There's an order to her story, a chronology, she's not giving up, she's not skipping over anything. She's growing up in front of me, childhood, adolescence. When will she finally become the woman I know? Time has no meaning—five hours in the past, a half hour in the present. I want to get to the future already. She waits with the new expression on her face that I've come to know over the past few days, ready to continue from the exact spot where she left off a few hours ago. I need to set Mrs. Rott aside, make sure the doors are locked and the phone's off the hook. Some tea, warm up a bowl of soup, she needs to eat something, or at least drink. I rinse my face, comb my fingers through my hair, sit down, get up—I want to touch her, what can I do? What can I do? I take a deep breath. We dive back in.

"In high school I understood that the formula for a simple, carefree life was to be in the middle. Something pushed me to the side, something heavy, invisible, and unknown, like a hidden speed bump. Back then I thought a lot about Yutzi, naturally: adolescence, the questions, the wondering. I sat in my room for hours, scratching out pages of colorful drawings, color on top of color, layer upon layer. I wanted to tear the picture of her out of my memory. Again and again I returned to those images. Sometimes I was angry and hated Yutzi, sometimes I was angry and hated myself. I thought maybe in the end I was just a little brat of a girl, and Yutzi simply didn't have any patience for me, maybe she had the right to want to rip out my guts. Something wasn't normal in my head. I was delusional. I thought that if I kept asking so many questions I'd lose my mind completely. My mother had been in Auschwitz. She smiled calmly; she'd risen above it. I needed to be calm, too. Was it really so terrible? Maybe she hadn't actually tried to kill me. Maybe I was sick. In my adolescence these fears would seize me in the middle of the day. I could control everything except my fears. I would go to public parks, watch children playing in the sandboxes, wandering about, kicking a ball around, strolling along in the care of older people. I tried to guess who was just pretending that everything was fine. Only at home, in my room, alone, did I feel safe.

"In high school there was a general aim toward the average, toward fitting in with everyone, being neither a genius nor an idiot, neither loud nor silent, in the middle. I sat on the side, quiet, with too much of everything: I was fat and had more pimples than everyone else. On tests I always received the highest grades, my answers were always the most complete. I lived too far away and my drawings were too strange — the more I tried to remain hidden, the more I stood out. Everyone was in the middle, I was on the sidelines, in a corner, where I stuck out like a fly on a white wall. I was so passive.

"At the age of seventeen I floated inside a bubble of armor. Nothing came in and nothing went out. I thought about death. At night I used to press a pillow over my face like Yutzi had done years before; in the mornings I'd wake up with a headache. I used to cross busy streets very slowly. In the evenings I went to the central bus station in Tel Aviv, wandered between the platforms, and took the last bus home. I wanted to define my fears, I wanted to know if I was afraid to die. Was that what this was about, was this why I'd kept these memories of Yutzi and the slaughtered cows? During the rare opportunities when I found myself home alone, I used to search through all the rooms in the house, as if someone had hidden the answers in the drawers, in the kitchen, in the yard, in the shed, next to the cypress. I burrowed and dug without knowing exactly what I hoped to find. Everything in the house was always clean, neat, pressed, numbered. I opened the medicine cabinet and took out one pill from every bottle, so it wouldn't seem like anything was missing: one aspirin, one pill for diarrhea, one for constipation, an antibiotic, a spoonful of cough syrup, a little something for heartburn. I washed it all down with half a glass of cognac. This was foolish—half an hour later I vomited everything up in the hallway. My parents came home just as I finished cleaning it up. They put me straight to bed, took my temperature. My mother said there was a virus like this going around and ran to the medicine cabinet to get me another pill. Two days later my father went to Haifa for some training; before he left he insisted I stay in bed for at least another day, even if I was feeling better, because viruses like this one could have complications if I didn't recuperate completely. So I stayed home, my sister went to school, and my mother sat in her armchair and read a book—after she'd finished the housework, of course. All morning I drew, and then ripped up the pages. I went to throw them away in the garbage under the kitchen sink. I drank a glass of water; my mother said, *Good, drink a lot of water.* I went to the bathroom and rinsed my hands. I did this three or four times. My meandering through the house was natural for someone in my condition; my mother acknowledged me with a smile every time I passed by.

"I went into the bathroom, looked through my father's shaving things, which were always on the right-hand side of the plastic cupboard above the sink. He had taken everything to Haifa with him. The empty corner contained only three rusty circles. I went to the kitchen, put an orange on a plate, opened the cutlery drawer, took out a knife, and went to my room. My mother gave me an approving glance and said, *Good, good, oranges are full of vitamins.* I closed the door behind me, sat down on my bed, bared my left wrist, guided the knife along the blue lines that were the easiest to see, and pressed down. Nothing happened. I made a sawing motion. The skin turned red, stripe after stripe, like the scrapes on my sister's knee after she fell hard. The knife stayed clean. I returned it to the kitchen, took another orange, and took the meat knife, too. My mother said, *Good, another orange, just be careful that you don't get a stomachache.* I went back to my room, to the bed, to my wrist, to the blue stripe beneath the skin. I guided the knife, pressing hard, and a red drop welled up, as if I were having an ordinary blood test. The drop swelled until it broke open and a thin line trickled along the groove left by the first knife. It looked like a little stream of red paint flowing from beneath my palm onto the blue cloth of my jeans, spreading out in a dark stain. Suddenly I was worried about the bedspread, which my mother had sewn for me by hand. I grabbed my sketchpad to catch the dripping. The paper looked like the decorations we made at Chanukah with the candle wax. I moved my hand around, drawing with the drops. I found this amusing. My sister came home, slamming the door behind her as always; my mother called me to come eat lunch. I wasn't afraid to die — it was something else. I bandaged my hand with a strip of a rag that I used for cleaning my paintbrushes, put on a long-sleeved shirt, changed into clean pants and went to the kitchen. My mother put her hand on my forehead and said, *No fever, but if you're cold it's a sign that you're still sick.* I'd folded up the page and stuck it in with the rest of the drawings that I'd decided to keep for the time being, on a shelf between my books and notebooks. I must have thrown it away at some point when we were doing our spring cleaning before Passover. I wasn't afraid to die, like I was when I was a little girl and Yutzi almost killed me. So what was I afraid of now? There were dozens, hundreds of Holocaust survivors; most of them didn't live in a constant state of fear. It wasn't death — death ended everything. It was the moment before, the powerlessness. It wasn't fear, it was powerlessness, the anger and shame you felt afterward. This discovery comforted me a little, and I decided that I was strong, I was in control.

"A month before I took my graduation exams, my father died. There was nothing symbolic about his death, nothing tragic in it. One day I came home from school and saw people in the yard. Our neighbor Yardena ran toward me, embraced me, and told me I had to be strong, especially for my mother. Inside the house, my sister raced around, her eyes red, all the while giving instructions for dividing up all the desserts to the volunteers who had come to help our family in this difficult time. My mother looked like a fragment of transparent paper, fluttering a bit in the air and then remaining prostrate, only her soft sobs tearing through the hearts of those around her. I hugged her and told her she wasn't alone, that I would always be by her side. I couldn't cry. I was neither surprised nor angry that my father had died. My mother needed to get used to thinking for herself, deciding how to spend money; she would learn to come up with answers to questions. My father wouldn't be there anymore to consult. I loved my father, I still miss him, but I understood the need to get organized, to get used to life without him; there was no use in crying about why or how. Just as they'd taught me—always look to the future. Not until a few days later did it occur to me that even a gaze turned to the future can be pulled back.

"After the funeral, while we were sitting shiva, my mother sought refuge in memories. We took two boxes down from the attic, and my mother searched through the old papers in tears. She sobbed and moaned; when she felt completely helpless she went back to her room and curled up on my father's side of the bed, holding his pillow as she fell asleep. My sister and I fell upon the boxes with curiosity—we hadn't even known they existed. They contained old pictures, documents, letters. My sister soon lost interest in the contents of the boxes and went to curl up beside my mother. I remained, alone. Two letters. Two letters from Yutzi.

"One letter had arrived about two months after we'd left for Israel. She opened with the word *drágaim*, my darlings, and continued for four pages, unwinding the events that had occurred after we had left her to her fate. '… and you remember, Mrs. Leona, that the same day that I stayed with your dear girls, my brothers didn't look kindly on my trust in your family, but you yourself know, dear Mrs. Leona, how hard it was for me, and that except for you I didn't have a soul to tell my troubles to, and you know the kind of nasty gossip that always made problems for me. I remember every wise word you ever spoke to me, but the rumors that Pishta and I were involved reached my brothers, and only after you'd already left did they start to talk about me and Pishta, because nobody wanted to slander your good name. Everyone respected you. After you left the stories began. Can you imagine? My brothers never were cultured men, they never bothered to seek an explanation. They went to Pishta's and they beat him so badly he had to stay in bed for a week, and you know that his wife just had a little baby girl and their situation isn't good, he was almost fired from the slaughterhouse. I always thought, what kind of wicked person could find it in their heart to make up a story like this? You remember that Ildiko was sick, and I told you that he had just stopped by to help me take care of her, but my brothers are such hotheads and nothing could convince them of this. When they were finished taking out their anger on Pishta, they came home like two lunatics and beat me without mercy; they broke both of my legs with a stick. The doctors say that one of my knees will never heal properly, I still hope that my limp will go away, because I have nothing left, it's very hard for me to walk to work, and everyone stares at me with anger. Pishta won't speak to me. I can't go to the slaughterhouse anymore. If you were here I'm sure that you would have helped me in my distress. My mother is still in the hospital and they say that her heart will give out soon. Her head is already a muddle, she screams like some primitive at the market. It shames me that she does her business in the bed. These sorrows have plagued me since you left, and I have nobody to talk to. Mostly I hope that all of you are well and adjusting to your new home. I'm sure you are, because you are good people. And how is Ildiko? Is she healthy?'

SUZANE ADAM

"...I didn't taste the sweetness of revenge. I read these lines, and between them I understood that she had left clues for me. That maybe I was responsible for her broken legs, because both of us knew what had happened between her and Pishta. The slaughterhouse workers saw her play with her hair as Pishta drooled over her. Of course they gossiped about it—I saw it but I said nothing. I didn't think about Yutzi's punishment with pleasure, and I wasn't surprised that my mother had never read the letter to us the way she had read us the other letters that arrived in those first months. When I read the letter Yutzi was already twenty-nine years old, what had happened to her since then, and what had happened with her legs I didn't know, and I didn't intend to ask my mother. Instead of returning the letter to the box, I ripped it into shreds and threw it in the garbage. The second letter was sent about a year later, and in it she told of her mother's death, her limp, that she had left her home, and that she was working as a governess at the home of an important family, party members, rich and very strict. They had three children and a big house, and she had much work to do; her leg really bothered her, but she had no choice, because no man would want her and she had already given up on the idea of a husband and children of her own, so she was putting all of that love and happiness into this new family, and she missed us so much and would never forget us.

"So she had come to no good, just as everyone had predicted. I put the letter back in the box and didn't think about her again for a long time, because I felt as though I'd freed myself of her. Just as I was taught, what had happened, happened. As for the entire truth, I knew nobody would ever believe me.

"I took my exams and needed to start thinking about what I wanted to do in the army. My sister had finally started

122

getting her period, and my mother was seriously considering learning how to drive. Everything else remained back
there, beyond the forests, in Transylvania. In Israel we had
orchards. So many times I thought about speaking of Yutzi
when the three of us sat on our balcony on pleasant days,
discussing memories of Transylvania. We spoke about my
father; my sister didn't remember Transylvania at all—she
barely knew enough words to carry on a basic conversation
in Hungarian. And my mother's Hebrew was...even today
she hasn't learned the language. What good would it do to
bring up the past again, especially since my mother always
summed everything up by saying *what happened, happened*
and that we needed to keep going forward."

It's late and I need to go to sleep. Tomorrow we'll get up
early. I made a doctor's appointment for her at seven-thirty
so they can check her stitches; they might need to change her
bandages and give her something to help her appetite, or at
least they can convince her that in her condition she needs to
eat. Gently, I interrupt her. She eats half an orange, brushes
her teeth, gets in bed. I'm happy, I don't say a word. I crawl
under the blanket, holding her, breathing her in: head, belly,
back, hands, feet — everything's in place, we're in our usual
positions. Night falls.

In the morning we pull ourselves together, the same old
routine. We leave through the back door so our neighbors
won't assault us; she doesn't look at the road, at the scenery.
I watch the traffic and then look at her. She says, *The tests
will take a long time. The doctor told me at least two hours.*
I want to stay with her; she encourages me to go and run my
errands. I call her sister, ask if she'll come to the parking lot.
We can speak in the car.

We have two hours.

nine

"Mother told me everything, what do you want to talk about? Ask. I really don't know what to tell you, I'm completely stunned. How is my sister? Is she in pain? Why doesn't she want me to come over? Now that she's taken care of, I feel like she's a stranger. Even though she's always been introverted, and she's never been a big talker, now that everyone wants to help her she's even more closed off. I don't get it. I thought I could read her like an open book. As far as I knew we were good friends. I told her all my secrets, intimate details. I asked her advice for every step I've taken in my life, even more than I asked my mother, because my mother thinks and weighs everything so scientifically. I have to do things my own way — *chik-chok*, onward, my life has a rhythm, this is how I live. Am I hearing an accusation, blame? Or does it just appear that way to me? You should know I don't have any regrets. She always told me not to get involved, she was the big sister, so I let her spoil me. A thousand times I offered to take her to a good beautician to take care of her pimples. Today she has a pretty face, but still, when we were younger she insisted on neglecting herself; she had all kinds of excuses. I told her, *Go on a diet, you're beautiful, you're smart, why do you sit alone in the house all the time, you're wasting away with the books and depressing violin music, you're like some kind of retiree, why don't you live?* I wanted to introduce her to the older brothers of my boyfriends; she always preferred to buy another sketch pad and more paint instead of dressing properly. My mother always kept her wrapped in cotton wool, told me not to bother her, we should love her just the way she was. Don't get me wrong, she wasn't sad, I never saw her cry. Even when our father passed away she shed a few silent tears at the funeral and that was all. How could I have known? Yutzi? She never even had nightmares. If she had screamed, called for help...but no, only silence. I thought, my sister is a quiet and calm person, she takes after our mother, what is there to discuss? I love to talk, I would speak instead of her if she would let me know the words. I would turn the world upside down. Yutzi enchanted me, to me she was a fairy, not a witch, who knew? And now? She's a grown woman, not a little girl. I was so happy for her when everything began to go well and I saw she was happy. She had a light in her eyes. Am I my sister's keeper? No sir—we were taught from a very early age that everyone needs to take care of themselves, and to respect the path each person chooses for himself. I studied in order to make something of myself, she studied so nobody could tell her that she wasn't doing anything with her life. I told her to go to art school, have an exhibition. She could have been a millionaire, but no, her paintings have always been something private, not for show, not to talk about, she wasn't proud of herself. I love her how she is, quiet, practical. She has the wisdom of an eighty-year-old woman, sitting on the sidelines, learning with her eyes—this is good, this is bad. I fell and got back up, like Humpty Dumpty. When I brought Yuval home she said he was the one for me, so I married him, and she was right. She told me to study economics and not social work, she was right again. So now, you tell me — with all of her wisdom, why is she screwing up her own life?"

I could talk to Zsuzsi for another two hours and never manage to explain to her the thoughts I have about her sister taking shape in my mind. She's in a hurry, busy, she hasn't got the time or patience. There's a problem, it needs to be solved, one two three. I say it isn't so simple. She says nonsense, we need to leave the past behind, I should tell her sister to stop speaking nonsense, she should just tell us what she needs, tell me what she needs, and other than that she should stay quiet. And besides that she's in a hurry, she has a meeting at ten, plus she'll take half a day off tomorrow so she can stay with Mrs. Rott. *You'll come with my sister in the evening, you can convince her, good, I have to run.*

I go back to the clinic. Everything is mending properly. Next week more tests. On the way home I tell her that I've spoken with Zsuzsi. She says not yet. At home she undresses, showers. I say maybe she should take a break, just half an hour. No. She's on the edge of the couch and she wants to continue.

ten

"In the army I got my name back. I loved the army. I arrived alone at the recruitment station in Jaffa. Dozens of blondes, brunettes, tanned and curvaceous, waited with their anxious parents, and their boyfriends who already gazed at them longingly. I arrived alone and found a quiet corner that made a good observation post. An energetic sergeant sorted and organized us, aided by two soldiers who acted like they were at a party: I'll dance with this one, maybe with that one, that one for sure. I didn't go to parties, but I nonetheless understood the inviting gaze that boys gave to girls. I was asked to get on the bus: *Ildiko Rott.* I almost didn't recognize my own name, everyone called me by the name my classmates had given me in third grade, or by a nickname, Chavatzi. I loved the army. There weren't any smart-alecks and the rules were clear. Ildiko was written on my identity card, so I was Ildiko. I sat on the bus and laughed to myself. Even my mother didn't call me *Ildiko* anymore; at home I was always Kitschi.

"In basic training I am officially declared a vegetarian, after I faint three times. I don't eat meat; I hardly eat eggs. Hungarian dishes have so many layers it's hard to see the meat. I haven't eaten cutlets of any kind since I saw the belly washers working with the guts. My mother thinks I'm simply spoiled—vegetarianism isn't in fashion yet—who had even heard of it? Neva Weissfish was a vegetarian, but she came from America. In Israel nobody is yet talking about cholesterol or ideological vegetarianism. Without even thinking about it, whenever I see the texture, the color of it, I can't eat meat. Sweets don't tempt me. It's funny, but in the army I didn't have anything to eat. Everything seemed so greasy, covered in mayonnaise, platters of shanks and chicken legs and haunches. I don't eat it, and without realizing it I eat only bread and what few vegetables there are. During a checkup they discover that I am practically malnourished. *Very funny*, I tell the doctor. I'm not on a diet, but he claims I've lost twenty-six pounds in less than three months and that isn't healthy. He gives me a note allowing me access to the large refrigerators in the kitchen. I eat a lot of green peppers for lunch, I exchange my clothes for size small. The other girls stand next to me in line and we trade long sentences. I grow thinner. Apparently this is somehow a sign that I care, that I'm human. I don't feel any difference as my hips diminish, it isn't important to me, my body has one simple function: to drag my head around. My head was still filled with heavy thoughts. I hadn't lost even an ounce of them. But the pretty, slim soldiers can't see these. When my stomach becomes flat, they become interested in how I spent my weekend at home. My hair hung in heavy curls down to my shoulders. I cut it short so I can see more easily who's in front of me and who's behind. This arouses cheers of admiration; the other girls crowd around me as if I were one of the wonders of the world. *Illy, what pretty eyes you have.*

"I noticed that Gidi Bender was making an effort to get himself posted to the same duty shift as me. He was a funny and exhausting guy. I learned to smile at him even before he began his strings of wisecracks and impersonations, which only stopped if an urgent call came for him over the radio. At meals he used to sing to me, *Illy, Illy, tra la la la la, peppers and tomatoes are her favorite things, whoever wants to marry her should give her onion rings*, and other silly songs about me being a vegetarian, my quietness, my seriousness. He sang like that and teased me until I thawed. He was like a little brother, although he was a year and a half older than me. Gidi had an urge to shake me up, to topple the careful order I'd created around me—as he said, to get me to snap out of my indifference. He didn't woo me with flattery or special attention; he wore me down, jumping up in front of me until I stopped pulling away, a clown who never tired of trying to get a smile out of me. On our long nights on duty he told me stories about his heroic feats. His revealing stories and scandalous descriptions awakened a dormant curiosity in me. Since I'd seen Yutzi dancing naked in front of Pishta, I'd been afraid to think about myself naked with a man. I'd seen movies, I'd read books, I knew that logically this was meant to be something pleasant and that someday I'd do this too. I wanted to, I was curious, I prayed that one day someone kind would caress me gently, and it wouldn't frighten me, and he wouldn't try to kill me afterward.

"One night I was alone in my room. One roommate was on holiday and the other was on duty. Gidi came to check out my place; when he finished joking around he trapped me in his arms and pressed his lips against my own dry lips. I was nineteen years old, almost as old as Yutzi was when she danced in the firelight. 'Why are you so cold to me?' he asked. I wanted to tell him that I wasn't cold, just lacking experience and a little frightened by the suddenness with which touching had replaced words. He didn't wait for an answer. With the skill of an experienced man he massaged my body with his hands and his lips like a child playing with a lump of plasticine, without worrying about the effect his actions might have. At first I was a stone, a lump. He kneaded me, dissolved my limbs, rolled me out into a precarious sheet; he plucked, squeezed, plumbed, I bloomed. As a spring breeze blew through the mossy cell inside my body, he peppered me with questions. *Do you like it? Is this good? You want more of this, yes? More, that's good, that's good, touch me, open up, turn over, turn around.* He divided me with instructions and attacked me with questions. At the same time, I thought that if I had died he wouldn't feel that my soul had left my body and he'd continue to twist and turn me around as though I were an inflatable rubber doll with holes for penetration. When it was over for him, his body was soaked with sweat. He lay beside me while releasing deep groans, as if he had just competed successfully in some athletic event. If I hadn't moved, I'm sure he would have slipped into a sweet slumber. I was completely mystified and didn't know what I was supposed to do when it was all over; I wanted to check the color of my sheets and see if I could stand; meanwhile I tried to relax myself by counting my toes. 'Was that good for you, sweetie?' he mumbled into the pillow. I said yes in order to leave things the way they were. 'We'll still be friends, right?' he asked before he fell asleep. The next day he got himself placed on duty with Ruchama, even though he had always claimed to me that Ruchama was not his type because she was too thin and she had that nasty way of always chewing gum. I wanted to ask him, *Why me*, but I was embarrassed. Things stayed like this between us for long months, which were filled with opportunities to run into each other. At first I followed him from a distance. I wanted him to talk to me, to tease me, make me laugh. I didn't know how to make him want me. He had lost interest. I could hear the giddy laughter of his flock of admirers coming from other rooms.

"I loved the army because I could sit in the gallery, salute the parade that passed in front of me, and still be considered part of the whole. We had uniforms, we spoke in code. Gidi left, I finished another course. Now I knew: I had done something my body wanted. And I drew. All the other possibilities I inscribed in colored pencil on pages of white paper. I discarded Gidi's naked silhouette that swam in front of me. His eyes were stalactites hanging in caves. I mixed colors, drew twisting lines, dots, filled sheet after sheet, I spoke. With my eyes closed I explained everything, just as Marishka had taught me. I could see further, yet with each step I took I examined the stable ground, made sure there were no hidden obstacles, that nothing would suddenly block my path. During vacations I equipped myself with a fresh supply of paper and exchanged a cardboard carton of files for more durable material, until at the end of my army service I had learned which components to mix together to create the color khaki, and a light apricot that expressed the color of my skin.

"My sister bloomed in a blaze of color: a deep burgundy, pale yellow, turquoise, black and white. She was tall and solid, her muscular arms were tan even in winter, her blue eyes were outlined in black, they shone in the dark and glittered in daylight. My little sister wasn't afraid of anything, everything was clear to her from an early age, she walked, ran, dove in, and then stopped to check. I don't know how many times she said to me, *Jump, it's so much fun to fly, it's no different than landing.* Even if she stumbled, she just shook it off and jumped headfirst off a new cliff with her eyes closed. In school, with her friends, at home with her chores—washing the dishes, helping our mother, farther, farther, what's next! In some ways she turned out like Gidi, but without the jokes. I told her once that if she kept up at this pace she'd run out of possibilities at age twenty; she replied that at my pace I'd still be stuck in my room with my drawings at age eighty, that my legs would never take me anywhere because my head was like a concrete block, I needed to loosen up a little. She pleaded with me, and even though she never was able to get me to alter my cautious way of doing things, she always asked me, what do you think? And she acted on my suggestions. *You're right, I don't know where you get all these answers, how do you know? You sit home all day and nonetheless you know.* She would sit and consult with me and then burst from the room, on to her next achievement.

"My mother had slowly become as blurry as a one of Monet's later paintings. She floated quietly on the surface of the water like a delicate pink lily; there was something so relaxed about the way she sat in her armchair. I translated her into colors. With pastels I illustrated her peacefulness, the completeness of her silences. On her fiftieth birthday I finished the drawing and gave it to her. As you know, this is the only work I've ever done that hangs on a wall.

"I signed up for two years in the army. This was very easy, relatively close to home—an hour's trip by bus. On the ride I could fall asleep and arrive home refreshed; this allowed me to be a worthwhile companion for my mother. My sister enlisted and asked to do her service far from home. This was a very stable time. Shrubs grew wild all around the house, climbing over each other, covering the house. Our neighbors made renovations and improvements. Every couple of years they painted the interior walls, the plumber repaired the leaks, we bought a set of new dishes for everyday use to replace the ones that had mostly broken, and that was that. The washing machine never broke down, the beds were comfortable, we ran into friendly neighbors at the grocery store, my mother read her books. After I'd finished with the army I registered for a class in textiles, my sister came and went like a volatile breeze, and everything was peaceful, routine, day after day. Our neighbors married off their children, became grandparents for the first time. I loved to sit with the Farkashes, to try to imagine how they managed the chaos of their lives. The brief course in textiles I took wasn't enough; I didn't find a job. Without an alternative, I registered at the technical institute. I say 'without an alternative' because I didn't like my classes, they reminded me of being in high school, so many enthusiastic young people. I wanted to get up in the morning and do as much work as I needed to do and collect a paycheck at the end of the month. To make the time pass. My sister threw herself into her studies, earned her degree, started a career; I had no expectations and no plans. I wanted peace and a routine.

"In the evenings I used to sit in the kitchen with my mother and a steaming bowl of soup. My mother always ate hers with little pieces of bread that soaked up the rivulets of thick, filling soup, so that she wouldn't be hungry. She still had a fear of hunger. She ate everything with bread, even though the refrigerator was full and there was always another pot of soup on the stove, she'd throw it out in two days, because the flavors needed to be eaten when still fresh. I told her not to make such big batches, but the vegetable market might have had a nice celery root or the parsley might have been fresh and not stringy, or it was the season when carrots were sweetest. 'How did I leave out the *nokedli*? I think I forgot to put in salt, my memory isn't what it used to be.' I thought about her memories, how she never spoke about them. She'd even stopped talking about my father, only, *What are you going to do tomorrow*, and, *Maybe Zsuzsi will stop by for a visit*, and, *Tomorrow I'm going to wash the curtains because it's time already*, and, *Tomorrow I'm going to find a good gardener because the light can't even get into the house anymore and the laundry gets dirty from the dead flowers and leaves blowing into it*. Tomorrow, tomorrow, I didn't have plans for tomorrow. I went to class. I was happy if the lesson was cancelled because then I could return home when the light was still good for drawing. This was enough for me. The style of drawing Marishka had taught me kept me awake during the day and helped me fall asleep at night.

"Understand that my mother was a princess, the armchair was her throne. I couldn't shake her from it, even my wild sister was restrained in her company. I learned about the Holocaust at school. Looking in my mother's eyes I gave up the idea of prying into my memories, her memories. I didn't want to make her dwell on sad things that would make her wrinkle up her face, twist her Sophia Loren lips into a frown. I'm so happy that you sit with her and keep her company, right now she really needs someone calming who can help her to understand, someone she can speak Hungarian to, tell her that she's not to blame. In time I'll be able to tell her this myself. And please don't bother my sister, there's no point. I've always been a strange bird in her idea of the world. I'm okay, I'm not in pain. Go talk to them if you want. When you come back, if you still have the courage to hear it, I'll tell you everything."

She's putting off the ending. Soon I'll see myself in her violet eyes and she'll tell the story of how we met; is this a painful story too? Another night ahead of us. I'm happy that she's tired, that she's not feeling pressed to continue. Tomorrow with renewed energy I'll have more strength. I help her into bed, she can fall asleep without a sleeping pill now, that's a good sign. She's encouraged me to go see her mother, why?

To get both sides of the story? To pass on a message? As soon as I think I'm beginning to understand something, to see a logical progression, there's suddenly a new story. Her mother also needs to sit with someone who will listen to her. I want to tell her about her daughter, make her understand, interpret it for her. A hidden door is opening, an enormous wave has broken, finally spilling out, engulfing me. If I'd been prepared I could have held onto something, nobody imagines a flood like this. I'm all mixed up in it, beaten, I'm not resisting. I feel like I've been listening to the same story in two voices. Her story has no shortcut, she's closing in on the present, with composure, with courage. I need to prepare for the ending. Mrs. Rott says that I'm a strong man. I trim trees, lift heavy bins, go to Ashkelon to hold everyone's hands. They're lucky I'm strong. In the car I turn on the radio, what are they talking about? Lebanon, accidents, the dollar has gone up, the humidity has dropped. Nothing is new out there, inside my head is chaos, disarray, damage.

At the house on Queen Esther Street all the lights are on, even in the yard. The big cypress is lit up from below by the spotlight I bought two weeks ago that sets it off nicely. In the sky the moon is almost full, hanging in exactly the right spot, close to the top of the tree and a little to the side, a postcard. This is all I knew about her, that she loved the cypress.

eleven

"Oy, good you here, Zsuszi come soon with Yuval and Tali, sit, sit, I to talk in Hungarian, yes? You understand everything...

"I can understand why my daughter doesn't want to see me. To tell you the truth I don't think I can find it in me to face her right now either. If this were all up to me I would declare everyone innocent of all charges, even though I've been made to understand that someone needs to be blamed so that she can come out guiltless. Everyone has a past, it's possible that my insistence on erasing mine, severing from it completely, not speaking about what was the root of evil... I never spoke about it either. I have nightmares, of course. I don't believe anyone who came out of there escapes the nightmares, in the dark, when the blanket falls to the floor and it's cold. In the light of day you see that it's all over. Almost every morning I wake up relieved. This is why I always say what happened, happened, because in the morning I see that I'm alive, that I survived. At that very moment I am filled with optimism, this is how I wanted my family to feel, even if it's difficult, to look ahead, to the future. She learned this from me apparently.

"At a young age I fell into the abyss. The Meyer Changre family thought it could avoid the approaching grasp of evil.

With all our money and culture, we sat in our fortress and waited for the chaos to finish, for the happy ending, like in a fairy tale. Today I know that we were completely cut off from reality. During those last months of the Meyer Changre family, before they came and took us in the trains, we spent our time in heated arguments — not about the threat that was becoming clear to anyone willing to see it, but about my desire to become engaged to a young and talented violinist who had neither money nor status. I was in love, my father was furious, my mother sobbed hopelessly, such a disaster about to befall the family — their bright and beautiful daughter was going to be disowned, she was erasing her own future. I battled with them over my love. Such foolishness was quickly reconciled as we stood in the town square, waiting to be loaded onto the trucks. How did the saga end? *Nu*, how do you think? I arrived at Auschwitz, I was separated from my family, I never saw a single one of them again; they were liquidated instead of another. Hand in hand I walked with my grandmother. I'd lost my parents in the massive ejection from the caravans. I held tight to my grandmother's hand, we stood in line. Mengele sent my grandmother to the left side and ordered me to go to the right. Of course I didn't want to and I followed my grandmother. Mengele took two huge steps toward me and dragged me back by my hair, stood me up in front of him and slapped me with the back of his hand, then pushed me to the right. This isn't an unusual story. Many people have stories about the selection, what could I tell my daughters — that Mengele saved my life? That we had to bathe in piss? That we stole food from garbage cans? And I have no explanation for why I survived and others didn't.

Afterward I met my husband. Did we fall in love? We were like infants, groping around for some life in the shadows. This wasn't the great love or the promise of romance or a storm of passion that helped me to breathe again after I was liberated from Auschwitz. But his hands were the ones that brought me water, wiped up my vomit; his fingers were the ones that rubbed goose grease on my frozen toes to warm them. So tell me, what good does it do to talk of what we went through? I know many people who returned from there who couldn't forget, and these images are braided through every aspect of their lives. Your mother, is she any better? We were young, we had the strength to look ahead. The small struggles of daily life didn't bother us. I wanted my daughters to grow up in an optimistic environment, without pain, without knowing. But if my daughter had told me, maybe I could have helped her, maybe I am guilty after all. What kind of example did I set, keeping everything hidden? We had so many difficulties blocking our path when we tried to leave for Israel. And here, too—those first years were terrible. My husband was unemployed; my daughters didn't know how we struggled. We thought it was better to hide it from them, they were young, we needed to fill the home with the spirit of optimism, *Everything's fine, everything's fine*—the important thing was feeling like everything was fine. Even when she came home from school with questions I told her, *What happened, happened.* From me she learned to hide her fears.

My husband always said, *One of them takes life in her hands and leaps ahead; one of them stands on the sidelines.* I love both of them, I respected their different ways—what should I have taught them? What can a parent do when a child decides to shut herself off? Should I have pulled it out of her with pliers? I didn't know. Did you know I survived the Holocaust? I can't cry about everything I didn't do the way I should have, can I? What's the use? And you? It seems to me you have a part in this, too. What do you say to her? This is all speculation, there aren't any facts, it's all possible, but maybe she's crazy. I think maybe she's simply lost her mind."

She gets up from the armchair in a slow and deliberate way, walks heavily to the kitchen. There's a clattering of dishes, she's crying. She comes back empty-handed, sits down, stooped, picking lint from the corner of her dress just like her daughter does with the checked blanket. Queen Esther Street is also quiet in the evening; I recognize the sound of a Volkswagen engine, tires scraping the curb, a door slamming, energetic footsteps. Zsuzsi, Yuval, and Tali burst into the house, taking charge of the quiet. Zsuzsi scatters objects around the room, tosses her shoes in the corner, Tali's blanket, a bottle. Yuval collapses on the couch, turns on the television with the volume muted. Zsuzsi is in motion as if she's still in the middle of her workday. "Oy, it's good that you're here, we don't have very many opportunities to all sit down together. Yuval, do me a favor and put Tali down in my mother's bedroom, she's starting to kvetch. The pacifier is in the bag, maybe change her diaper? Who's drinking what? Mother, you're pale—have you been crying? I spoke with Amnon. He's not worried, it's possible that everything's already history. I've postponed what I could until next week, but I suggest that we start trying to get back to some kind of normal life, I can't cancel everything. Mother, what are you doing tomorrow? Can you pick Tali up from daycare? Tell me the truth. I'll explain exactly how to get there. No, Yuval can't do it. Yuval! What about tomorrow? No, that's it, I knew he wouldn't stay home for another day, a half day is the same thing. Mother it's not a big deal, Tali loves you. Just play with her a little in the backyard and I promise I'll be here as soon as I can, what do you say? Great—you'll see that it's not so hard, maybe this will be just the thing to help you clear your mind. And how is my sister? Is she in any pain? I don't understand that concrete head of hers. Tell her I'm not going to hold myself back much longer. Like it or not, I'm going to tear down those walls of hers and come in. She's making me crazy, she's still talking about her childhood? Patience, you say, patience. Let's get to the bottom of this already. Yuval claimed a long time ago that she needed professional help. Don't get all offended, you know I love my sister to death and I'd do anything I possibly could to get her out of this mess, but she has to cooperate. Amnon says that in the meantime it's good that she's being quiet, but I'm worried about her, even if it all ends well, I need to understand what happened there. Mother, stop crying, that's the last thing we need now, for our strength to leave us. Mother, we have to think about her. Guilt, guilt, let's say you're guilty, let's say we're all guilty, let's say she's lost it. Maybe that's what this is about, don't look at me with those cow eyes, let's take a little action, can we? Is the baby sleeping? She's completely upside-down from this, too, she doesn't understand all the commotion. Yuval, could you please watch the news later, we need your perspective on this, you can be at least a little more objective than we can. This is exactly what I'm talking about, to calm down and see how things develop. So you sit all day and talk? She tells you about herself? Finally after all these years we could know what's going on in her head, and she doesn't want us to know? So why are you telling my mother? To hear her side of the story? You sit here torturing my mother, what for? No, let me talk for a minute, let's put the cards on the table. We're family, we want to help, okay? Amnon says we have to keep it together, so that's what we'll do. Say something, Ephraim, maybe you know her better than anyone does…"

twelve

The circle of eyes pins itself to me in concentration, drying up, in the tense hope that something will come out of my mouth. *You know her better than anyone*, they tell me, pressing me with a long *nu*? Then silence, they're waiting. I clasp my hands together so tight my fingers whiten around the stripe of dirt lodged beneath my fingernail. I dig through my brain, trying to dredge up some useful word or phrase, and just as always when I'm thrown into an unexpected situation, the tape hidden in my head switches on, and the Beatles burst into an appropriate song: *Bright are the stars that shine, dark is the night. I know this love of mine will never die*... They sing these words at a melancholy tempo, my muscles relax, the armchair beneath me turns into a stack of dry leaves. After a silence of two minutes and twenty-eight seconds — the length of the song — the atmosphere in the room loosens up, everyone is deep in their own thoughts, everyone seems to understand my reticence. They're used to it. In a more relaxed atmosphere I can think. The pictures draw themselves in my head; I don't even need to close my eyes to see them, as long as I'm not asked to speak. I can't find the words. I need to look back, too. Why do they think I know her better?

I can picture the first time I saw the house at 23 Queen Esther Street. The Rott home stood at the end of the street, bordering an orchard. One day I'd gone to the grocery store to get rolls and yogurt for breakfast, and the grocer told me the Rott family was looking to hire a gardener. He recommended them, they were a good family, he said. The father had died some years earlier, the wife was refined and reserved, quite cultured and well-spoken. *You understand Hungarian, don't you? So go over there, their garden is neglected.* I wanted more information. The grocer said, *What's with all the questions, it's not like you're going to marry one of her daughters.* I asked him, *Daughters?* He said that the younger one didn't live at home. *And the older one?* He got angry and said that maybe it wasn't such a good idea, sending a young man like me over there.

Mrs. Rott was standing in the doorway, surprised, reaching a hand up to her braid to make sure it was neat, smoothing her dress, saying, *Oy, sorry, I wasn't waiting to anyone, sorry I'm not arranged, please who to looking for?* I said, *I'm the gardener.*

Ahh, yes, yes, good you came, there is much mess, sorry, please be coming into the house. I told her to speak Hungarian. She reacted with one of the biggest smiles I'd ever seen in my life, her lips stretched endlessly, revealing white teeth. She laughed with her eyes as well, her shoulders lifted. After this moment of interior calm she burst out with a breathy, *Oy, this is so nice, you to understanding Hungarian, please, to sit, please, good, good, my Hebrew no good, sorry.* The whole time she kept apologizing. She offered me cookies and a cold glass of grapefruit juice. *Maybe you not like grapefruit? Sorry, there is nothing else, coffee?* I reassured her, *Thank you, thanks, don't worry.*

Oy, nonsense, she continued, taking a few extra little steps toward the refrigerator, toward the sink. *This isn't hard work*, she continued. In the end she remembered to speak Hungarian, and then she relaxed, sitting down across from me with her wide smile. *Tuesdays are best for us, you can feel at home here.* I wanted to ask her all kinds of questions to satisfy my curiosity. She didn't even ask about where I'd learned Hungarian, like all the other Hungarian speakers, who always asked right away. Mrs. Rott was so pleased by the fact that I understood Hungarian. She said there was much work to be done, and she wasn't expecting anything special, just that it be neat and clean.

Everything is growing wild; it has been years since anyone cared for this garden. I take a turn around the yard, alone. She stays inside the house. *You know what to do*, she told me, *so that it will be neat.* The cracked one-story building is imprisoned by a jumble of plants holding all the other plants in their grasp, battling each other, dried out. Thickets of oleander and bougainvillea that have taken on the appearance of trees cover half a dunam of the Rott family's dry ground. Ivy stubbornly blankets the walls of the house, holding inside their roots the air beneath the cracked irrigation pipes, knitting into dry frames around the windows and the eaves, climbing onto the roof and twisting between the shingles. The backyard is a field of weeds invading the neighboring orchard, wild raspberries are encircled by a dripping pipe. Three trees seemed cast from the hard ground: bitter orange, lemon, and grapefruit, all barren. In the farthest corner a cypress grows. Asparagus bushes surround it, a cape with thorny sleeves on the shreds of the wooden fence rotted by many winters, unprotected by waterproofing. The cypress is growing like a miracle above it all, a complete miracle, because wild creepers love to entwine themselves between the branches of trees and around light poles, climbing far up with the help of others' height and strong trunks, strangling the trees beneath them, forming giant human sculptures, hands outstretched, clad in green cloaks, the crucified among the plant kingdom.

I start working on Tuesdays. I trim around and around the oleander and the bougainvillea, I collect the branches of the tree in two large black garbage bins, taking them to the municipal dump, and there is more. With a pitchfork I turn over all the dirt, I tear the ivy from the walls, especially the tough roots, and the moss and the thorns. I am scratched and cut, covered in dust, and bits of dried leaves prick the sweaty skin of my sore back.

Little by little the house is revealed.

At every opportunity, Mrs. Rott tells me, *Oy, this is lovely, oy, this is wonderful, clean, tidy, I can sit in the garden, just like when I was young, you have made me feel so good with this garden.* The garden that I am creating from the Rotts' imagination is still empty and bare, but the earth is moist and fertile, the roots of the trees sucking up the plentiful water that fills the rubber hoses around their trunks. I have already designated a square in the backyard where I will plant a border of grass—the kind that does well in shade—that I've brought from the orchard next door, a strong grass that quickly grew wild in the orchard. It won't cost Mrs. Rott a thing; the owners of the orchard are happy to have the rows of trees weeded voluntarily. Under the open windows of the house I will plant colorful daisies and dahlias. At the front of the house I'll plant miniature vines, and when the garden begins to take shape I'll have time to give Mrs. Rott a treat by planting a small herb garden for her below the kitchen window.

I work in the Rott garden for weeks yet never manage to run into her older daughter. I know that she comes and goes through the rusty gate, but I don't see her. The window of her room faces the backyard; it's always open. During the winter, a white awning shadows its contents: A narrow bed covered by a colorful patched quilt, a small round rug made of some synthetic white fabric in the middle of the floor, a simple wooden table—a plank and four legs—and a chair nearby with rounded armrests and a seat covered in worn brown corduroy. On the other side of the room, in a corner, stands a large easel on a nylon drop cloth, squeezed tubes of paint and rusty boxes of paintbrushes in many different sizes on a stool below it. A tall wooden bookcase leans against the adjacent wall, the two higher shelves lined with books arranged in perfect order. On the lower shelves are stacks of paper, pamphlets, boxes of figurines, rags, cans of turpentine and paraffin, small plastic cups of paperclips, scissors, stacks of letters, a large wastepaper basket lined with an orange plastic bag. Her room. Apparently she is an artist.

I peek inside her room many times; once a week I examine it for changes. Everything is always the same; the only things that change are the tubes of paint on the stool and the size of the stacks of paper. The pages rest on top of each other, I can see colors moving back and forth in waves on the papers in the corner; these are her paintings. Sometimes the corner is empty and the wastepaper basket full.

And the fragrance—apparently once I miss her by only a few seconds, when I am unloading my large sack of tools from the truck, across from the gate. Between the leaves of the bougainvillea, over the thin branches, blossom tiny molecules of her scent. That day I can't do anything to the entryway; I am afraid that if I trim anything, the molecules will drop away, sinking into the cracks in the sidewalk. The fragrance also hangs in the air of her room, and despite the fumes of turpentine and paint thinner I sense that her fragrance has been absorbed into her bed, on the walls or by the shirt that she has thrown over the back of the chair. I know more about her.

In the backyard, behind the square strips of grass I'm tending, stand two columns, each with two hooks, between them stretch clotheslines. On the lines I see her clothes. I recognize her mother's dresses easily—every Tuesday, when I take a break, she brings me something to drink, so I've seen those dresses strung on the upper line, most of them without buttons. The jeans and all the purple and blue and gray t-shirts would not fit on that body, so they have to belong to her daughter. I know they are hers. Her underpants are medium-sized, I easily read this on the label, all of them white except for a few with a grayish or bluish tinge that apparently got mixed up with a load of colored laundry; originally they were all white, I am certain of this. Her underpants always hang from two clothespins and wave back and forth. When the group that hangs in front is narrower, they stick to the ones behind, her bras hang in the middle, cup to cup. When the wind fills the fabric it seems like a balloon is stuck to the line, floating around on ribbons. I am afraid that one day someone will catch me examining her clothes as they dry in the sun and won't understand what is going on in my head, my neck outstretched toward the clotheslines, my nostrils quivering in their attempt to draw in the scent of the laundry detergent. Sometimes a guest's underpants hang on the line, strips of black lace, or shiny red silk; I am not curious about these. I love to examine the clothes of the older daughter, it is as if we already know each other, already we've composed an intimate poem between us because I've seen her clothes, her underpants. I could identify them from among a million others. Sometimes on my breaks or before I start working, I speak with her mother, I receive my instructions. Mostly

she says, *Just make it so that it's clean, maybe a few flowers?*
I am stunned that she always asks, instead of demanding,
like the rest of my clients. Once she says, *My daughter is
bringing her boyfriend's family to meet us for the first time,
so make sure the backyard is nice and tidy; if the weather
allows, she'll want to entertain them on the lawn.* I sink into
despair, someone is whispering to her, someone is rubbing
against her underpants, someone has taken her; without a
single logical thought or the pull of reality I want her. Later
I understand with relief that it is the family of the boyfriend
who wants the other daughter. Once, her mother says to
me, *You're an artist, it's such a pleasure to watch you while
you take care of the garden. My older daughter is a painter,
she has the soul of an artist, she loves the big cypress in the
corner of the yard, she's even painted it a few times, but she
never shows her work.*

Nevertheless I start to clean up around the cypress, driving
myself crazy wondering what to plant around it. Nothing will
grow there, twigs and acorns are the only decoration. Even
fencing in the hedge near the cypress is difficult. I rack my
brain, considering all the different seedlings, poring through
books. What can I plant for her there that she will notice,
that will make her ask about the gardener? I almost neglect
the rest of the garden. I consult her mother. *It's good the way
it is*, she says, *you don't have to bother with it.* I tell her, *This
is my job, so I want to make a nice garden, I'll plant flowers
around it, in the spring there will be so many colors and nice
scents in the yard, maybe you could ask your daughter?*

*My daughter? Which one? The younger one is busy, she
doesn't pay attention to things like that. The older one? She
wants it wild, to be a jungle, like it was when you came here
the first time, she doesn't like everything trimmed and orderly. I told her once that anyone passing by on the street who*

peeked into our yard would think that the house was aban-
doned, and plus who knows what kind of pests could be hid-
den in that big thorny mess. In the end she said that maybe
we needed a gardener to clean up the weeds, my daughter
loves only the cypress tree, so God forbid you should do
anything to harm it.

I want to plant flowers for her so she can paint them. I
don't think about her in terms of flesh and blood; she exists in the fragrance that remains where she has been, in her
empty room, in the changes that take place on the stool next
to the easel, in her clothes hanging on the clothesline.

I work and work, week after week, but I don't meet Mrs.
Rott's older daughter. I ask if I can change the day I come
to work. *Whenever you want to come, come — it doesn't*
matter to me at all, Mrs. Rott says. I try every day of the
week, and I don't meet her daughter. I arrive at seven in the
morning instead of nine, ask if I can work in the afternoons,
intentionally forget my tools, come in the evening, apologizing for the disturbance, looking all around, but she isn't
home. Her window is dark, she's never home.

According to the paints on the stool, the laundry, her
fragrance, she lives with her mother. When will I meet her
already? I've run out of strategies to invent. I leave gifts
beneath the cypress, colored pebbles that I collected at the
Kinneret. A week later I find them piled up beneath the bitter orange tree. I leave a flowerpot of spiderwort under the
cypress, maybe this will have a higher status. An unknown
hand moves the flowerpot, placing it beside the entryway. I
ask Mrs. Rott if she is satisfied, and if it disturbs her that the
ground next to the cypress is bare. She says, *No, no, leave it*
the way it is, without anything, that's my daughter's tree.

You're an idiot, Ephraim, I scold myself, talking to the
cypress, hiding my questions in whispers between the folds

of its bark, maybe she will hear. I water the ground, leaving
my fingerprints behind. The most foolish thing I do is leave
my work shirt under the tree and go home in my undershirt.
The next time I arrive, Mrs. Rott bursts from the house with
my cleaned and ironed shirt. *You forgot.* She hands me the
fragrant cloth. *Thank you, thanks,* I say. *It's nothing,* she
says, and I imagine her daughter's clothes mixed up with my
shirt in the laundry machine and try to guess what had hung
next to it on the line. I don't have the nerve to ask about her
daughter, I have to meet her without any assistance.

Once a week I come to take care of their yard. Their
house is not like any of the other houses where I've worked.
From the moment I took the first tour of the yard, from the
moment I reached the end of the street and walked through
their gate, in just thirty seconds, a few heartbeats. Maybe
this time I will manage to meet her. I used to say to myself,
*Ephraim, you're an idiot, how do you fall in love with a girl's
fragrance? Maybe she's a terrible snob?* I try to push her from
my thoughts, because they don't make sense. I used to park
my truck across from the gate, and the emptiness would hol-
low me out, once again she wasn't home. She is never home.
*You've fallen in love with a ghost, Ephraim, go and look for
someone you can hold in your arms. One day she'll be standing in front of you and all your fantasies will sail off into the
air like a weather balloon.* I have no control over this incomprehensible desire; it buzzes around in my brain like a fly and
won't leave. I think about her, I don't hope for anything, I
only know that she is the woman I am searching for.

Nobody waits for me at home, only the bare walls, a
stack of dishes in the sink, a refrigerator that needs airing
out from the rotten smell of spoiled frozen dinners.

In the evenings my friends drag me out for a beer. *What a
monk you are,* they scold, *what's the point of sitting alone at*

home? Go out, have some fun, life is short, the world is full of nice pieces of ass, you only have to choose one. With your looks you could screw anyone. I want love. A wife. To plant something that will grow. Maybe an artist, who will want me for my brain, not just for my tanned stomach muscles.

Get out of here, you romantic, my friends tell me after the third beer, *today we have free love, take our word for it.* I want to build her a house with my own sweat, to plant an herb garden for her beneath the kitchen window—parsley, chili peppers. The smell of her cooking will lead me home after a day of work. *You'll go after her in time, my friend,* they tell me, from experience. *Today women go around braless, they want their space, cooking and having children isn't in fashion, all of them become professors, they have Kabbalah groups, you have to be able to quote some genius at least once a day. You're a gardener, not a philosopher, what do you understand about that life? What are you going to offer? A garden? Money, make a lot of money, then you might have a chance, you're fooling yourself, no woman is going to want to be shut up in the kitchen with your herbs, today everything is free, you can't lock her up in the house and toss out the key, what kind of dreams are these, my friend? Nice girls want more, layer cakes don't make women happy anymore, you can buy them ready-made, we're done with the fuss and muss, there's no time, they get dressed in a hurry in the morning, drink coffee on the run, toss out some instructions, disappear for the whole day, come home tired in the evening with a headache, sweetheart. Today a woman wants more from a man than to put bread on the table, you're second in line, right after a James Bond briefcase, a shiny office, you'll get half an hour from her busy schedule, to get a woman like that you need to make an effort to improve yourself, really improve yourself. Look, the truth is that they look good, they always take care of themselves, look after their own interests, and earn a lot of money, because of the money they have in the bank you have to have more, to get a word in edgewise, open a business, have a tailored suit, trade in your old car, and hire a gardener to make a garden for her. You'll do the dirty work, then she'll kvetch in her robe and slippers that you're boring her because you're never home. No, my friend, you're fantasizing about something that doesn't exist anymore, you don't know anything. Education, baby—read some books, listen to classical music, get a manicure, look at your fingernails.*

My friends are good people on an individual basis, they work at a packaging plant, a beach hotel. *There's a lot of nice pieces of ass on the beach, tourists—live a little, you're still young, what do you want now with a wife and kids?*

I want a wife to erase the bitter taste of married life that my parents left in my memories. My mother says I don't understand anything about life, maybe because I left school after tenth grade and went to work for the city, trimming the trees in people's yards. I wanted to work, I wanted to be myself, self-sufficient. Whenever I asked her for money she always wanted to know what for, when I told her, she reacted with anger, *What do you think, it grows on trees, where am I supposed to find it for you? Under the ground? Your father should hear this.* But my father didn't hear, he was careful to not be ambushed by her words, he tried to come home late. *Don't go around in your filthy shoes,* she used to say, driving him out of any place in the house. The living room was reserved for the small handful of guests who kissed and hugged and spoke without reservations or rules. I thought they were relatives who had survived like my parents. At school I loved to say that for my vacations we'd gone to my uncle's house, or we'd been visited by my cousins, to make it sound like I came from a big family. Later I understood that they were only acquaintances from the camps, the trains, the motherland. They had a common language of suffering, they shared the same tragedy.

The more overbearing my mother's extreme moods became, the less she wanted to have guests in the house. Nobody ever came over, except for her sister. *Nu, of course, who else would come over,* she used to hiss at my father, *if you had listened to me we would be all right, too, but no, you're so smart, you went to work at the port, now you're an old man and you have no strength, and you think I have the strength to clean other peoples' bathrooms? You've never known how to get along.* My father didn't know how to get along? He did know, but he didn't want to. He told me once that he had no strength for struggles, he wanted to live in peace and quiet, to get up in the morning and bring a little bread home to put on the table in the evening, none of the rest was important. *Give me a pillow and a blanket, someplace dry, give me a cigarette and a little glass of cognac and I'm satisfied.* He told me I was still young and maybe I'd want other things, and that was fine, why not, I could shoot for the moon if I had it in me. He said to my mother, *We have a house, children, food, this isn't enough? Have you forgotten where we came from? A house, a house, did you ever think you'd get out of there and have children and food on the table?* My father was quiet until he started to scream back at her, in the simple language of a laborer. When nothing worked and she kept at him, he started to beat her, slapping her across the face, she gave him two in return, he shoved her. She horrified him. My brothers and I tried to separate them and got pulled into it instead. Once she broke a glass and made us get down on our knees to pick up the shards. My brothers went to live in Kfar Giladi, far from her. I went into the army. I bought a book, a bestseller about the ornamental plants and flowers of Israel by D. Tsafrir. During my spare time I learned everything in it by heart: the proper time to prune rosebushes, how to trim trees.

My mother said, *For this I survived that place, so that my son could be a gardener?* After the army I went around the neighborhoods of Ashkelon, peering into all the gardens and imagining what I could do with them. At the grocery store I put up flyers: "Industrious Gardener Seeks Responsible Work." I learned to know people by their yards, both front and back. From the money I earned before I enlisted I bought an old Susita pickup truck and some tools; my father helped me with a little money, encouraging me to show my mother that money did grow on trees and under the ground. I couldn't even speak to her anymore, couldn't deal with her tears, her groaning *jaj istenem* constantly. My father also left home. He rented a two-room apartment in Ashdod, near the port. His female friends spoiled him with dinners, always inviting a lovely widow or divorcee, maybe he'd find her attractive, he had much to offer. I asked once if my mother had always been like that. He told me how they'd met at a refugee camp in Cyprus. She arrived there like some kind of puppy that had been saved at the last minute from a beating, her parents had been shot to death right in front of her, she and her sister were raped, later they were sent to the train, bleeding. She always pressured him, she always wanted more. *Because of everything that happened*, she said, *I deserve this.* My father had nothing to give her, so he married her. He said, *I'm yours, now you have something.* Later she complained that she had to feed us from her floor-washing money. Her sister used to come to our house and together the two of them would weep and wail for hours, regretting that they were still alive. Especially on Holocaust Day, it

SUZANE ADAM

was impossible to comfort them, they used to scream and pull out their hair, cursing the whole world and agreeing between themselves that it would be better to swallow rat poison and end everything once and for all.

Now she lived with her sister. I visited them at least once a week for a few minutes. On Rosh Hashanah I would bring a huge bouquet of flowers, she would toss the festive blooms on the kitchen table, sit down again on the couch next to her sister, shaking her head from side to side, *jaj istenem, I have nothing in this life*. Her sister asked me if I was still a gardener. *And how can you live like that? I hope you're not taking money from hooligans, that would kill your mother*. No, no, I'm earning money on the straight and narrow. They insisted on speaking with me in Hungarian, I no longer remembered how to speak, but I understood every word. I got up to find a vase for the gladioli, so that they wouldn't wilt. *Take it, take it back with you, give it to your young lady, for me it's not so important*. Every year my mother gave me back the bouquet. *I have no young lady*, I told her, I'd brought the flowers in honor of the holiday, in honor of her. *I have no holidays left in my life, you can bring flowers to my grave.*

I wanted a wife I could bring flowers to, she would hurry to put them in water with a few drops of bleach, she would trim their stems every two days to keep them fresh, I would fill the whole house with flowers. I'd had women. In the Afridar neighborhood in Ashkelon there were many gardens, they spoke Hungarian at the grocery store, the neighbors were from Hungarian Transylvania, rich Ashkenazis who had managed to do well. In the Migdal and the older neighborhoods it was different, they squandered money on food and necessities, there were beatings, stress, honor killings, homes were neglected, there was no housing committee, the

158

city didn't take care of the lawns, they needed a decent market and bus service for the workers. In Afridar the streets were clean, there weren't enough children to make a mess of the small commercial district. There was a delicatessen that sold pork for the rich Hungarians who missed the taste of Europe—like the Debretzeny family.

The fortress of the Debretzeny family stood on an artificial hill. The children were grown and gone, each of them had their own palace. The enormous house crouched in a sterile silence. A tall white wall with an iron gate surrounded it; there was a separate, gated building for the car, with a roof. Everything was paved, trimmed, clipped—not even an ant wandered out of line. There were ten steps to the front door, the house stood on columns. Why build a house in the air, dragging baskets up the stairs if it was possible to leave the house and walk directly onto the lawn? A wolf-like dog was tied up in a lair beneath the house, bored in the darkness; one of his ears flopped down and his tail was chewed on. He was never let off of his tether so that he wouldn't ruin the lawn. When I came into the yard he didn't bark, he wagged his injured tail at me. *Set me free*, he pleaded with his eyes. I petted him and promised him he'd be fine. Joschka Debretzeny stood at the head of the stairs, observing his estate. *Spray it, spray it so that it doesn't get pests, and trim the branches of this tree so that it makes an exact circle.* He bought me a secondhand lawnmower in good condition because I fussed over every blade and he didn't have the patience to watch this. He asked me to cut back the blanket of rose bushes that covered the slope of the artificial hill, because too much pink bothered his eyes. I offered to walk the dog when I'd finished working, he didn't want me to. *Don't spoil him, piddleh, kratzyeh, first he needs to learn to guard the house.* After giving me my instructions he squeezed his bulk behind the steering wheel of his gleaming American car.

I closed the gate behind him and was surprised by Mrs. Debretzeny in a transparent cotton robe, a cup of tea in her hand. She breathed in the cool morning air, stretching. Her robe parted into two wings, beneath it only her translucent nylon nightgown enfolded her shriveled breasts, she wanted to take flight, watching me as if I were a helicopter that could fly her somewhere. They all gave me something to drink: tea, coffee, juice, cold water. Mrs. Debretzeny invited me into the kitchen, set half a layer cake in front of me. *Eat, eat, it will give you strength, there's not that much work to do, eat slowly, there's time until my husband comes back, you can finish it all.* She fluttered around me, pleading with her body, she kept pulling her chair closer, bending over me, stretching, yawning, rubbing glycerin cream into her hands, offering some to me so that my skin wouldn't dry out. *Let me see your fingers*, she said. Her hands were cold and damp and slippery, her touch made something in me start to tremble. She was an attractive woman, hungry. She had enough money to buy anything she wanted. One day she wouldn't be able to restrain herself, one day I would take the dog and they would look for a new gardener.

I wanted a wife with warm hands, and flannel pajamas that would keep her from being cold. I would plant a lawn for her feet, and our dog would sit beside us and we would pet him. His fur would be shiny, and his eyes mischievous. I wanted a wife who would be hard to say goodbye to in the morning.

Over beers, my friends tell me, *Hey, you look beat, who's been sapping all your strength?* They wink at me, drunk. *Have another beer, life is short, why are you always so deep, on Friday we're going dancing in Tel Aviv, there'll be a lot*

of nubile young things there. I go with them, but my dreams
stay behind with Mrs. Rott's daughter, at home next to the
vase of white tulips.

At the discotheque, a tall girl in a miniskirt sways her
hips in front of me, her bright hair clinging to her cheeks and
neck. She sees I am looking at her and smiles; she comes and
stands next to me. *Why aren't you dancing,* she asks. I laugh,
embarrassed, and ask her for a slow dance. She clutches me,
hanging on. *Where are you from? I'm from Ashkelon, too.
A gardener? What kind of profession is that? I thought that
all gardeners were old retirees.* I tell her that today gardening
is a profession like any other, that one could study landscape
design, there is such a profession, making gardens. I tell her
that I studied on my own, I don't have a degree but I am
very good at my job and I have many clients. She works for
the city government as a secretary, nothing too exciting, she
says. *Are you Ashkenazi? Ahh, Egen migen. Hogy vagy. We
have lots of Hungarians in Ashkelon, do you know Hungarian? You have an accent.* I tell her my parents speak only
Hungarian to me. I offer to give her a ride home. My friends
wink at me with envy. *You've caught a nice piece.* Her name
is Miri.

My truck smells strongly of organic fertilizer. She wrinkles her nose, *Oof, what a stinky job you have.* When we
aren't far from her house she asks if I can drop her off on the
corner. *My father will for sure be looking out the window,
and your truck, what can I tell you? Don't be insulted, don't
worry about impressing anyone, certainly not my father.* I
ask if I could take her to a movie some night. *Great, wait for
me on the corner at eight o'clock, ciao*!

In the evening I dress up to go out, I put on aftershave,
Aqua Velva. I feel clean, Miri looks good. After the movie
we'll have something to talk about for sure. When the movie

is over she says she's cold. I offer to take her home; she says it's too early. I ask her, *Do you want to come up to my place?* She smiles. *On one condition: it's just to have something hot to drink, that's all. You won't try anything with me.* I promise her I won't.

She stands in the middle of the living room like a city inspector, even examining the ceiling, glancing at the walls and the floor. There isn't much for her to look at. She peeks in the kitchen, the refrigerator is working again, she closes it. *Who brought you flowers,* she asks, noticing that the place was lacking a woman's touch. She runs a finger along the stereo, leaving behind a transparent stripe in the gray plastic. *So, who brought the flowers?* I tell her I brought them myself. *Oh, of course, you're a gardener.* She wears tight jeans and high heels, she stretches out on the quivering bed as if it were the living room couch. I put on some Moody Blues, "Nights in White Satin." She says, *What's this? You like classical music? You don't have anything with more of a beat?* I tell her I have the Beatles. She says that will be fine, I sit down next to her. I don't know what to talk about. She doesn't touch her coffee. She licks her lips, digs her hands into her pockets, then clasps them under her breasts? *Are you cold?* I bring her a blanket, on the way I turn off the light. I sit down next to her, the blanket covering both of us, the Beatles singing about Michelle. Beneath the blanket I slide my frozen fingers along her thigh, stop after half an inch, waiting for her reaction. The song is two minutes and twenty-seven seconds long, the words and the melody don't move her at all. She licks her lips, leans back in stages until she is lying down. John Lennon, Paul McCartney, George Harrison, and Ringo Starr shout in desperate harmony. *I want to be your man, Help, I need somebody.* This isn't for me, it isn't for me, I don't love Miri. She wriggles around,

I am inside of her, she screams, bites, scratches, her legs fly up into the air, kicking. I feel like an actor in some kind of porn movie, I can't keep going, I stop moving, resting all my weight on her. She tries to push me off. *What happened? Is something wrong?* Her voice is insistent; I don't know what to say. I ask her something logical. *Do you have protection?* She says, *Don't worry, it's okay as long as you pull out.* I don't want to, I don't want to, I can't tell her now that I don't want to. I feel sick.

A month, two months this went on. I hate myself because of Miri, but I don't want to be alone. Once I bring her a perfect red rosebud, to blur her hard edges a little, so she will whisper, so her body will soften. She looks at the flower indifferently and asks, *Where's the rest of the bouquet?* Another time I say to her, *Next week I want to travel up to the north, to the Kinneret, do you want to come?* She is enthusiastic. *Which hotel?* I say, *No, we'll sleep on the beach, in sleeping bags.* She says, *Are you insane? Not for me, darling—I'm spoiled. I need a bed and sheets and hot water, you're always coming up with the weirdest things to do for fun.*

I called this my Kinneret test. In tenth grade we learned the poetry of Rachel. She loved the Kinneret, she wept and suffered and was buried there. The teacher tortured us with the rhyme and the meter, so we all thought Rachel was some kind of weepy consumptive *nudnikit*. The book was very expensive, so my mother decided not to throw it away with the rest of my books when I left school. The plumber found it in the crawlspace under the water heater. Up to page 82 all the pages had rotted from the dripping heater, which my father had never managed to repair. The rest of the pages were patterned with greenish-gray dust, and their borders had yellowed, but the letters were clear until page 253. A few years earlier I had started sleeping at the Kinneret, on the stones beside the peaceful water.

My head was bursting from my parents' constant shouting. I traveled by bus and by hitchhiking, as far away as I could get. One night I was stuck in Tiberias without a lift, so I went on foot. I left Tiberias. Suddenly it was quiet. I walked, listening to my own footsteps, to the dry leaves of the big eucalyptus trees rustling on the branches. I heard the waves gently washing the trembling pebbles over and over, churning into miniature bubbles that broke apart when they reached the open water, then again rose up and fell with the soothing movement of a cradle. I sat with my feet in the water and felt that perhaps not everything was lost. Since then I've always traveled to the Kinneret for solace, taking a backpack and the decaying book of Rachel's poetry.

Only to myself do I know what to tell, she wrote on page 128. Inside of her complicated words I looked for lines that said exactly what I felt. I used to know a soldier in the reserves, at Camp Tzrifim; I told her once I was going to the Kinneret. *Wow, sounds great, I'm going with you.* She brought a bottle of wine and a joint. By sunset she was drunk and wouldn't stop laughing, she threw up during the night, later she fell asleep and snored until morning. I hid the book from her. None of my friends knew that I searched through those poems, either. *What a brainiac we have in our midst*, they would have said if they'd known.

Miri also knows that she didn't pass the Kinneret test. One Friday I drop her on the corner; she says she has a headache. I go home feeling clearheaded. On Saturday my friends come by for coffee. *What's going on—did you break up? Last night she was dancing alone.*

In the evenings, alone in front of the television, I make plans to earn a lot of money and take a trip around the world. Decisions like this hit me when I feel like there is no point in getting up in the morning for another day of work, yet I make myself do it. I make a list of clients asking for more of my time, come up with original ideas, remind myself to hang up more flyers: *Polite and responsible gardener offers customized, innovative work.* I add a new telephone number that I haven't started to use yet. Miri doesn't know this phone number; I will send it to Mrs. Rott in case her daughter is ever looking for me.

I call my mother. She says, *Now that you can talk to me from far away, you'll disappear on me too, don't give me that, you know what I'm talking about, I don't matter to you anymore, you'll only come to my funeral, when I already won't have the strength.*

My father had already been courting Mrs. Amalia for almost a year. She was a large woman who dressed according to the latest magazines; her fleshy lips were always painted a fiery red, her hair piled elaborately high on her head. She wore a gold chain around her neck, and she always placed a colorful kerchief clipped together with a large, sparkling brooch precisely over her wide shoulders. She called my father by affectionate pet names, filled his rooms with vases that gave off a sweet perfume. I was confused, though not surprised, by this woman who showered my father with love.

I was the glue of the family. I visited everyone, passing news between them all. Gadi and Menashe, my brothers, were pals in Kfar Giladi; I visited them every few months. I told them that our mother was slowly losing her mind along with her sister, that our father had found someone who took care of him as if he were a baby bird. My brothers preferred not to speak of family matters. They took me on trips to the farms, the quarries. We drove in my truck to

Nimrod's Castle or Banias—places where we didn't need to talk. Ephraim, Gadi, and Menashe. In my fourth-grade Bible class I understood what was being hinted at in our names. My mother didn't care about names, because even if you were named after a bear or a wolf, even if your name meant *life*, you would still die anyway. Ephraim was the name of my father's father. Once he'd been part of a large clan, from a well-known group on the border between Hungary and Romania—men, women, old people, little children were squeezed into cattle cars, and my father didn't have even a photograph to remember them by, only the names. Gadi and Menashe, who might have multiplied and populated the earth together with me, with the tribe of Ephraim. I think that my father hoped so, or maybe not. One day I'll ask him, and I'll insist on being called Ephraim Marcowitz, and not just Ephraim the gardener.

thirteen

On Tuesday I'm on my knees in the Rott's garden, trimming the unrulier parts of the lawn, pruning the bougainvillea around the gate into an arch, dragging out the large garbage bin. I take my pruning shears so that I can tend to the raspberry bush that refuses to relinquish the hedge I've made in the backyard.

She sits under the cypress, on a piece of an old towel, her back straightened by the shape of the tree's trunk, her head leaning back against the bark, her hair lifted a little by the breeze, catching on the sticky little piles of severed branches.

Her eyes are closed, her lips joined by a bright thread of moisture. Her hands rest loosely on her bent knees, her bare feet anchored in the curling shapes of the pinecones. She's asleep. She breathes deeply and steadily, her lips parting when the air escapes from her lungs, a thin thread of saliva quivering between her soundless breaths. I know this is Ildiko, because I know.

The shears drop from my hand, thudding to the grass. She blinks. Her head pulls away from the tree, tearing the hidden threads of a spider web from between the wrinkles of the cypress. Her eyes open wide, two violet circles focusing on me. She gets up nimbly, supported by the tree, stands straight and takes a few steps toward me. A doll grown into a woman. Her chocolate-brown curls spill over her neck and rounded shoulders, her pale skin is hidden beneath a loose blouse and old jeans. I know she is soft and warm under that rough cloth, I simply know. I can smell the perfume that the sun has blended with her sleeping body. She examines me, everything is a blur, she is the focus. *Hello, you must be Ephraim, yes? I'm Chavatzelet, Leona's older daughter.*

At that exact moment I have only one thought: to take her to the Kinneret. *It's nice to meet you,* I say, *sorry for waking you.* She says, *That's okay. I really like what you've done with our garden, thank you.* Words, words, quick, I've forgotten how to speak, I've thought of her so much, we've never spoken. I've only smelled and watched the empty space where she's been, what can I say to her now? I bend down to pick up the shears, searching for words in the grass, what would Rachel say? "The shape of my world seemed like an ant's world." So I stand up with a long *ohhh.* I meant to say *Oh, thanks,* and talk to her about the garden, but the only lines that come into my head are from the Beatles' "Oh Darling," and in my despair the melody jumbles up with my thoughts and I can't come up with a single word. I can only hear them playing at full volume in my head. *Oh-darlin'.*

She stands patiently, eyebrows raised, a smile beginning at the corner of her mouth. She is already starting to walk away, what's the point of continuing to stand there in front of me and the idiotic expression that is apparently on my face? She gives me the kindness of another few seconds, but I can't find a way to put some words together into a logical sentence. She lets out a sigh, as if she has just heard a long story with a clear and wise message and doesn't have any-thing to add. She says, *Okay, I don't want to bother you while you're working*, and walks away from me, toward the house. Her steps are slow, as if she has a journey of many miles to go. I call after her with the rest of the Beatles song: *Oh-oh darlin', if you leave me.* The shears bite at the edges of the raspberry bush; in my head I switch to side B. The next song clarifies something important for me. *How could I dance with another.* I am in love with her. *I'll never dance with another.* I know all these songs by heart, I mutter them quietly to the little worms that escape the blades of the shears. *Love, love me do.* Every now and then I glance toward the house, worried that maybe she can see the songs coming out of my head, and I want to be original, to tell her in my own words that she is like something out of my dreams, that she is perfect, that I will build her a house, plant her an herb garden, Ildiko Chavatzelet Rott, Ildiko and Ephraim Marcowitz, and the children. Of course she will want children, how many will she want? If not children, then dogs and cats. Birds I don't like to see in cages, but I could compromise—Kartschi could help me build comfortable cages. The sound of my friends' disdain is mixed up with the wailing harmonicas: *Are you lost in a fantasy again, Ephraim?*

I sit where she sat, under the cypress, wiping away sweat, thirsty. Her mother comes toward me with a tray piled with cookies and grapefruit juice. *Ephraim, you don't need to work so hard, you're all flushed, the work isn't so urgent.* She leaves, and I take a short break in the shade of the cypress. The juice rejuvenates me, cooling my thoughts. *Enough! Enough, Ephraim, you're making a fool of yourself, choked up like a seventeen-year-old boy, Ildiko, Chavatzelet. You never make a great impression on anyone.* I thought that the fragrance and the paintings belonged to Ildiko, and the clothes on the line belonged to Chavatzelet. I part from the

Beatles with a last song in which they suggest, *Hey, you've got to hide your love away.*

Now I know what she looks like, yet I continue to dream about her without colors and without an outline, just two violet searchlights that scanned my face for only a moment. Every time I close my eyes I see her violet ones. At least the curiosity and ignorance that has been scraping my nerves raw has been replaced by a confirmation: *She is exactly, I mean exactly, as I imagined,* I tell myself. *Ephraim, you were right, you haven't just been sniffing around after her for months, she's exactly right.* I hear my friends giving me a hard time. *And where do you get this knowledge from?* I say, *From gardens, from front yards and back yards. A doctor checks people's blood pressure; I check their plants.* It was as simple as that — a girl who feels such a connection to a cypress tree is the girl for me.

The urgency vanishes. I arrive at their house relaxed. Just the fact that I can reconstruct the movements she made while getting up, the empty space that cloaked the cypress has her shape. I don't even have to close my eyes, they are wrapped in her curls. I collect three strands of her hair that caught in the folds of the cypress's bark, two of the same length, a shorter one tangled between the other two. The tip of the second one ends with a tiny white dot, the root of her hair that was plucked out when she separated from the tree, when she woke up. She wakes up in front of me every time I stand next to her cypress; every time I want to see the violet of her eyes, every time I want to say something to her, a new sentence — something more successful, something brighter than *I'm sorry I woke you.* I see her clothes on the line, they keep me company in the backyard, fluttering in the same gentle breeze that evaporates the sweat from my body.

There is time. I hoe, fertilize, plant, water, weed, examine the buds with a strict eye. I wait for days. It takes time—to keep the pests from spoiling the soft new edges, to make sure the wind doesn't push anything over, to water everything just the right amount so that the roots don't rot from excessive moisture. It can't be rushed; you must be patient.

Days pass. I work in the gardens. I have a lot of work. I trade in my pickup for a Peugeot, I buy some brand-new tools. I have a reputation already, people know my work. The sun rises every morning; in the evenings I return to my empty house, put an album on the stereo, let the music drain the stress from my muscles. When I settle into that softness, I think of her. Ildiko Chavatzelet, she exists, there is time, I relax. When my friends come over for coffee, they joke with me, offering to put me out of my misery, suggesting a strategic conquest. I'm silent, because it's impossible to draw a map that will lead me to her heart. They say to me, *Ephraim, enough with this indifference, one Miri doesn't represent all girls, there are a thousand more like her, come to the sea with us, just for a few laughs, some conversation, you'll see that there's something out there for you, you're a good-looking guy, such a waste — believe me, if I had muscles like yours I'd get laid without a second thought, God doesn't give everyone teeth like yours, but first you have to play the game a little, girls love to play hard to get. You're so serious, soon you'll have to start talking to a matchmaker, someone who can find you a girl who's just as serious, some dried-up monkey, you'll marry her because she's serious, and then you'll start coming to the sea with us just to get away from her.*

I tell them I don't have the energy and they should go ahead without me. They're worried about me. *You're in bad shape*, they say.

When Menachem comes to sit alone with me, he tells me he wants the same things I dream about. I tell him he needs to be patient, not to compromise. He asks me, *But how do you know what you're looking for?* I tell him everyone knows, it's just that we don't have the nerve to follow the dream to the end, so we get desperate and make compromises. He ends the tiring conversation with a foolish thought: *It's just too complicated, this idea of finding the right girl is simpler than trying as many as you need to until you fall for the right one.* I tell him that everyone has his own system, he has to do what he thinks is right, we're not in high school anymore, and that I've known since childhood what kind of woman I want to be with. He says, *Next month I'm taking a couple weeks of vacation, going down to Eilat to have some fun. You should come too, Ephraim, it'll clear your head to get out of here for a while.*

fourteen

On Tuesday I work in the Rott's garden. I am on my knees, trying to fix the sprinkler. Mrs. Rott approaches me, stepping daintily on the lawn, bringing me a bottle of cold water. I thank her, adding an explanation about the broken sprinkler, offering to replace it with a modern irrigation system. I warn her that it will be expensive, but also an opportunity to design the garden from scratch. She hesitates with her opinion, and is suddenly seized with concern, *Oy, sorry, you trouser the house to speak, not stand like this on your knee-shoulders in sun, in house to speak also Chavatzelet, good?* I smile and follow her. She insists on speaking Hebrew, the words she invents always amuse me, she asks me to correct her mistakes but I couldn't improve upon her inventions; I understand it all.

Chavatzelet is at home. Mrs. Rott wants us all to sit down together and talk. Mrs. Rott, Ildiko Chavatzelet—I want to live with them. I'm sweating, mud sticks to my shoes, my hands are filthy, under my fingernails are dark lines of red loamy dirt that never come out, even after a good scrubbing on Fridays. My face burns, my hair is glued to my forehead. What do I have to offer them? In the doorway I try to clean the soles of my shoes on the small welcome mat whose short fibers are entwined with a greeting to visitors. Mrs. Rott waits patiently. I wipe away my sweat with a sleeve, sorry that I've agreed to leave the familiar territory of the lawn. I'm not ready. Then I remember that I've been invited into their home to discuss business. Never mind, so my clothes are dirty, she's seen me, and it's not important anyway. I am who I am, with or without the scent of aftershave. I am still wiping my shoes, unsuccessfully trying to buy myself a little time to organize my thoughts. Mrs. Rott finally loses her patience, pats me encouragingly on the shoulder and says, *Good, enough, enough, clean, my house isn't museum, please to sit on the couch, you speak on your water plan, Kitschi, gyere ide, come here.* She calls to her daughter. I sit in the middle of the clean living room, my feet on the soft rug decorated with interlaced flowers and leaves that form geometric patterns. Mrs. Rott sits across from me in an armchair that seems to envelop her whole body. Through the open window I see the cypress standing tall, only shuddering and shaking its prickly leaves a little from time to time.

I hear footsteps, her fragrance draws near, she emerges from the dark tunnel of the hallway and stands on my right in the light of the living room. She sits down next to me. I feel how the couch cushion sends a wave from the place where her body sank down to where I sit, stone-like. She turns to me casually, her voice direct and clear. *Hello, how are you?* I turn toward her gaze, meet her two violet spot lights. I want to jump inside her eyes. Before I can come up with something logical to say in reply to her greeting, Mrs. Rott says, *Kitschi, maybe Ephraim wants something to drink?* Another wave goes through the couch when she gets up from her place and takes a few steps toward the kitchen. Halfway there she turns back to me. *What would you like to drink?* I remind myself that this is a meeting about a work

174

matter, and say, *Black coffee with one sugar, thanks.* I try to concentrate on Mrs. Rott's comforting face, explaining to her how the sunken pipes would work. She is very impressed by the technology and says that maybe this is a good idea. On the other hand, she wants the garden to stay simple and, above all, tidy. She doesn't want anything fancy or big, she just doesn't want it to be a jungle again. Something simple and natural. Kitschi stirs the coffee she has prepared for me, serving it in a matching cup and saucer, a plate of cookies in her other hand. Her mother asks for her opinion, and she answers simply, *This is Ephraim's profession, he's the expert, if it's good for the garden I'm for it.* I ask for a sheet of paper so that I can sketch out the design. She pulls a sketchpad from the pile of newspapers beside her and leafs through its pages. The cypress tree, red and orange stripes and dots, the cypress tree, woolly clouds, green vines scattered inside rows of black and white cubes, purples, the cypress tree, a clean page. I can't manage a polite conversation, something like, *Are these your drawings?* Because I know, I know she is the artist. I explain the changes that would take place in the garden. Mrs. Rott nods her head after every word that I say. I wonder if she can understand my Hebrew, or maybe she doesn't care. She hovers over me, Kitschi concentrates her violet spotlights on my hands, following the lines that flow from the nib of the pen, her body leaning over the table that I hunch over, explaining every detail. She is so close, I feel the warmth of her body on my bare right arm. She says, *Yes, no, interesting, looks good, this will be over here?* Her words caress the nape of my neck with a warm vapor. I want to leap up and shout, grab her in an embrace, hold her tightly, absorb her into me. She says, *This is important to you, isn't it? You can imagine how it will all look. When will you start?* I tell her that at the beginning of the month I am taking a two-week vacation; after that I will begin work. Her mother, hovering nearby, glances strangely from me to her daughter, her smile stretching wider and wider, as if to say something. Kitschi, she has nicknamed her daughter. Ildiko Chavatzelet Kitschi Rott. Ildiko of the paintings and the fragrance, Chavatzelet of the clothes, Kitschi to connect mother to daughter. Which name would I use? I want to know the name that would embody all of her. A two-week vacation, she ponders aloud. I say, *Yes, this is a good time.* And with a strange daring I add, *Two weeks in the north.*

The north is big, she says. I tell her I am going to the Kinneret. She straightens her back the way she did when we first met. I am afraid she is losing interest. In my overstimulated state the Beatles are cracking my head open with a mixture of tunes, what would they say? What would they sing about? I can't absorb any comforting words. Mrs. Rott shakes herself as if she's just discovered the solution to a difficult problem. *Kitschi, you could use a little vacation, too.* Ildiko Chavatzelet Kitschi rolls her eyes at her mother, with a smile. Mother, mother, mother, she says, her voice rising. I try to understand the meaning of this. I am bewildered, what are they discussing with these hints? I offer an itinerary to clear the air. *My brothers live on a kibbutz, Safed, Rosh Pina, there's a lot to see in the north.* I talk about the Kinneret, though they didn't really ask, about the big eucalyptuses, the wild beaches, the quiet, the distant lights of Tiberias that twinkle on the other side, the pebbles. I am swept away in the confusion of my own words. I feel like they are being pulled from me. Instead of shutting up I continue with my descriptions. Where are all these words coming from? What am I talking about? They sit in stunned captivity before the explosion of words, as if I am telling them something. Some emergency spring is activated, forcing my feet toward the door. I'm a polite person; I am confused by my sudden escape. I thank them, and then I thank them again, what else can I do? *See you soon, in a couple of weeks.* I need to say something else, I am already at the door, thanking them again, I am holding the doorknob.

Mrs. Rott is suddenly standing next to me, patting my head. *You're a good man.* She smiles at me and asks me in Hungarian what day I am leaving on my trip. I'm completely confused; I tell her I haven't decided yet. *Wonderful, you to work truly hard, you are deserving it.* She has again switched to Hebrew. *You are warning-light not to burn your head in the sun.* I smile at her as best I can. I feel as if standing by the door intensifies a feeling of uprootedness; I am scattered into fragments. I can't pull myself together to start working in the garden and perfect the irrigation system for the Rotts. In the end I can only nod my head at her and stumble away with uneven steps, staggering a little, turning toward her, stretching, scratching. I'm already in the middle of the yard, she is still standing in the doorway. I'm far away, putting up a screen to shade the basil plants that are already drying in the sun. I'm such an idiot, I think, even a sophomore in high school has better moves than I do.

At the end of my workday I collect my tools. The window of her room is open. As usual, she's not there. If she'd been sitting on the couch, looking out at the cypress, she would have seen the top of my head, coming and going. I have already gathered up my tools and loaded them into the truck. I slam the back door of the truck and say in my heart, never mind, be patient.

She stands with her arms crossed on the sidewalk, a few steps away from me. Her eyes are lit up by the sun, I am dragged inside them. I scratch the back of my neck. I really don't have any words left. She smiles at me and speaks in an amused voice — amused but not unkind, I feel. In no way unkind.

She says, *My mother suggested that I join you on your trip north.* I wait for her to continue the sentence, to keep talking. I haven't digested whatever Mrs. Rott has in mind. Facing my puzzled gaze she uncrosses her arms, plucks a leaf from the oleander with the red flowers, and rolls it between her fingers, tasting it, gently gnawing on it. *What do you think about that?* Her words tumble out, mixed with laughter. I tell her to be careful because the leaf has a bitter and poisonous milk inside. *I would like to travel to the north with you,* she says without lowering her gaze. Oy, oy, oy, I'm not used to being spoken to so directly. Dreaming about a conversation like this is easy, if only I could remember how to arrange the words of my response. She waits patiently. I say, *In sleeping bags.* She says, *Should I bring a sweater? Does it get cold at night?* I say, *Don't worry, I'll make a campfire.* She laughs. *Should I bring potatoes?*

Not that kind of campfire, I tell her, *although why not, if that's what you'd like. On Friday I'll pick you up at four o'clock; that will give us enough time to get there before sunset, to get everything set up before dark.* She asks, *What is there to set up?*

I understand that she is challenging me, that she is simply having a little fun with her replies to me, that a conversation like this could only take place between people who already know a previous text, that she is only reproaching me because she knows it by heart. It's okay for me to smile broadly at her; we are speaking the same language and about the same thing, no danger of misunderstanding, and yet when this happens I am stunned, confused, insecure, I want to bite my nails, to ask her, *Are you sure? Do you really understand? What will this be like?* She says, *I'll be ready on Friday. Are you a punctual kind of person? Because I don't like to wait.* I promise her I'll be there at four o'clock exactly. I am grateful for the chance to escape in my truck until the following week, to catch my breath, control my excitement. At home I have a strange attack of butterflies in my stomach, I can't think of any song to explain this situation I find myself in. Just a few more days, in the Kinneret with her, she and I, the two of us. *Ephraim*, I tell myself, *you're like a kid in a candy store for the first time.*

When was the first time I tasted candy? At the age of three, in Jackie's nursery school, on Rafi's birthday. He cried the whole time because he didn't want to put the wreath on his head, not even for a photo, and there was nothing for his complaining. His mother stood behind him, trying to sneak the wreath onto his head; his father stood ready with the camera in front of him. Rafi was nervous, he tried to push his mother away with his little hands in a clumsy gesture, she moved toward him instead. He took the boxcar from the candy train that decorated his birthday cake and threw it to the floor, next to the doll corner. The children were all stunned. Jackie tried to calm them down, *It's no big deal, no big deal, next year.* Amid the chaos I spotted an orange piece of candy under one of the doll chairs; it had decorated the window of the train. I bent over, picked it up, and put it in my mouth. At home we never had candy because it ruined your teeth, stuck to the furniture, and children made a mess with it and spoiled their appetites. Ildiko Chavatzelet Kitschi Rott. The second piece of candy I was about to try.

fifteen

On Friday at exactly four o'clock I shut off my engine in front of the Rott's gate; I don't know whether to get out or to wait. A tall young woman comes click-clacking toward me on a pair of black high-heeled shoes, her solid body packed into a yellow two-piece outfit. She takes off her sunglasses, leaning into the driver's-side window. Her eyes are blue. She extends her carefully groomed right hand to me, her nails long and sharp, glittering with red lacquer. *Hi, I'm Shosh, Ildi's little sister, she's on her way, she's been ready since yesterday, I had to see the exceptional and extraordinarily lucky man in whose company she would agree to spend time, don't let her frighten you, she's insanely sweet when you figure out how to act around her, don't tell her that I gave you that tip, she's really a sensible woman, she's a quiet one, you have to push her a little, don't be scared, I've heard such nice things about you, the garden is absolutely flourishing in your care, oh here she is, you already know my mother, Ildi don't make those faces at me, it's time I also got to know this young man who's always roaming free around our house and gets so many rave reviews, Mother you didn't tell me that he was so hunky too, we'll all get together, you two have a good time and don't do anything stupid, I have to run, kisses kisses, Ildi, did you pack that new towel that I bought for you? Mother, I'll try to stop by tonight so you won't be alone, it depends on Yuval, oy I'm late, see you later kids.* Shosh hugs her mother and her sister and then walks with a swift and commanding grace toward the red Polo parked in front of my truck. Her mother calls after her, *Zsozsika, you don't need to stop by if you're so busy.* She has several names, too.

Ildi throws her small backpack under the seat and gets in next to me. Her mother waves goodbye with a big smile. She waves energetically, as if her daughter were going on a trip around the world and nobody knows when she will return. This is bizarre—on the one hand, this is apparently normal family behavior for her daughter's overnight trip. On the other, up until a week ago I was just a hired hand, likable, of course, but nonetheless paid for my services. Now I've been entrusted with the daughter who sits beside me; they are counting on the generosity of my actions, and what is bizarre is the feeling of worry this stirs in me toward the object of my care—their daughter and sister. How pleased they are with this strange exploit of hers, traveling to the north, alone with a young man. I am certain that I love her, but what if I were someone else? Would that be okay too? There was no worry at all in her mother's goodbye; I am unnerved by her sister's cynical encouragement—it is as if they are handing her over to her fate without even holding onto the end of an emergency cord that they could use to pull her back to safety if, God forbid, something terrible should happen. Miri's father, for example, stood at the window and observed the cars that came to collect his daughter. She had a secure connection—her father held onto the end of the cord, letting it out little by little. When he thought that something harmful was happening to his little girl, he pulled, bringing her back safely to shore. At least that's the way I heard it from Miri, when she used to talk about her parents. Certainly Mrs. Rott's daughters are more mature; the younger daughter is rolling in money, she lives with her boyfriend. But the older daughter sits next to me in the truck, and her next of kin wave goodbye to her without a care. What if she doesn't come back? Then again, I'm not a total stranger, they know me, maybe they have sensed for some time that I love her and they are happy about it. I turn on the engine. I haven't yet managed to utter a word. Ildiko Chavatzelet Kitschi Ildi sits, self-contained, in her seat, her hands busy with a long cotton thread coming loose from the edge of her purple T-shirt, which the sun has already bleached most of the color from. From the corner of my eye I see that she's smiling, then she grins and eventually she bursts into laughter. *Did you enjoy my sister's show?* she asks. I smile at her calmly and say, *No. Do you want to listen to music or do you want quiet?* She says, *I know who put the stones under the cypress.* I say, *Well, so now you know. Once I thought that your sister was you.* She laughs. *My sister would never go to the Kinneret with you. To Wall Street, maybe. Collecting stones is my job in the family. My mother is too fragile to drag around that weight and my sister doesn't have time.* I ask about her collection of stones. She says that she started to collect them at the age of five, that she had a special chest she kept them in, only instead of stones they were pages and paints, these were easier to drag around. I asked her about her paintings. She said, *I think that painting for me is like the Kinneret for you, like a tidy house for my mother, like a successful business for my sister, like death for a sick man who has suffered a long time. At any rate there are stones that are so heavy it's impossible to move them; there's nothing that can be done, they need to be left behind. This much I've learned—to walk forward with my hands empty and my back straight, because there's no point in dragging around heavy sacks of stones.*

I say, *That sounds sad.* She says that stones are stones and it's not possible to attach those kinds of descriptions to them: sad, happy, afraid. They are just symbols, stones are just stones.

Despite the relatively large number of words that we are releasing into the truck, there's still a feeling that we are actually quiet the whole time. She turns on the radio to a soft volume, leans her head to the right, and closes her eyes. The breeze scatters her curls, which look like a frame of brown sunlight around her clear, smooth face. We travel on without exchanging another word, inside a tunnel of light that slowly softens the brighter colors of daylight into the gray-orange of twilight. The best time to arrive at the Kinneret: Slowly wrapped inside the dark, waiting until all the sharpness of the daylight is reduced to a blur, the edges blend together, reaching the lake after the wind ceases stirring up the water, tossing around the torn and empty plastic bags that people have forgotten to throw away. In the winter it is best to arrive at the Kinneret a few minutes after sunset, when the sun makes bright stripes of orange and blue and gray in the woolly clouds. In the summer, the blazing orange of the sun disappears behind the third hill to the right at the tip of Arbel Peak, the warm vapor rises from the surface of the lake, blurring the edge between the water and the sky, and there is a feeling of endless softness that invites you to rise up, to fly unafraid. The blood that flows through your body synchronizes with the melody of the bubbling arrangement of the water on the pebbles. Maybe a baby feels this way while still in its mother's womb. Then the night comes. The summer sky is black, a million festive stars sparkling with the elegant shine of a heavenly chandelier lit by the same unknown hand that keeps order among the living. The moon rises, sometimes a modest crescent, sometimes full and spherical. Today we know that there's nothing but soil and sand on its surface, but if you don't think about what it's really made of, you can feel the peace and quiet that poets have written about. Children see the moon smiling, making faces; at the Kinneret I try to feel like the moon, brightly quiet slowly blending, caressing, oh, my Kinneret, Rachel's Kinneret, the Kinneret of the families at their barbecues, joined in modern comfort, gathered in a circle around the meat that eases a primitive hunger, which attacked our fathers' fathers exactly the same way, as it has for years, a warm fire to help the cooking process, the whispering embers fill the conch shells with the rule of syntax and grammar, tongues lick each other with a hypnotic gaze.

I'm learning how to be the moon, and water, earth, and fire, and she is traveling with me to the same place where all this exists for me, in me, and I don't need to tear my hair out in search of the right words, and she doesn't have to say anything either.

After Tiberias I keep driving toward the Kinneret's eastern side. Some miles after Kibbutz Ein Gev, I turn left, driving down a dusty path between some banana plantations. The swaying and the dust wake her from her sleep, from her silence. *We've arrived*, she announces instead of me. Another few meters to the left, my eucalyptuses are standing straight in thicket after thicket, the treetops touch each other, old branches stoop toward the water, trembling leaves caress the silent foliage below, which rises toward the little waves. In the embrace of three wrinkled stumps with intertwined roots I spread out a heavy wool blanket and put the sleeping bag on top of it. We do everything without words.

Ildiko Chavatzelet Kitschi Ildi Rott is even quieter than me. She puts our sleeping bags close together, sits down with her back straight, her gaze detached, breathing deeply through her nose, releasing the air through her parted lips, twice, then turns her head toward me, resting her chin on her left shoulder and flooding me with her violet gaze.

I'm stunned, trembling, dim, quiet—the upper half of my body moves slowly toward her, my right hand reaching up, her curls tickling the spaces between my fingers. I pull her to me gently, turn her face to mine, her eyes are shut again. My dry lips press against hers. I keep my eyes open so that I won't lose this image of her for even a moment, a shudder crawls along the length of my spine, every nerve ending in my body wakes up: in my toes, in my knees, in my spine, my whole front, my loins are burning up, oh, my darling, my woman, my beloved, so close. I melt and harden in turn, and only from the touch of my lips to hers and the locks of her hair that are wrapped around my fingers, a woman breathing next to my own nostrils. I inhale the warm air that escapes from her nose, I can't hold back, I surrender to this pleasure and I close my eyes. A night bird startles us with its cry, she pulls away from me carefully and returns to her place.

Let's stop this, Ephraim, she says quietly, gazing again into the distance. *I've been in this situation before, it's not right for me, I'm so easily emptied out. I like being with you, I don't want this to end with sex.* I say, *So let's go in the water.* We undress without embarrassment, stepping naked onto the stones. She is very careful, sinking into the smooth water. I run in quickly so that she won't see the hardness protruding from between my legs. I dive in far away from her and float, trying to relax my tense body in the cold water. Nearly whispering, she says, *I'm scared,* but in the quiet

I hear a whirlpool forming around her, I swim to her quickly, wanting to hold her. She reaches out her hand. I help her to the shore. We dry off, dress quickly, back to back, make a campfire, some black coffee in the *feenjan*. She slices up a cheesecake. The stars, Tiberias twinkling across the lake, the moon rising—just a small bite missing from the white ball, relaxed, relaxed, peace. *My name is Ephraim, how many names do you have?* She laughs, embarrassed. *You don't even know them all yet; you can give me another one if you like, you have my permission.* I said, *I don't have any ideas yet.* The cool wind makes us get into our sleeping bags. She says, *Hold my hand until I fall asleep.*

We are at the Kinneret for three days. Alone. Quiet. We also speak. She tells me about the snow in Transylvania that she almost can't remember anymore, about Bokshi her dog, about trying to catch storks in the village with a handful of salt, about Jesus, whom she knew from her friend Bijou's church, about the amazing smell of the flowers that stunned her on the day she arrived in Israel with her family, about the new name that was given to her in third grade, about her father, who died suddenly. She tells me every story in no more than one or two sentences. She says, *What happened, happened, and who can figure out if what I remember really happened or if maybe I'm making it up. What's important is what I am now, not what I was.*

Three days we are at the Kinneret. Once a day we go to Ein Gev to fill the big jerry can with drinking water, to buy dry rolls and leben at the little guesthouse convenience store. Apart from this, we sit on the stones, we are quiet or we speak, she allows me to caress her head and her hand. I take out my book of Rachel's poems. She doesn't laugh at me. She says that next time we go to the Kinneret she wants to put flowers on Rachel's grave because she is practically forgotten. Sometimes, when she disappears between the banana trees with a roll of toilet paper, I say to myself, *You're alone, do you see? You're alone, there's nobody here, pinch yourself, wake up, you're dreaming*. Then she returns with a shy smile, puts the roll of toilet paper in her backpack and goes to wash her hands. On the second night I am tense, painfully hard. I swim far off, dive, and masturbate. I return calmer but trembling, she dries me off, puts our sleeping bags close together, hides her head under my arm and falls asleep.

On Sunday afternoon I accompany her to the bus station in Tiberias. I will stay in the north for another week. I hold her, near the bus station, feeling as if she has turned over a new layer inside of me, that even when she leaves I won't be alone. The image of us holding each other in a tight goodbye hug doesn't particularly excite the mass of people filling the bus station. Only we know these feelings, here and now, beside the rusty steel gate that keeps the line straight. We put a comma in the sentence that begins on the stones of the Kinneret, the rest to be continued. Anyone observing us from the sidelines cannot guess that this embrace is the embodiment of our hesitant future.

sixteen

Under no circumstances would she agree to discussions of fate, the hand of God, or any other kind of deities hovering in the air and descending to create order or chaos in our lives. Now I sit directly in front of her mother and sister. They say I know her better than anyone, and I have only one stupid, simple response. She is my beloved woman: Ildiko Ildi Ili Kitschi Chavatzelet Chavatzy Rott Marcowitz. I haven't created another name for her, one that might include them all, now there's no point, especially after what's happened, what would I call her? Most of the time I simply say to her, *my woman.*

After the Kinneret she is always home on Tuesdays. She offers me something to drink, tells me the garden is coming along nicely. I go back to work as if we didn't spent three days together at the Kinneret, yet something has changed. One day when I finish working, she asks me to join her and her mother for lunch because her mother always makes enough for a regiment. Fresh, homemade food. *A million flavors in these sauces, dripping between the layers*, said Mrs. Rott. *When I was a child I loved to spend time in my mother's kitchen.* She remembers how to prepare traditional dishes. *People think that Hungarian food is goulash, they don't know that there is goash soup, and what about rakot krumpli, and rakot kapusta, and palachinta—my grand- mother would be spinning in her grave if she knew what Israelis did with palachinta. Oy, filling them with mush- rooms? Blintzes? This is palachinta: You fill them with low- fat white cheese, egg yolk, grated lemon peel and sugar to taste, what's with this cinnamon and raisins?*

I don't know anything about real Hungarian food; my mother didn't like to cook. The next week they say to me, if you're in the neighborhood stop by around noon. They feed me, say I should take a shower so I can feel refreshed. Everything is in Hungarian, this seems natural to me after the first time. Even when Kitschi has to work late in the eve- nings I eat with her mother every couple of days, until Mrs. Rott says, *Why didn't you come by yesterday? We waited for you, tomorrow we're eating at two o'clock, will that be convenient?* So I shower and eat at the Rott's house.

Sometimes, as if justifying myself, I tell them about my mother's problems, about the distance of my father and my brothers. I am ashamed by how hungry I am, and that they've adopted me so naturally. Kartschi Farkash says to me, *Nu, young man, any developments?* Embarrassed, I tell him, *It's not like that. Mrs. Rott and her daughter have ad- opted me, you and Siddi also like to pamper young people.* I don't think very much about how they fuss over me, but at the end of the month I don't know what to do with the mon- ey that Mrs. Rott hands me. I don't know if I should refuse it, switch things around and offer her money for her hospi- tality. Instead of complicating things, I buy them presents. Useful things for the kitchen, like an electric can opener. I show Mrs. Rott how easy it is to use, so she won't have to strain her delicate hands. I replace the light bulbs that burn out, the shower curtain, the fence. I put a better antenna on

the roof, I install a gate with an electric bell and an inter-
com. A box of Holbein Professional colored pencils, sheets
of watercolor paper, an eraser for charcoal. They already
feel free to ask me things like, *Maybe next time you'll bring
your power drill, because the screw that holds up the heavy
mirror in the entryway needs to be tightened.*

Summer ends. At Rosh Hashanah I am invited for the
holiday dinner, with Zsuzsi and Yuval, who are to be married in another month. *Of course you're invited, Ephraim.* I
am already part of the family. On Saturday mornings I stop
by for a cup of coffee in the garden with Mrs. Rott, as I am
careful to call her, and Ildiko at her home is Ildiko.

Since I took her to the Kinneret we've gone five more
times, always the same: we speak like brother and sister, we
sit with our arms around each other, we fall asleep holding
hands. We kiss, too, our lips a little less dry now. I know the
feeling of her skin under my hands, her breasts are large and
solid and sometimes I suck on her nipples, moaning, but she
just strokes my head, and I know it isn't time yet, that she is
still afraid of ruining everything with sex.

Her mother gives me sweet Madártej to drink; when the
weather starts to cool she insists that I stay until evening,
telling me to lie down on the living room couch, bringing
me a pillow and blanket. *Relax, take it easy—what do you
have to hurry home for*, she says, laughing. *What, are you
shy now? You're like my own son, Ildiko will be home soon
and we'll have supper together.*

There aren't many guests at her sister's wedding. The
newlyweds go to Eilat for their honeymoon, and Mrs. Rott
goes to Haifa to visit a childhood friend who is also widowed.
This is unusual; Mrs. Rott is anxious and asks me to stop by
and see Ildiko every day, because even though she is grown
up, she is still afraid to be home alone. The refrigerator is

full—she's been using the new oven I bought them with my most recent wages. At first Mrs. Rott was angry. She scolded me: *I'm supposed to take this big present from a boy? Isn't this your house, too?* I tell her it's for everyone to use, and in honor of the holiday.

I don't see my friends much anymore. They say to me, *That's it, then, you've found yourself someone, but who?* They insist I tell them, but I say, *Listen, guys, it's not what you think.* I keep it all a secret because I don't want my friends to scare her off. At night I toss restlessly between the cool sheets, finding release from the physical pressure, going to her with my body relaxed.

On Monday night I shave, put on clean clothes, go to Malka's fancy flower shop and buy a huge bouquet of red roses wrapped in cellophane, and go to see how Mrs. Rott's daughter is getting along by herself. When she opens the door she also smells as if she's just taken a bath. She is cheerful and relaxed, unlike me—I am suddenly seized with a wave of tremors. Automatically she places a hand on my forehead. *Are you sick? Nervous?* Those direct questions of hers. She says, *Come in, you're freezing out there—there's hot soup, that will warm you up.* She puts the flowers in a vase with fresh water, arranging each bloom in its own place. We eat in silence. She takes my empty plate and turns toward the large pot to give me another helping. To her back, I gather the courage to say, *Ildiko, I love you.* She returns with my plate filled, sets it before me with controlled hands, and sits down again across from me. Time passes, maybe a million years, and I say to her again, *Ildiko, I love you.* She turns away from the table, wipes it off, leaves the kitchen. I follow her, turning off all the lights on the way to her room. Despite all the months that I've been a welcome guest in her house, this is the first time I've set foot in her room. She stands in the middle of the round rug, and even though it's dark and the tremors have again seized my body, I can see that she is lost, that she doesn't know what to do. With trembling fingers I touch her shoulders; they are tense. I grab her and turn her toward me. She looks down. With both hands I hold her soft, burning cheeks; in the dark I see that her round, violet eyes are wide with fear. *Ildiko I love you*, I tell her again and again. I hold her, I cling to her, I caress her back, I kiss her forehead, her eyes, her lips, dripping with tears. I lick them away. I say, *I love you, love you*. She softens, I gently lie her down under the patchwork quilt and embrace her; together we tremble. I say to her, *Love me, if you can*. I stroke her curls, grope around for her buttons and zippers. I try to do everything slowly and tenderly. I feel like she trusts me, she is yielding to me. She helps me take off my pants, my shirt, she pulls off my socks. We are naked, clinging to each other.

For a long time we lie together without moving, the only sound our intense breathing. She moves first, bringing her lips closer to mine, her tongue entering the space in my mouth. I close my eyes and suck in her sweet saliva. Then we are like dough, she is inside me I am inside her, moving like the little waves on the Kinneret, again and again in perfect harmony. *Oh, my woman, my woman, my beloved*, I whisper to her; she whispers back, *You are my man, my beloved man*. We cry until the end, then we are suffocating each other with the strength of our embrace, and suddenly we burst into laughter. She laughs, her whole body shaking. I lie on my back and laugh and laugh, waves of laughter rolling out of me until I nearly run out of breath. After we calm down we lie in each others' arms quietly. She snuggles close and entwines her legs in mine. Again I whisper to her, *My woman, my beloved*, and she whispers back, *My man, my beloved*. She says to me, *I'm going to fall asleep, is that okay?* I am surprised that she still isn't sure. I tell her, *Whatever you want, my love.* She asks in a whisper, *And then what?* I tell her that then we need to choose one of her names, because it will be impossible to write all of them on the wedding invitations. She says, *Ahhh, then it will be Chavatzelet, if that's okay with you?* I love her understanding, her body against mine, our thoughts that fit inside each other, and again we wake up and, blended together, licking, sucking, until sworn to each other, we fall asleep.

Ephraim! Did you fall asleep! Zsuszi is shaking me. Apparently I did fall asleep, I'm tired, suddenly I was asleep. I wake up in a panic, look around the room, their eyes are stabbing me, no, no, I wasn't dreaming, she is my wife, my woman! Hurry, fly to her, I escape from the warm armchair, I fly. I was in the clouds, it was an accident, everything is coming apart, scattered, the ambulance, the investigation. I'm a gardener, not a pilot, worried eyes examining the pieces, how much time has passed? Five minutes, five minutes and I don't know anything more, a few days ago they were asking me if we had already decided which model of gate to use to close off the yard, now they want me to explain what happened to her? I don't know. She's my woman, and I don't care what she did, what could I say now to their stabbing eyes, she is my woman and I don't care what she did. I want it all to be over so that we can walk barefoot again on the lawn I planted for her. We have cypress seedlings in the yard that still haven't taken root, she's expecting them to grow, to be able to look up at them, if only this could all be over. I tell them all goodbye, I go home. She will surely tell me the ending some time, and then we'll all understand and know if we need to save her or be angry with her. In any case I am going back to her.

seventeen

Oh, my woman, my woman. I won't leave you unsupervised anymore. In the morning she wakes up gloomy. Folded inside of herself on the couch, she begins to speak.

"... One day you knocked on the door, my mother was stammering with excitement, even though she could have spoken Hungarian with you. I sat at the living room window, soothed by the sight of the cypress. My mother knew that it was forbidden to touch my cypress.

"I saw you, our gardener, struggling with the plague of weeds, pulling and ripping the strangling limbs of the parasitic shrubs that had taken root everywhere, yanking out the thick roots of the wild plants that were sucking the life out of the soil. You trimmed the dry branches from the trees, you dug up and aerated the hard dirt that was suffocating the tree trunks, you unclogged the rusty sprinkler system. You struggled in our dusty garden without a word until it was bare and clean. You didn't touch the cypress.

"Neighbors passing by exclaimed, 'How lovely! It's long overdue, *nu*, what are you going to plant?' I had the sense that you didn't need any guidance, that you would always know exactly what needed to be done. I followed you, watching as you walked, drawn into yourself and yet still upright, tall and handsome, gentle, simple. You didn't have the tiniest bit of arrogance in your strong body. People say the eyes reveal the soul, but I couldn't see your eyes. I saw your short hair, your muscles. I thought about all the women who'd been tangled up in your arms. I imagined how you touched them—shyly, gently, the way you smelled the laundry, the way you caressed the cypress, the way you stole quick glances at my room. I didn't want you to stop. I knew you were looking for me. My mother was always saying, 'What luck we have, Kitschi, don't be impolite, go say hello to Ephraim, he's just a wonderful young man, just go and say hello, he's an artist, he has such sensitive hands, go, bring him something to drink.'

"My mother. She caught me peeking at you from the kitchen window. I told her, *I will get to know him at my own pace.* Some old feeling that had been closed off inside me for years was awakened, as I observed the way you took care of our neglected garden. For years I hadn't thought about Yutzi, about the curiosity she awoke in me, about the intense desire to be close to her, to attract her attention, to be loved by her—once again it tickled my fingertips. I wanted to touch this man who was wiping away the dust, clearing out a place through which the sunlight could pierce the windows. You concentrated on your work, as if you'd been sent to our yard by the highest authorities. And I couldn't push aside the foolish feeling that you were the one who had taken on the mission of waking the one who'd been asleep for a hundred years, clearing away the vines that closed up the house and all the while searching for the place where the sleeping one lay, waiting to be awakened by a kiss. You aren't the prince, and I'm certainly not Sleeping Beauty.

"I was entertaining myself with this idea, painting the possibilities, examining you from every angle. I was quite an expert at following you. From the little window in the bathroom I saw you peeking into my room, the first time you were hoeing under the window, your back stooped. Only when you straightened up to wipe the sweat from your forehead did you sneak a glance into my room. You alternated these hesitant glances with brave sniffs, which you took when you popped your head over the windowsill. When you were in the backyard I watched you from the kitchen window; when you worked in the front yard I peered at you through the peephole in the front door. I collected the gifts you left me under the cypress, and I waited to see if you would give up in despair or keep bringing me more. I encouraged you from the dimness of my parents' bedroom, I helped you pick out my laundry on the clothesline. *The white underpants are mine, you're right*, I told you from inside the house, you identified the fragrance correctly. Early in the morning I went out to the grocery store, got what I needed and then returned home to hide in the house. I saw your truck pull up, I saw how you closed your eyes, sniffing for the scent I'd left in my wake. I couldn't laugh, even though you looked like a hungry animal in a cartoon movie being dragged around in his sleep by the smell of fresh pastry. I was afraid I didn't understand properly what I was seeing, and I didn't have anyone to ask. *Danger, danger*, there were sirens in my ears. My mother liked you very much, always patting you, pampering you, scolding me that I wasn't being polite. She wanted me to wait on you, to entertain you in our yard. This reminded me of her blind affection for Yutzi. I told myself that this was exactly the opposite, you were cleaning up the mess, making things beautiful, and you wanted me, you were looking for me, it was the opposite.

"For a long time I didn't have the courage to admit to myself that I was looking for you, too. You contrived all kinds of plots to try to meet me, and this seemed like a suspicion worth investigating. I thought, *He won't see me before I am sure.*

"I couldn't even fall asleep anymore without thinking about you. I ached for Tuesdays to come. I had graduated with honors. Days wasted on complicated calculations. At the textile factory where I worked they didn't make use of my broad knowledge of chemistry; I sat for hours at a drawing table and sketched patterns for linens, for children's pajamas, for curtains, napkins and bedcovers—designs that repeated themselves every quarter of a meter: elephants for children, guitars for teenagers, hounds-tooth plaids for adults, flowers for young couples. Four, six, twenty-four, forty-eight, pair after pair for miles. Mr. Nathan, the factory manager, was a religious man. He believed in restraint. *Chavatzelet, I really like your work,* he told me. *Today all the linen designers try to be original, but you stay inside the lines, you understand that it's impossible to fall asleep inside red and green and black scribbles.* Maybe because of this he was among the first to lose his shirt when the textile industry collapsed in Israel. Mr. Nathan, I told him, On Tuesdays I want to work in the afternoons, I won't disturb anyone and I'll be very responsible and lock up in the evenings.

"On Tuesdays I was always home, drinking my first cup of coffee to the scratching, sawing sound of the rake in the dry leaves. The pruned hedge started to grow leaves, the grayness was replaced by green, the bald spots filled in with grass, the overturned earth was a deep, saturated brown. Even the bitter orange trees seemed more optimistic, as if toward winter they might manage to produce sweeter fruit. My mother was so happy; she sat in the revived garden and stared off into the distance. I wasn't sure yet if our gardener was more than just talented at his profession, if his presence in our lives was more than just a business matter.

"At every opportunity, Siddi and Kartschi insisted to me that the gardener we shared was not just talented, but also very good-looking, a nice man, shy, and didn't I know what chutzpah young men had today. Siddi said to me, 'If I were a young woman I would set my sights on that one, before some tart has him under her spell.' They had your address under a magnet among all the other forgotten reminders and mementos on their refrigerator; Kartschi once gave you a used couch that had been sitting in their garage. 'Such a good man, such a gentle soul.' They wanted to encourage you, too, so that you would become part of this crazy household. But you were shy and serious, maybe even a little frightened sometimes when they showered you with their affection. You weren't used to it.

"My sister was shocked one day when I asked if I could borrow her car. 'Why don't you buy yourself a little used car, get out of the house sometimes. Why did you even get a driver's license? How can you stand to take the bus all the time, Ildi. I really don't get you. Mother has offered a thousand times to buy you a car, it would be good for her, too, you could go on little road trips. You're rotting away in the house.' My sister. It's impossible to talk to her without her breaking into some kind of agitated speech about all the different things I needed to do to get moving and put my life in order. Do this, go there, see that, jump, swallow, do this, it's important—my isolation drove her crazy. My mother placated her, *Nu, nu, Zsuzsika, don't pester your sister, if she wants something she'll get it in her own fashion, at her own speed. Not everyone is like you, you need everything immediately; she has time.*

"Time was something I had in excess. I couldn't sink any more hours into my paintings; work had grown almost monotonous. My mother was very good at keeping herself busy with her books; I had lots and lots of time. *Ephraim, Ephraim, Ephraim*—you occupied my thoughts most often. What does he do when he's not working at our house, where does he live, who are his friends, what does he eat for breakfast, what music does he listen to? I don't remember exactly when I started to feel something pleasant wash over me at the appearance of our gardener. For hours I used to stare at the white paper of my sketchpad, and I didn't believe I was allowed the privilege of feeling something so pure and intense for a man I didn't know. I felt happy, as if I had arrived at the start of a maze, and an endless landscape lay before me, where I could run in all directions, and that someone would be at my side, keeping me safe. I don't know why you stirred up this feeling of security in me. Nonetheless I scrutinized you very carefully before I found the courage to appear in front of you.

"I took my sister's car, and I drove to the address that I had copied from Siddi and Kartschi's refrigerator. I drove past five times. I stopped at the grocery store on the corner, buying a loaf of brown bread so I wouldn't appear suspicious. *So here is where he buys his groceries*. I tried to guess whether you paid by check or cash. That evening I left my sister's car at home and returned on the bus, the stop was across the street, precisely in front of the entrance. Your truck. I wondered which floor you lived on. Maybe the fourth.

"I got used to taking three different buses: one from work to the central station, another that went through your neighborhood and returned to the central bus station, and the third from there back to Queen Esther Street. I had to do this, because I could barely keep myself from going to you out in the yard on Tuesdays. I was afraid that at the moment I took your hand you would drag me to some slaughterhouse.

"My mother turned to my sister for help, because I wasn't eating and I was pale and couldn't concentrate and I had stopped painting. I wanted to tell them I was in love, but this sounded irrational; the more I saw the despair in your eyes as you searched for me, the more dedicated I became to following you. In the evenings I disappeared from the house, my mother worried but tried not to ask any questions; only her praying eyes accompanied my silent exits.

"One Friday I saw you disappear into the dilapidated entryway with a young woman wearing high heels. I hid three buildings away, behind a large garbage bin filled with the remains of what women had been cooking for the Sabbath. A half-bald kitten acted as my host; he was full of scabs and nicks, and fleas hopped by the dozens through his mangy fur. He was hungry. I tried to pet him and he bolted in fear, but nevertheless came back. An hour passed; with his eyes the kitten pleaded with me from a safe distance. In the end I quietly opened the garbage bin and rummaged among the greasy bags until I found a piece of chicken skin; the kitten made off with the food, and I didn't see him again. I actually considered taking him home, cleaning him up and arranging a warm bed for him under the table in my room. Another hour went by. How could it be that we didn't have a cat or a dog? I tried to remember Bokshi; I couldn't see her face, but I could feel her fur beneath my hands.

"A light in the stairwell. She is first, then you, slouching behind her, walking as if iron bars were attached to your legs. She was busy with her hair. There is nothing intimate between the two of you, that was it, I'd had enough. I decided to end this torment. On Tuesday I let you find me under the cypress…"

eighteen

She's talking about me, and I feel like I was somebody else. We never bring up memories of how we met and when we fell in love — the way I hear Shosh sometimes, talking about how she pursued Yuval, and how at first he was indifferent, even to this day, but then she worked very hard to catch him, she wasn't such a bad bargain, was she? She needles him: *Yuval doesn't have a lot of time for cuddling, whatever, I saw exactly what I was getting myself into with him.* They talk as if their relationship began like some kind of battle that ended in a tie, and then they got married. With us it was different. I knew before I even saw her that she was the woman for me. Now it turns out that for all the months that I tortured myself with the thought that she wasn't home, she was actually encouraging me with her gaze, but afraid of me. We've never spoken about the past. We sketched our future, adding detail after detail — creating such a beautiful picture.

Once, in high school, they took us to an art exhibition. The artist was present, and tried to explain in complicated words that art was a language, and if we learned the language we would better understand the artist's intentions. Someone asked him, *But tell us, for example, what's the story behind this painting?* The artist snickered and said the answer was very simple, behind the painting there was a wall. I remember being disappointed, even angry—he could have revealed a little more to us if he'd wanted us to understand his paintings.

Now, as she speaks about me, I feel as if she is revealing to me all the things hidden behind the picture. There's no wall, there's an enormous hall, she's taking me almost nonchalantly on a guided tour behind this picture. *You see, this is what I was like when I was five.* She leads me onward, *there's me curled up in my bed, soaked with urine, Yutzi, a little plastic closet with rusty circles of paint, Gidi Bender, here you are peeling away the garden, the Kinneret, there we are making love for the first time, the dusty, still-unpaved path that leads to the little house we bought at the moshav.* I can see Mrs. Rott wiping away a tear of relief under the chuppah at our wedding, a lovely wedding, *Look, Ephraim, even your mother is at peace.* I'm wandering along with her, trying to see the images through her violet spotlights, and not the way I know them.

Since that embrace at the Tiberias bus station, after that first time we spent three days together at the Kinneret, I feel for the first time that she is separate from me, standing across from me, that I've had a miscarriage, I am an orphan, she has jumped and broken apart and now she's licking her wounds alone, not letting me touch her. In the newspaper maybe they would write that even the husband she lived with for many years never knew a thing. At the grocery store they interviewed the neighbors: *Such a nice woman, quiet, kept a perfect home, a diligent worker, a sweet young couple with an herb garden, why this, now? We heard she was in her fourth or fifth month. Bizarre.* Ildiko Chavatzelet and the rest of her names, I needed to make more of an effort, to insist on finding her a name that encompassed them all, my wife, my love, even this is only part of it. I see all that she imprisons within herself behind the table, my woman. Inside her womb our baby is growing, the future.

Why did I think about my mother at that particular moment of happiness, when she announced to me that the results were positive, we were going to have a baby, that soon I would be a father, have a family. In a steady, calm voice, she said to me, *I'm pregnant*. We spoke about it many times before it happened — we examined, considered, we were afraid, we encouraged each other, we quizzed ourselves. *Yes, we're ready*, we'd made a decision, we were strong, certain. We were pregnant, we were on our way to the Kinneret to celebrate. Alone.

On the way, she told me she had almost the same sensation as when she got her period for the first time, except she had celebrated that turning point alone, and now this belonged to the two of us, together. I felt the way I did the first time I saw her, we laughed at the comparison. Our one-month-old fetus was traveling with us to the Kinneret, sleeping in the sleeping bag, splashing in the water. The next day we took him on a hike to the Upper Galilee. Toward evening we headed back, still thinking about whether we might get to Ashkelon at a reasonable hour and stop by her mother's house to share the happy news or wait until the next day. By nine o'clock it was already dark and we were still on the road heading toward Kibbutz Gonen. Chavatzelet was asleep. I must have been lost in thought. The road was empty, no traffic at all at that hour; it was just a small, unimportant road between the kibbutzim. I didn't feel the collision, and I didn't know that I had hit anything. I stopped, thinking that there was a puncture in one of the tires. Chavatzelet woke up in a panic. I told her, *I guess we have a flat*, I got out of the car, checked each tire in turn, everything was fine. On the front fender I saw a large smear, on the grille. I thought that I'd hit a chunk of mud, but the ground wasn't muddy. In the middle of the road, about two meters behind the car, I saw a lump of something. Chavatzelet got out of the car, came and stood beside me. I said, *Stay here, I'm going to check this out.* In the red glow of the taillights I saw that I'd crushed a wild boar. *Don't come over here*! I shouted in spite of the fact that she wasn't very far away and this was all happening on a little-used side road in the silence of the evening. The boar lay on its side, its eyes wide open, as if it were still looking at something even though it was already dead. Its glassy white eyes looked like ping-pong balls in an island of red mud, surrounded by a dark wetness that was spreading into the ditch on the side of the road. I stood close to it; I couldn't move, the blood streamed under the soles of my white sneakers; I didn't know there was so much blood in just one boar. I was hypnotized, I couldn't turn my eyes away from the slow trickle.

Before I heard her, I felt her warm body beside me. I couldn't turn to her. Strangely, I was worrying that my sneakers would get dirty if I moved too suddenly, in that same split-second, or minute, or maybe hour, I was stuck in the middle of the puddle, at that moment any activity seemed almost intolerable in my mind: the Beatles were playing something, my friends were laughing and telling jokes. Was I sad? Confused? Did I feel guilty? I killed a boar, it was only a boar—a cat or dog would have made me feel worse. But it was dead, I was to blame. Shots fired, hunters—I needed to warn them, so that they wouldn't shoot us by mistake. Ildiko, protect her, where was she? Ildiko was sitting under the cypress, Ildiko, was standing next to me, hunched over, more like folded in half, and throwing up on the boar. It was crushed, how could it be crushed from such a little hit? This is what I thought about, and I still couldn't move. It seemed natural to me that my pregnant wife was throwing up on the image that I myself couldn't stop staring at. I'm certain that not very much time passed—it just seemed that way to me. I wouldn't have let her stand there next to me alone without calming her, without comforting her. We stood there, the two of us. I didn't know what to do, I didn't hear the Jeep's engine coming closer, light, the light came closer, descending with the road, widening and growing brighter. It stopped with its headlights exactly on the boar. Three men jumped out of the car, the two younger ones stood next to us, one holding the right shoulder of the other. *What happened? Is everything okay? Zevik, come look, right in the middle of the road.* Zevik wore denim overalls and black rubber boots. They were kibbutzniks from the area; I recognized them by their appearance. I knew kibbutzniks from Kfar Giladi. They looked like this, they would know what to do. The third one—the older one—had already seen the surprise from farther away. He came prepared, with a knife. *Did you run it over,* he asked us, poking a bit at the boar's head with the blade of the knife. *Take your wife over there, give her something to drink, can't you see something's wrong with her? Ma'am, calm down, this isn't pleasant, but don't get hysterical. What, you've never had a steak? Think of it as a fine cut of meat. Believe me, they suffer more at the hands of the butcher.* The younger men helped us away from the scene. We stood on the side while the hunters consulted each other and went about their business like professionals. Zevik said, *I take it by the look on your face that you don't want it, right?* I held onto Ildiko, she trembled and mumbled something. We need to get into the car and

SUZANE ADAM

escape from here, I convinced myself, and yet in shock I still didn't move, I just nodded my head, I don't know what I was waiting for. We were a group, and I couldn't remove our presence from around the boar. The older man examined it, turning the boar's doughy head from side to side and said, *Died on impact*. The younger men were busy with the guts, poking around in the organs with a stick and discussing something. Zevik got up first and said, *It's completely smashed, it's shit*. The second one said, *Looks like it was an old, sick boar, let's get out of here*. The older man agreed that it was an old boar, possibly sick, and it was still the beginning of the night, *and we're out here to hunt, not go to the supermarket*, and then he laughed, they all laughed and slapped each other on the back. *Yalla, let's get out of here, what are you standing there for? Get your wife out of here already, maybe you're going to bury it? Mourn it?* They left, laughing. Again the boar was bathed in red light.

The sudden change in the light, or in the chill that had descended, brought me back to reality, where I hadn't been for several minutes. Again I was in charge. I urged Chavat-zelet into the car, I took the emergency cables out of the trunk—I wanted to tie the boar's legs together and drag it into the ditch. I couldn't leave it lying there spread all over the road. But the cables weren't flexible enough and the metal grippers got all mixed up in the boar's guts. In the end I gave up, what could I have done? The boar was too heavy. I wiped the nastiness off my hands in the grass that was wet with dew. I needed to take care of my wife, too. I calmed her, caressed her, kissed her, soothed her. We were quiet. What was there to say?

We traveled in silence almost all the way to Tiberias; then she whispered, *I wet my pants*. I laughed and stopped.

I would have wet myself too if I hadn't gone earlier, I told her. She wasn't laughing. With heavy steps she walked around to the trunk to take out a change of clothes; I went to shield her so that nobody passing by would see. I tried to joke with her again, because I didn't want to suddenly start talking about what we'd seen, I wanted to forget. I hoped that by tomorrow, when we'd returned home, she would have forgotten, too. Quietly she said, *This is blood. I'm bleeding.* After that everything sped up, I don't remember any of it, the road there, the emergency room, the women's section. They said, *This happens to one in every three women, spontaneous miscarriage.* In my mind the word "spontaneous" is always associated with happy events, interesting things, adventures. The doctor said that if she had had a great fright within the last two hours that this might be the result, but we shouldn't worry, we should take heart, we were still a young couple, we would try again. We went home in the morning. We made a silent pact that we wouldn't talk about what had happened. That was easiest, not to speak of it. Nobody else had known about it because we'd gone to celebrate alone, what was the use in talking about it? The doctor was right; the best thing was to try again.

Four months later Ildiko was pregnant again. I thought about my mother, I wanted to tell her, to say, *Look, you see? There's no need to despair.* The second pregnancy we took to Grandmother Rott and Aunt Zsuzsi, to the family. It seemed to me that at first the two of us were afraid to wander too far from the house.

One Friday we put on happy smiles and went to announce the good news to Mrs. Rott, her younger daughter, her husband, and their baby. We were excited, we didn't relax our grip on each other's hands for a minute. We wept and embraced and even her sister was at a loss for words, and just sat in an unusual silence, every now and then kissing her sister and stroking her head, as if to say, *Some peace, at last you have some peace.* Mrs. Rott shakily placed glasses of wine on the table and announced in a choked voice, *Today we have twice the reason to celebrate; I've got a surprise for you all, too.* She disappeared into her room for a moment and returned with an envelope addressed with her name written in a foreign language. She waved the letter in front of us with excitement. 'You'll never guess, never in a million years will you guess who this is from.' Her cheeks reddened with excitement. From the sudden slackness of her grip on my hand, I guessed that the mother of my child knew the answer. From Yutzi. For months she had been corresponding with Mrs. Rott; in another week she was coming to Israel. Mrs. Rott had invited her to live there with her, she could be a house-companion until she found some kind of work in Israel. 'Oy, Ephraim, you don't know Yutzi at all, the girls were small, they certainly don't remember her anymore, she was beautiful and clever, our foster child. Did you know that once, Ildiko was lost, and Yutzi brought her back from the devil only knows where, to this day I haven't forgotten how frightened we were, until Yutzi brought her back to us safe and sound. What do you say, Kitschi? Isn't this wonderful?' Suddenly we were all looking at Kitschi; her eyes were closed and she was very pale, her body limp.

I spoke first, *She's fainting, bring some water, quick.* I caressed her, dampened her face, not again, please, everything is good, there's nothing to be excited about, I didn't run over a boar, don't get excited, I'll take her home. Mrs. Rott laughed, *I have a princess for a daughter, throwing up and fainting, it's natural in her condition.* She didn't know her daughter had already had a miscarriage, we hadn't told anyone. It was better not to tell anyone, I was hysterical enough for everyone already. I dampened her shirt with some of the water. Shosh said, *You're going to drown her*. We didn't give Ildiko room to breathe until her eyes opened a bit. *I'm fine*, she mumbled, *I was just a little weak, suddenly*. We smiled at her in relief. This was natural in her condition, too much excitement for one day.

We toasted, *L'chaim*, sweetening the happy news with warm apple cake. I worried about my wife. Mrs. Rott repeated the details of her excitement, encouraged by the curious questions from her younger daughter. She spoke in a mixture of Hungarian and Hebrew. 'I don't tell about the letters with Yutzi, until I am no sure. Today they let Romanian citizens go to other countries to earn money; apparently Romanian government needs dollar. The Debretzeny's have a Polish girl and they're very satisfied with her, but I don't want Yutzi to work as a maid, no absolutely not, and what is here to do that I no can alone? No, not because I am to being alone, God forbid I'm not complaining. I'm happy that everyone has a house his own and you are young couples not needing old lady going around between your legs, absolutely. Of course it's not hard for me to be alone in the house, but it will be nice when Yutzi will live here, I thought your room, Kitschi, it's just empty. You don't care, do you? You have the moshav house. We'll make it nice and comfortable, she deserves it after all that's happened to her. Yutzi isn't young anymore, and according to what she told me in her last letters, her life has been trashed—isn't that what you young people say? She needs now to be something like forty or more, Kitschi, you were five years old and she was about sixteen or seventeen, right? I really don't remember already. I hope she won't be boring to live with an old bird like me. Anyway, I wrote to her, it's a temporary situation, she can check if this suits her, need to find some nice job and not tiring. I understood she's not so healthy.'

Over the next few days, my wife grew paler and quieter than ever, as did I. Three months, said the doctor, you need to look after her, not too much excitement, not too much exertion. I worked in our garden, she sat in the yard and watched how I made it more beautiful all around her. I planted cypress seedlings and more grass. Two stray dogs had adopted us. We needed a fence so they wouldn't run around in the neighbors' yards. On the moshav they didn't like dogs to run around loose; the last thing I needed was for someone to poison them.

She brought me something to drink. I scolded her, *Sit down and relax*. We both knew she needed to be careful. We didn't talk about it. At night I stroked her belly, promising this second baby that I would take care of its mother, soothing them to sleep. I lay awake for hours, watching my beautiful wife. Did my father watch over my mother like this when I was growing inside her?

Hesitantly, I suggested that we visit my mother; maybe she would be happy to hear the good news. But my mother was hard to please. And Ildiko said to me, *You go, alone, maybe it will make her happy if you go to her alone, tell her that this is your child, her legacy.*

From the very first time I introduced Ildiko Rott to my mother I knew that I would go on visiting her and her sister alone, for a few minutes every week. I'd been prepared for the first meeting, Chavatzelet didn't like surprises. I told her, *My mother is ill, this is how she relates to the world, she's just like that, and her sister suffers from the same symptoms.*

To my mother, I said, *There's a woman I love very much, I want to build a house for her, I want you to know her, she speaks Hungarian.*

Right away my mother wanted to know about Ildiko's parents' experiences in the Holocaust. I said, *I don't even know if they were there; at her house they don't talk about what happened.* My mother said, *Must be rich snobs from Afridar, they're the only ones who can let themselves forget.* Ildiko was worried from the beginning, pale and anxious. I said, *She's my mother.* My mother received us with an impenetrable expression on her face, threw the bouquet that I'd brought her on the kitchen table, as always, and reclaimed her place beside her sister on the living room couch. Ildiko stood frozen until I sat her down in the upholstered armchair that was covered with an old sheet. We sat in an awkward silence until I said, *Auntie, Ildiko speaks fluent Hungarian, you can have a conversation,* and that was when they started giving her the third degree: *What town is your mother from? And your father? Ahh, he's already dead? You were born in Transylvania? That's not Hungary; we are real Hungarians, you're actually Romany, and that's something else, your parents must have had some sense, after everything we were also in Cyprus; they brought us to this primitive desert. How is it that you don't know anything? A few years and they'll be saying we were in resorts, it's a shame, a shame how young people don't care about anything, we old folks can rot and nobody cares, better we should have stayed there, at least they don't know how it feels to be a survivor, nothing, I have nothing left to live for, if you'd gone through half of what we went through you'd never sleep another night, ahh, what can you understand, going on with your life as if nothing ever happened, we'll die and that's it.*

I tried to make the best of the situation, saying, *Ildiko and I are getting married, we're going to have a family, a future—this is what makes staying alive worthwhile, to see your family continue.* My mother responded by saying that this didn't mean anything to her, and for her personally nothing would change.

After that visit Chavatzelet told me she wasn't ready to come with me again, I would need to take care of my mother without her. Of course we invited her to the wedding, also my father, Gadi, and Menashe; everyone met for half an hour before the ceremony, only Mrs. Rott smiled and tried with all her might to meet my family on their own terms, and celebrate accordingly; with a million tiny steps she ran around between the frozen guests like a fairy that long ago lost its book of magic spells. Nonetheless it was a beautiful wedding, on Queen Esther Street, in the yard, with many flowers, good weather, and Zsuzsi made enough noise to fill in any silences left by the others. My friends and Siddi and Kartschi contributed their laughter.

Meanwhile I was postponing a visit with my mother. Chavatzelet was barely pregnant; there was time. I told my father on the telephone, and he took the opportunity to suggest we come for a visit, finally he could get to know my wife better; they had met only at our wedding. I knew this wasn't normal for relatives. Amalia was very ill, he couldn't leave her even for a minute, she needed him. I told him, *It's no big deal, Dad, I know that my happiness makes you happy, take good care of Amalia, she deserves it.*

The truth of the matter was that I wanted to be alone with my wife, to grasp together this amazing thing that was developing in her belly. I expected happiness to buoy us, to buoy me. I had a wife, a house, I was an adult, proud of myself, successful—I had struggled and succeeded. I wanted a moment of peace, to wrap myself in medals, to enjoy the feeling that at this moment in my life everything was perfect. I wanted to go to the Kinneret, to bury the tortured book of Rachel's poetry, to tell her, *Rest in peace, I don't need you anymore, poor Rachel. My head has already been crowned with a laurel wreath.* I was victorious.

My beloved wife sits across from me every morning with a cup of coffee, beside the table that was once in her bedroom. We are wrapped in the warmth we carried from our bed, from a peaceful night of sleep, our bare feet fit together under the table. Soon the cypress seedlings will grow and peek at us through the window. When the season comes I'll plant herbs. She walks me to my car, another kiss, and another, we'll speak another three or four times by telephone over the course of the day. In the evening we'll soap ourselves together under the warm water in the shower, she decorates the house during the day. It's good that in the meantime she's stopped working outside the house. She does something to every corner, I bring her all kinds of things: a shelf, a mirror, a curtain rod, she sews a new cover for the bed, I strip the paint from an old chest of drawers. I bought good wooden boards to make a bed and dresser for the baby's room, which will be ready before too long, we found an empty steamer trunk that we haven't managed to open. In the meantime it's a useful place for our collection of stones. Everything is good.

We don't have many friends. We have each other. Batya visits sometimes, tells us what's new and then sits quietly. My friends are discreet when their girlfriends are around, drinking coffee politely, talking about the sea. Menachem got married, too, and went to live in Haifa near his wife's parents. We don't need friends, we have each other. Sometimes I go see my friends on my own, I say, *This has turned out very well, married life is good, my wife is wonderful.* They don't laugh at my dreams anymore, and I am embarrassed to tell them just how good everything is. I laugh with them at the same old jokes, I make excuses, saying, *We're still a brand-new couple, we have a lot of love still.* They say *Nu? It looks to us like you have a few more years ahead of you.* In a few more years I envision children, big and small, running around on the lawn; the cypresses will be tall. It's hard for us to leave each other in the morning.

nineteen

Now she sits across from me. I already know, I can describe how she felt when we went to the airport to bring Yutzi home in the yellow Volkswagen Transit I had bought a month earlier. It still smelled like the plastic I'd peeled off the seats when I bought it. It was roomy, everyone who got in could sit comfortably, and there was still enough space for luggage. I'd gotten a good deal; it was a car big enough for a large family and guests, and it was also good for work. Chavatzelet stayed behind to wait for our visitor at her mother's house. We told her, *It's no big deal, it's really not necessary for you to make the effort, the plane might be late, and traffic, in your condition it's best to stay here and rest.* Yuval also wanted to stay behind, with little Tali, but Shosh decided that everyone except for Ildi needed to participate in the experience.

"Here she is!" Mrs. Rott shouted with delight, and pointed to the woman who appeared on the threshold of the automatic double doors that opened around her. At first I thought the baggage cart she was pushing in front of her was about to flip over, even though the cart carried only one narrow suitcase. It looked light to me, but it must have been filled with heavy stones. Later I understood that the skewed image was due to her bad limp. "Oy, she hasn't changed at all," Mrs. Rott said with excitement, and was already taking her tiny steps toward her foster child. They fell into each other's arms, kissing and embracing, laughing and wiping away tears. When she had calmed down a bit, Mrs. Rott turned to the rest of us, and Yutzi fell on Shosh. "Zsuzsika, jaj drága Zsuzsikam." Everyone was speaking Hungarian, and Yuval, who couldn't understand a word of it, held the astonished Tali in his arms and tried to explain to her in baby talk that this was her new aunt, called Yutzi, and Tali, who already knew how to imitate new words, repeated the name out loud, *Yutzi, Yutzi*. Then Yutzi came and gave me a hug. *You're Ildiko's young man, Ildiko the little imp, how is she feeling*? I understand every word but I don't know how to answer, Mrs. Rott comes to my aid, explaining her older daughter's condition to Yutzi. Never mind, Yutzi comforts me, but I don't understand why.

We drive to Ashkelon, to Queen Esther Street. There is noise and chaos in the back seats. Yutzi wants Tali to sit on her lap, and at this Tali bursts into tears. Yuval tries to calm her down, and everyone speaks in a loud mixture of voices. This is how Hungarians are when they get excited, anyone who doesn't know the language would think they're arguing and screaming, but the atmosphere is pleasant, with eruptions of laughter, especially when Zsuzsika tries to speak Hungarian. I'm quiet, I need to concentrate on the traffic. Occasionally I check my passengers in the rearview mirror. I haven't yet made up my mind about Yutzi. There is something cold about her, despite the fact that she is always smiling and touching everyone around her. Her black hair is interwoven with strands of dull silver, stretching behind her, collected into a tight, high bun. Her face is smooth and white, her eyes black and radiant; without the limp I would have considered her a stunningly beautiful woman. But when she stifles the cries of amazement that come from her painted red lips, I see her age in her hands. Her fingers are thin, almost transparent, but there is nothing delicate about them. They look like broken glass that has been glued together carelessly. Her hands, her hands disturb me, and also her sudden appearance. I'd never even heard her name and now everyone is as happy to be around her as if she were some long-lost relative who'd suddenly been found. But I didn't ask and I didn't investigate, because they didn't pry into my family either. On the way home from hearing the news of Yutzi's arrival, Chavatzelet said to me only that it was good that her mother wouldn't be alone in the house, and that was all. My wife isn't given to extreme displays of enthusiasm, and she doesn't like surprises—I'm used to this. So a guest was coming, and in a couple of days everything would return to normal.

Chavatzelet sits on the living room couch next to Mrs. Rott's armchair, under the light of the floor lamp. What a pretty picture my wife makes. I enter first, Yutzi's suitcase in my hand. Chavatzelet is pale again, or maybe it's the light. I go to her, help her get up for the guest, and I think that it seems too early for her to be rising with such difficulty, as if she were already in her ninth month. In the commotion that begins again as soon as everyone crosses the threshold, I observe that Ildiko and Yutzi do not embrace; they barely exchange a nod of the head. Behind the chaos of celebration, Mrs. Rott becomes a blur in the riot of happy voices; she is thrilled by the image of a large family crammed into the small room. I sit down next to Chavatzelet, I want to take her home. It wouldn't be nice for me to take my wife away from her family on such a joyful occasion. Another half hour, an hour at the most, and I'm taking her home. She's pale, I'm worried about her. I try to listen to the conversations. Yutzi is talking about the grim economic situation in Romania, about the ungrateful family that threw her out into the street, even though she'd cared devotedly for their children, especially the one who'd been very ill. After the child died, the family moved to another town, but they didn't want to take her with them, and she was forced to go from place to place looking for work. And her two brothers were in prison, and how everything had changed and everyone was always looking to the west, they wanted to move to America at any price, but she always longed for Mrs. Rott and her warm family, and how sad it is that Mr. Rott was no longer with us, and she sheds a few tears in his memory.

Ildiko does not participate in this lively conversation. Occasionally she says yes, no, or I don't remember. Again her hand clutches mine, sweaty—sweaty and cold. Worriedly I study her face. She is very pale. I suggest that we go home, she nods in agreement. Suddenly she jumps up and runs toward the bathroom, I follow her, my wife, *What happened*, I ask her from the other side of the bathroom door, she is throwing up, everyone stands around me. Yutzi asks Mrs. Rott, *She's still like this? She didn't grow out of it?* She throws up again and again, I shrug, as if to say, *What can I do? It's natural.* But I'm afraid, I can't get the boar out of my head. Everyone relaxes, smiles. This will pass by the fourth month, it's natural. Before we leave, we make plans to host Yutzi. Zsuzsi will take her here and there, Yuval will find some time to take care of the paperwork, I will take her to see our nice new house. Mrs. Rott says, *There's time, we don't need to do everything in one day, let her rest a bit, I'm going to take care of her, spoil her a little, then you young people can take her out and show her a nice time.*

On the way home Chavatzelet is quiet. I attribute this to her condition and suggest that maybe she stay home the next day and rest in bed. She says, *You're right, maybe you can take a day off and stay home too?* My wife, pampering herself? This is something new, and I again connect it to her quiet, delicate state during the pregnancy. I promise to stay with her all day. She has a restless night, getting up twice more to throw up. I bring her water, stroke her hair, tell her, *I wish I could throw up instead of you, for you,* and this finally brings a smile to her face, and before she falls asleep she says, *You can't feel bad instead of me.*

twenty

We sit in our locked house, in the living room. She's on the couch, I'm across from her, and it seems as if I'm also talking, but I'm not. I am the audience, she is talking about us, I am there, but nonetheless missing. I want to tell her, *I remember it differently, I didn't know.* We're getting close to the end, everything is connected. *My woman,* I tell her, *you are my woman.*

"...What went through my head when I learned she was coming to Israel? And afterward, when I met her face to face? I was five-year-old Ildiko with a baby in her belly; I felt powerless. As if the spring weather had suddenly ceased, repelled by a frozen wind that smashed and shredded and shattered everything, everything. Now you know. It's not logical, maybe that's why I didn't say anything. I was a five-year-old girl again.

"I convinced myself with a million positive thoughts that I didn't need to faint, that there wasn't any real danger, that I had a husband I could hide behind, that I had everything. What happened, happened; I hardly ever painted anymore and that was a sign that everything was forgotten. But the fear, the powerlessness—these things I had not forgotten.

My mother was excited and happy again, you were all re-laxed and at ease, my sister was busy, released from all her worry. Yuval? Yuval was a distant relative, baby Tali was enrolled in some special toy club that had been sending games to develop her intelligence since she was an infant. You, my husband, I convinced myself I shouldn't ruin this peaceful picture, from the hope that I would be able to over-come Yutzi's restored presence in my life. *She's a crippled, lonely woman, I thought. I'm safe,* I told myself in my heart. Okay, bad memories, nightmares from years ago, now ev-erything is different, she's on my territory, what could she do to me now? It wasn't logical. I wasn't a little girl, but when I saw her, that hell returned.

"On Friday my mother invited us for a celebratory din-ner, Yutzi's first Sabbath in Israel. *The Sabbath is ours,* I thought, *she should go to church in Jerusalem or Bethlehem.* Jesus certainly wouldn't want her in his neighborhood, and I didn't want her sitting next to our Sabbath candles, either. But she sat, at the head of the table no less, and ate and drank the food that my mother lovingly served her. I wanted to flip the table over on her, to throw her out. This was our honored guest, everyone was happy. I sat there, my fears seemed detached, they didn't belong. In my heart, I thought, *Enough, what happened, happened, she's pleasant company and she has undoubtedly forgotten about Ildiko, the little devil who followed her around, who is responsible for her broken legs.*

"At the end of the meal she volunteered to help clear the table. I began rinsing off the dishes. I heard her limping behind me, my sister said that as soon as she had a chance, she'd take Yutzi to Tel Aviv to buy her some nicer shoes that would make it easier for her to walk. She pressed close to the sink and dropped a handful of silverware into the warm water where my hands were submerged. Then she raised her icy, chapped fingers and pinched my cheek. I didn't move, as if I were a cow tied up before the slaughter. She pinched hard, just like before, and laughed. We stood there alone beside the sink, close together.

"Amid the aromas of the cooking and the peaceful ruins of the festive Sabbath meal, there were also the rotting quinces … her gaze.

"I felt the warm soap bubbles bursting around my knuckles, the bubbles were rising like a broken washing machine in a cartoon movie, the foam rose and rose to the edge of the sink, filling the kitchen, reaching my hips and continuing to rise, and I knew that soon I would dive in, and I thought about my baby and how it was perhaps forbidden to hold my breath when the baby was so young. I tried to hold onto something, my hands were closed around a stack of knives and forks at the bottom of the sink, the metal that was already starting to grow warm from the water strengthened my resistance in a surprising way. I released the silverware from my fingers and felt around in the cloudy water for the serrated meat knife. I held the wooden handle and I felt safer. Maybe two seconds had passed. I know that my sister was in the middle of a story about Tali's latest display of cleverness, this certainly wouldn't be something long, we knew all of Tali's new displays of cleverness. Yutzi limped back to the living room, leaving me with the knife in my hand.

"The fear that woke up inside me was so enormous I didn't feel safe anywhere. I was afraid for my guts, for my baby, for you, for the young cypresses. A thousand times I'd been on the verge of telling you, and on our trip with the boar, it had all came back to me. You were in shock, we grieved together, and there was comfort in this, in the fact that I wasn't alone this time. I didn't want to make you sadder; we didn't talk about it. I thought, *I actually prefer that we don't talk about it.* I'd made a vow to myself on the day I decided to be your wife that I wouldn't hide anything from you, that you'd be able to read me like an open book, and you wouldn't think you had made a mistake. I am who I am, I am the person you know, but I am the way I am because of what I'm telling you now, this is clear, you never pried or looked for explanations about who I am; you are also who you say you are. Never mind, tomorrow, even your mother didn't succeed in replacing your history with her own. I didn't want to talk about the boar, about the miscarriage, you didn't insist. You escape, erase, wait for it to be over somehow, for tomorrow, what happened, happened. I said to my unborn child, don't be ashamed of me, I will find a solution to this problem.

"I was afraid of her. My age had no meaning — illogically, I felt like I was five years old. And just like many years before, I wanted to know where she was at all times, so she couldn't surprise me. And she was everywhere. She wormed her way into our lives within a matter of days, as if we had always been saving her a special place. She slept in my room, she cooked and baked and did laundry, she sat and rested in the backyard, she gave my sister advice on how to raise Tali. I was used to all of this, the loving embrace that she extracted from everyone, she even worked her charms on you — no, no, don't deny it, I saw how she wrapped you up in her flattery. I knew Yutzi, she could work her hocus-pocus and then when nobody was looking she stabbed me with her threatening gaze, and I didn't know what she planned to do to me, and if the desire to rip out my guts still lived inside of her. She had insinuated herself into every aspect of my life, she had become an inseparable part of our daily routine, just like in Transylvania. My mother was always pressuring me, *Why don't you invite Yutzi to visit the moshav?* I tried to put it off. First we'd have to pave the road, then the path, we had to put in a fence, and a gate. I was afraid her mangled legs would make their way to our home, she would put some kind of curse on us that she'd brought from Transylvania. I thought she must have killed the sick boy; he couldn't have just died, she must have suffocated him with a pillow, now it was my turn. I was afraid she wasn't finished with me yet, she had come to finish me off just as she'd promised when I'd seen her for what I thought was the last time. I was afraid to be alone with her, without protection. I was angry with myself, angry that I was still powerless, and she acted as though nothing had ever happened, as if someone had forgiven her. All this time I was planning to tell you, but I waited, another day passed, everything was fine. I thought, *Maybe what happened, happened, and anyway who would believe me?*

"On that day, I was outside, hanging up the laundry. I saw my sister's red car approaching. I was happy. I thought I would have an opportunity to talk to her about Yutzi, to tell her everything, or at least hint at it, get her to notice how Yutzi had begun to control my mother. On an earlier visit I'd seen my mother's pearl necklace around Yutzi's neck. My mother said, *You don't like jewelry, it's not modern enough for Zsuzsi. I'm already an old lady, look how happy it makes Yutzi, look how pretty she is, it brings out her eyes, she's still young and it's not too late for her to find herself some decent young man. A new country, a new life* ... And Yutzi wasn't looking for work anymore. My mother said, *For what? Yutzi is like my adopted daughter, our family is small, who is left? Why should she have to go away again? There's no need, we have enough to eat, enough space.* She suggested maybe they'd take care of Tali together. Already Yutzi had stopped saying please and thank you, and one day she was sitting in my mother's place beneath the floor lamp, and my mother was sitting on the couch. It was hard for me to see this, but I didn't say anything, because it would have sounded like envy on my part, and what did I care, as long my mother was happy in her company? Her gaze was the only thing I couldn't stand.

"My sister turned off the engine, got out of the car in her usual precise fashion, and helped Yutzi straighten her legs and set them on our property. Yutzi was wearing new shoes. One elegant shoe looked normal, a polished black leather with four perforated lines that formed the outline of a butterfly; it was not yet creased from walking. The second shoe looked just like the other one, except that if you examined it from the side you could easily see it had a special heel, higher than the other by an inch or so. And a cane. Yutzi steadied her new shoes on the ground and then stood up straight and tall. The height of the shoe corrected the way that her body leaned; her shoulders were even. My sister handed her the cane—a column of polished wood whose handle she gripped. Yutzi leaned on the cane and took a step toward me, then stopped, and then another step, feeling her way on her new soles through the gravel for a flat surface on which she could make her way with a more certain stride.

"My sister fluttered about with excitement, saying, 'Look at the surprise I brought you, Ildi, we're back from our shopping trip, what do you think about Yutzi's new shoes? Aren't they nice? You'd never know that there was any kind of problem, would you? She needs to get used to them, that's what the cane is for, the orthopedist said that the limp was bad for her back, the shoes and the cane will help her learn to walk straight, without a limp, won't that be wonderful? Okay, I have to run, I have a meeting at six, my office is a madhouse, sticking me with a meeting in the evening, what can I do, all day I was running around with Yutzi, now I'm paying for it, I'll work a little, I spoke with Ephraim, he'd stopped for coffee at Mom's house, what a treasure you have, he never ceases to amaze me, he said he'd come home early and he'd be happy to take Yutzi home in the evening, or you could invite her to spend the night with you, that would give you lots of time to chat, listen — she's a woman with her head on her shoulders, she has a lifetime of experience that I never knew about — enough to choke a horse; too bad I don't understand Hungarian better. Ildi, tell Yutzi that I enjoyed spending time with her, I'm not sure I managed with my pitiful Hungarian to make it clear to her how welcome she is in our home, you wouldn't believe how Tali has fallen for her, this woman has a special touch with children, oy, and Mom is in heaven, okay, good, yalla, I have to run. Have fun you two, bye-bye Yutzi, *szeretlek dragám*, kisses, my sister, too bad I can't stay, have some fun for me.' And she vanished.

"I never asked for help, I never screamed *save me* and my sister didn't hear. She's not to blame, she didn't know, she wanted to make me happy. I thought you were on your way home, because you know me, you know I don't like surprises, you'd be there soon, you'd rescue me. I stood on top of the hill, in Transylvania, with Yutzi, alone.

"Your damp work shirt was still hanging on the clothes-line, attached by a single clothespin; I held the second one in my hand, and I felt as if this were the last picture on a roll of film, and soon the film would start to rewind and the scenes would be replayed, and then all of you would see the photo album of my memory: on the first page a smiling girl with curls and violet eyes, on the last page a pregnant woman with a clothespin in her hand."

twenty-one

I'm not to blame. How could I have known? I myself volunteered to help arrange for Yutzi's visa. Yuval and Zsuzsi
were very busy as usual. I myself went to take care of Yutzi's
paperwork. Everyone agreed to this. We bought her new
clothes, we fed her, we pampered her, Mrs. Rott took her to
a hotel at the Dead Sea to put mud packs on her injured knee,
Tali learned songs in Hungarian that even her grandmother
hadn't been able to teach her before. Yes, it's true that my
wife kept her distance, it's true, but quietly, and without
protest, and without tension, and without voicing all her
reservations about the loving care we were giving Yutzi.
How could I have known? Now I understand my woman,
my beloved. I'm amazed, her bare feet that wandered on the
soft lawn that I planted for her, her violet eyes that painted
my world, her touch, the child she carries. Ildiko, Ildi, Illi,
Kitschi, Chavatzelet Chavatzy Rott Marcowitz, my wife, she
didn't trust me, she didn't feel safe with me, she didn't reveal
herself to me, she had a double life. I was the shell she was
wrapped in; I was only the shell. I protected her cypress in
vain, I took her to the Kinneret in vain, Rachel, Rachel, she
cried in her poems, she spoke, she screamed. At the Kinneret
she used to hold me. I rescued her, she rescued me, I believed

the two of us were saved. We have a house, dogs, a child. Why are you alone? What about me? Where am I?

"… Yutzi stood two steps away from me. *Nah, Ildiko*, she said, *now we're alone*. I stared at her. Instead of a pillow she had a cane in her hand. I felt like I felt when I stood looking at the boar's guts. My baby, I couldn't lose him, I wasn't allowed to get excited, to be scared, to cower. I needed to take deep breaths, but my mouth was filled with saliva. If I couldn't spit or swallow it was going to drip all over my shirt and make my neck all wet, like when I was a child at the slaughterhouse. I didn't take my eyes off her for a minute, I waited for her laugh, her gaze. I was five years old, she was beautiful. She lifted the cane into the air, took another small step, the distance between us was the length of the cane. With the black rubber tip of the cane she touched my shoulder, *Nah, Ildiko*. It was a light touch, like a warning. She touched me again, this time a little harder, leaving a dusty round print on my shirt, *nah, Ildiko*, and she touched me again, the way children will sometimes poke gently at the corpse of a poisoned mouse. *Nah, Ildiko*, this time I could feel the cane pressing into the flesh of my shoulder.

"*What do you want, Yutzi*? I could barely hear myself. The words were all mixed up in my saliva, forming bubbles that burst with every word that reached the air. I tried to hear what she was saying. Yutzi laughed, or screamed, *What do I want*? She stabbed at me again and again with the cane, a succession of unending blows, *What do I want? I'll tell you what I want, I want to finish with you, I've needed to finish with you for a long time, I haven't forgotten, no, no, no, Satan, you think that you can escape me? Ahh*! She laughed her familiar horse's laugh between her words, laughing and speaking, just like on the way to the slaugh-

terhouse, just like when she tried to suffocate me with the
pillow. I didn't understand the words, I was little, what was
she saying? She stabbed at me with the cane. I'm a big girl,
I'm hanging up the laundry, I'm a woman, not a girl. Her
face hadn't changed. Yutzi the fairest of them all. The belly
washers all said, *Can't you see that the girl doesn't feel well?*
You're not allowed to frighten her like this. Yutzi winked at
the belly washers, saying, *In a bit, I'm not finished with her*
yet. She lowered the cane, marking the air near my belly,
and at that moment I didn't know if she was aiming for my
guts or for the fetus in my womb. I stood frozen, holding
the clothespin, gripping it tightly, I needed two clothespins
to hang up Ephraim's work shirt, or else the wind would
knock it to the ground and it would get dirty, and he needed
a clean work shirt. This is what suddenly went through my
mind, the laundry. I turned my back to her, pinned the shirt
to the line. She stuck the cane into my back, between my
shoulder blades. *I'm not finished with you yet*, she hissed,
do you hear me? I'm not finished with you yet! I still held
the clothesline in my hands, I turned my head to look back
at her, and just as I'd forced myself to do in so many bad
dreams, I said to her quietly, *Go away, go away. Go away.*
She burst into laughter and almost lost her balance, righted
herself with the help of the cane. I took this opportunity to
hurry inside the house; she came after me, limping, almost
skipping on her good leg, dragging the along the injured
one. She screamed after me, *Ildiko, where are you*, or maybe
something else. I heard the calves crying in the neighbor's
barn, they were hungry. I burst into the house, the hinge on
the screen door stretched to its limit and then slammed behind me. Yutzi stabbed her cane between the screen and the
doorframe and pushed, then stood gasping in the doorway. I
already gripped the doorknob in my fingers but I couldn't get

the door locked, she was standing in the way. I said to her, *Enough, I'm not a little girl anymore.* Maybe she didn't hear me screaming *enough.* Maybe I wasn't screaming. Again she lifted the cane, I retreated from her, from her gaze, her gaze. I was afraid, I grabbed onto my head. I was afraid, I screamed, *Help, help.* I was a stone, who can hear a stone?

"Behind her stood the locked trunk that we'd found on the street, the blue trunk with gold horseshoes in the corners. Apparently some new immigrants had packed it with things they brought to Israel, and they didn't know that at the flea market they sell these to hip teenagers, you remember how we tried to smash the lock. In the end we decided to leave the trunk empty. I covered it with an embroidered velvet cloth we bought at the flea market. We came back from the Kinneret with stones and put them on the trunk. It was supposed to be temporary. We traveled to Maktesh HaGadol and brought back more stones; we went to Safed; we brought home coral and pebbles from the Red Sea, sandstone; we arranged a pile of colorful stones on the trunk in the entryway of the house. My mother said once, *I've never heard of this, I understand collecting seashells, but stones? What is this—something modern? And how do you clean them? I don't understand,* she said. But we loved our pile of stones, expanding in the corner. On every trip we collected another stone to add to the heap.

"Yutzi stuck the cane in my belly and pushed, I wanted to move to the side, I caught my elbow on the doorknob, stumbled, the latch of the door pierced the flesh of my arm, breaking the skin, I fell behind the door. As I fell I held onto Yutzi's cane. I was afraid of falling. I was afraid I would lose the baby. I held onto the cane. I'm large, heavy, I held on tightly. Yutzi held onto the other end and stumbled after me. It took so long for her body to fall, I saw that she was falling toward me, I was afraid she would hurt the baby. I lifted my hands up to defend it, Yutzi caught the hand that I held up. I pushed her away, she fell to the side, striking her head on the wall behind the trunk. Her body spilled onto the floor, her head falling into the space between the trunk and the wall. I was on the floor behind the door. It was quiet.

"In the distance I heard the cars traveling on the main road. On the neighboring farm they were preparing the low-ing cows for their evening milking. Where were the dogs? They'd gone after the neighborhood bitch in heat that be-longed to the Yahalom family, or to bother the chickens. Soon the phone would ring and Anat would say, *Chavatzy, I understand you don't want to tie up your dogs, but it's not working out this way.* I'll ask her for a little more patience, Ephraim is almost finished with the backyard fence; next week he'll put in the gate. The refrigerator is running — is it normal for a new refrigerator to make so much noise? Qui-et. It seemed pleasant to me, on the floor behind the door, I couldn't feel a thing, it seemed as peaceful as if I'd woken up from sleep. Someone was dead. Was I dead? No. I was breathing, was something else breathing with me? Yutzi! Suddenly I sat up, a sharp pain in my back, a burning on my arm, blood, my blood was warm, a twisted clot on my arm like a bracelet and rings on my fingers.

"It was almost dark. I got up, supported by the door-frame in the hallway. I felt around for the light switch, *click,* a pale twenty-five-watt light shone through holes meant to resemble stars, a handmade metal lampshade, a housewarm-ing gift. We lit this lamp every night, turned it off in the morning, so it wouldn't be too dark at night; I was afraid. A dim light so that I would be able to sleep. In the light I saw Yutzi. She was dead. An accident. Self-defense. Her new shoes. She tripped. I bent over her, and like in a horror film her eyes opened. I came closer, the saliva that had again begun to accumulate under my tongue dripped onto her, making a dark blue stain on her thin blouse, which had come untucked from her belted pants. Her gaze, she died with that gaze, but she still wasn't finished with me. The skin on her face twitched, as if controlled by some supernatural phenomenon, her cheeks lifted, burying her nose between them, her nostrils quivered, her eyes were covered in dozens of wrinkles, her lips formed a hill of creases that bordered a hole, like the mouth of a volcano, it all moved in subcutaneous streams, slowly changing into a glassy white under her wrinkled eyelids, sinking into her concave red cheeks, turning over like a ball on the water, her pupils screamed at me, wide and black. She was looking at me, she saw me, it was her gaze, her gaze, she wasn't finished with me yet. *Enough! Enough!* I screamed, how many times? For every time that I'd wanted peace—a million, trillion times, who could count all the times I'd said *enough* since the age of five? Her gaze, she stabbed me with her gaze, forever. I grabbed her hair, lifted her into a sitting position. Her body was loose, only her gaze still had life, I was five years old, eight years old. I was a calf at the slaughterhouse, I was my parents facing Hitler, I was your mother on the transport, I was Jesus, I was Marishka, I was Nissim Pitosi's mammoth, I was my baby, I was the cypress tree, enough! With all my strength I struck her head against the brass corner of the blue trunk where we piled our stones. I killed her."

twenty-two

A man comes home after a day of work. His muscles are weary, his skin scratched. He's ready to be coddled a little in the embrace of hot water. His stomach grumbles, squeezing itself inside, flexing itself in the areas that will be filled with a million soft flavors of juice, the taste of nipples waking up at the tip of his tongue, my woman, my beloved, playing a tune in my thoughts.

The house is dark, has she gone out? Is she sleeping? The dogs aren't in the house. Quiet. A weak light in the entryway. The house is unlocked. The springs of the screen door creak. On the floor, in front of me, lies Yutzi... *Ildiko! Ildiko!* I scream, a kind of madness in my movements. *Ildiko!* I run down the hall to the bedroom, the bathroom, the studio, the kitchen. On my way I turn on every light in the house. I pass Yutzi, in the light I know she is dead, her eyes are open wide, she stares like the boar I ran over. *Ildiko!* I scream. In the living room, on the edge of the couch, she sits shrunken into a little ball, tiny, a tiny little girl, how could she possibly shrink into such a small ball? She is hurt. I examine her with my hands, kiss her, weeping. She is alive, breathing, I reach a hand to her stomach, it's warm, *Ildiko*?! I weep hysterically, she doesn't move, I listen to her, she's whispering something, repeating forms of "fall" and "push": *I fell, she fell, we fell, I pushed, she pushed.* I shake her like a rag doll. *Ildiko!* I hold her. *What happened, my woman, what happened?* She whispers, *I killed her.* I scream, *No, that's not true, what do you mean, she fell, tell me that she fell.* She says, *She fell, I pushed her, she pushed me, we fell, I fell* . . . I kiss her dozens of times, her face, her hands, enough, enough, everything's fine. I'm crying on her neck, an ambulance, quick, *Hello, I don't know what happened, I came home, my wife's pregnant, she fell, she's injured, she's in shock, we have a houseguest, she's dead, she fell, an accident, I don't know what happened, I just came home, hurry, my wife is pregnant, she's hurt.*

I sit beside her, my arm around her shoulders, with my other hand I'm holding our baby in her belly. I grab the embroidered tablecloth, use it to bandage her arm, the vase of flowers spills onto the table. She's mumbling something, *shhh,* I tell her, *you don't know anything, don't get excited, please just relax.* I'm crying, I'm begging her, *an accident, it must have been an accident.* The boar and Yutzi are all mixed up together, I ran over the boar, it was an accident, it wasn't my fault, the baby, she didn't run over Yutzi, the baby, please don't let us lose the baby because of Yutzi. *I killed her, I killed her,* she insists. *You don't know what you're saying, shhh, you don't have to speak, enough, enough, it's over.* Sirens, the ambulance can't find the house, it takes two trips around the moshav, the door is open, two paramedics over Yutzi, a doctor, they're examining the corpse, I scream from the living room, *Here! We're in here! My wife is injured*. . . . They speak into a radio, the doctor turns to us, examines Ildiko, they need to stitch up her hand. *She'll be fine,* he assures me, *does anything else hurt?* He raises his voice as he asks her this, as if she's deaf.

238

Can you walk? She doesn't answer, he tries to lift her up. I help him, she rises slowly from the couch. I scream, *Doctor! She's bleeding! She's pregnant!* The doctor orders a stretcher, there's a throng of people next to the door, blue lights flicker into the house, they're examining Yutzi. I say, I plead with one of them, *My wife, hospital. . . .* He says, *You can go to her later, sit down. Kobi, bring him something to drink.* Another policeman arrives. *What about my wife!* I scream. I want to run after the ambulance, the police stop me at the door. *Calm down, sir, we have a few questions, you can go to her after, don't worry, they'll take good care of her.* The house is noisy: an officer, the precinct captain, the crime scene investigators, the coroner, six detectives, all of them going around in a big muddle, speaking in a kind of code, a shorthand, many people. Very slowly words are spoken, the neighbors are curious, a police officer asks them to please leave the premises, there's nothing to see. Yochanan is insisting on coming in, they won't let him. I'm crying, shouting, no, I'm not shouting, if I'd been screaming someone would have come, they're standing crowded around Yutzi's body, consulting each other in whispers. I don't make a sound, I just cry, *My wife, my wife*, I need to protect her, she's not allowed to get excited, why did she say *I killed her?* I need to tell her it's not her fault, it was an accident. I'm crying wordlessly, nobody knows my wife, she's afraid of everything, I need to reassure her. They cover Yutzi, speaking quietly. Plainclothes detectives arrive, someone touches me, a warm voice asks me in a caring manner, *What happened? Do you know what happened?* I shake my head fiercely from side to side, *My wife*, I'm crying like a child, *I don't know, they fell, we lost a baby, she's afraid of losing this baby.* The detective understands that I don't know anything, he leaves, whispers with the others, they take Yutzi away, everyone goes with her except for two plainclothes detectives. Questions. I answer, what do I know? *Yutzi is a friend of the family, a guest, they love her, like one of the family, Chavatzelet is a quiet woman, she's good, an accident, they fell, a cane, a bad limp, a cripple, Chavatzelet is weak, pregnant, they fell, they tripped.* I'm weeping, begging them to take me to my wife, the one with the pleasant voice wants me to drink some more water. I'm not to leave the area, tomorrow they'll be back, don't touch anything, maybe sleep somewhere else tonight. I say, *How can I sleep?* They say, *It's a tragedy, be strong.*

I call Mrs. Rott, *Chavatzelet is in the hospital, she fell, something disastrous happened, Yutzi fell, I don't know how, she hit her head, no, not Chavatzelet, Yutzi, she's dead.* Zsuzsi's in a meeting, I leave a message, there's a knock on the door, my neighbor Yochanan is alarmed, I fall onto his shoulder, *Take me to the hospital, I can't drive.*

She's pale, sleeping, bandaged. I'm running around in the hall, the doctor on duty gets angry, orders me to calm down, I scream at him, *What did you give her?! She's pregnant. He says, Everything's fine, she's resting, she had a shock. We gave her an ultrasound, the baby is alive, we saved it.* I'm trembling in a chair at the nurses' station, I burst into tears, they offer me a sedative. Suddenly I'm not alone, Mrs. Rott collapses against me, Zsuzsi attacks me with questions, tries to get into the nurses' room; they ask us to go to the waiting room. I tell the family everything I know. We speak in a jumble, when it's quiet we can't hear each other. *Ildiko says that she killed Yutzi.*

What? What are you talking about? It can't be, you didn't hear right, I'm crying, *She swears that she killed her... What kind of nonsense is this?* Shosh says, *the most important thing is that she's okay, she'll recover, my sister*

is a strong woman. Mrs. Rott is speaking in her *istenems:
Yutzi, what a catastrophe, she hasn't got any family, who
can we tell? Where will they bury her?* I cry, *Ildiko killed
her.* They scream at me, *Put that idea out of your head, do
you want them to lock her in a mental ward? She was in
shock.* They don't understand, they don't know anything.
I know my wife, she doesn't just say things, she killed her,
why would she insist? I don't know, don't know, my wife,
she should sleep, it's good that she's sleeping. Tomorrow
she'll feel better, tomorrow she'll understand it was an accident, tomorrow. Hours pass, it's almost morning. Zsuzsi
takes Mrs. Rott home, I wait for my wife to wake up.

I fall asleep on the bench, what the hell, they gave me
a sedative—why didn't they wake me? The detective with
the velvety voice is sitting with me, offering me a cup of
coffee. *Listen,* he says in his optimistic voice, *your wife is in
shock, it's hard to investigate when she's in this condition,
I couldn't understand much of what she said. There's a lot
of despair in her eyes, they were full of tears, but she wasn't
able to speak, she's frightened. You'll be able to take her
home tomorrow. I'll be in touch.*

I take her home after two days. She's like a baby bird, I
take her gently from place to place, worrying the whole time
that she's not too cold, keeping everything quiet, dimming
the lights. Gently, gently I take care of her, at home she insists on sitting in a corner of the couch, where I found her.
I flip over the pillow so she won't see the bloodstain. The
baby is out of danger. I cover her with the warm checked
blanket she loves so much.

At home she's relaxed, like after a good sleep. She hasn't
spoken another word. She refuses to see her mother and her
sister, she won't let me touch her, she doesn't want water,
she won't eat. I don't want anything either, I only want to

be near her. Never mind, we'll talk tomorrow, we'll sit in the yard and talk. She sits on the edge of the couch, I straighten up around the house a little, throwing the flowers in the garbage, wipe the table, cover it with a clean cloth, bring her tea. I want to sit by her.

She says, *I killed her.*

I start to speak quickly, *What are you talking about, an accident, you fell, she fell.*

She says, *I killed her.*

I start to cry, what can I do? I'm crying like a little boy. When I was a little boy I never cried, now I'm crying. I'm begging her for some reassurance, *What do you mean you killed her?* She has to explain, to speak, just not this silence. I want my wife back.

She says, *I'll tell you everything, from the beginning...*